He'd been watching her again....

She wasn't sure of many things right now, even her own identity. But she was certain of that one thing. He'd been watching her, with those eyes like deep, dark wells that beckoned her to dive in...to drown.

She darted inside the house, locking the door behind her, pulling all the curtains closed. Even then, she fancied she could still feel that dark gaze on her, piercing her...drawing her to him.

And she had to fight an impulse to let him in.

For her blood surged through her veins, her heart thudded impatiently against her ribs. She knew he was coming to her.

For good or evil, he was coming to her. She was waiting for him.

And the waiting was almost at an end....

Dear Reader,

The year is winding to a close, with bare tree branches reaching for a cold gray sky, and chill winds howling around corners and through alleys. It's a bleak season, a perfect season for curling up under a thick blanket—and in front of a warm fire, if you have one—and seeing the old year out with the newest offerings from Silhouette Shadows.

This month we bring you two more of the eerie, goose-bump-inducing tales you've come to expect from the line: *False Family* by Mary Anne Wilson and *Shaded Leaves of Destiny* by new author Sally Carleen. As always, our talented writers have combined irresistible romance with spine-tingling spookiness, just for you.

And next year we'll be back, with more chills, more thrills, more darkly sensuous loving, right here in the shadows—Silhouette Shadows.

Enjoy!

Leslie Wainger
Senior Editor and Editorial Coordinator

Please address questions and book requests to:
Silhouette Reader Service
U.S.: 3010 Walden Ave., P.O. Box 1325, Buffalo, NY 14269
Canadian: P.O. Box 609, Fort Erie, Ont. L2A 5X3

SALLY CARLEEN

SHADED LEAVES
OF DESTINY

SILHOUETTE® *Shadows*™

Published by Silhouette Books
America's Publisher of Contemporary Romance

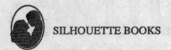 SILHOUETTE BOOKS

ISBN 0-373-27046-1

SHADED LEAVES OF DESTINY

SALLY CARLEEN

has supported her writing habit in the past by working as a legal secretary, real estate agent, legal assistant, leasing agent, executive secretary and several other things. She now writes full-time and looks upon those jobs as research for her real career of writing. A native Oklahoman (McAlester) and naturalized Texan (Dallas), Sally now lives in Lee's Summit, Missouri, with her husband, Max, and dog, Samantha. Her interests, besides writing, are chocolate and Classic Coke.

For Alfie, Carla, Gwen, Laura, Marcia and Mary,
for their criticism

PROLOGUE

Dressed in black, wearing a black ski mask, blending into the cloudy, predawn darkness, he strode onto Amanda's porch. Sliding a credit card through the ancient lock on her front door was easy, but he'd known it would be.

The door opened smoothly on the hinges she'd cleaned and oiled, and he stepped inside. An unexpected creak from the wooden floor caused his breath to catch in his throat, but he reminded himself that she'd be in her bedroom upstairs, and the approaching thunderstorm would cover any noises he made. He could take his time and make a thorough search before attending to her.

He pulled a small flashlight from his pocket and methodically explored the downstairs area—all the drawers in those little tables she'd placed so precisely, the antique secretary, even the kitchen cabinets; any of the places she might have hidden it.

Logically, she would have put it in the bedroom she'd turned into an office. But she wasn't always logical, and that failing constituted the core of the problem. She insisted on letting her emotions take charge. He could not allow that.

Failing to find what he'd come for, he crossed the foyer to the stairs. The growling rumble of thunder in the distance burst forth in a loud clap, and he halted midstep, momentarily startled. Just the storm, he reminded himself, irritated that he'd lost control even for a split second.

Moving slowly, carefully, he climbed the stairs, stepping over the boards he'd previously noted would creak. He thought he'd been silent, but when he reached the landing, he saw she was awake. She looked hesitantly from her bedroom door, then walked slowly and uncertainly into the hallway.

He permitted himself a brief, mental curse as he moved back, deeper into the shadows, and waited. He hadn't planned on this, had hoped to catch her asleep.

But he could be flexible, could change his plans when necessary.

She was beautiful, he thought regretfully as he watched her come down the hall. With her blond hair flowing above the white, gauzy gown that came only to her ivory thighs, she was a bright, almost luminous figure in the darkness.

As she neared the landing, lightning flashed, and he held his breath, fearful she'd seen him. She hesitated, but came on, looking carefully around while clutching a glass lamp base in one hand like a club. He couldn't help but respect her courage. It was a shame it had to come to this.

Actually, this would work out better than his original plan, he thought. As he moved up behind her, for an instant he had a strong, sudden feeling of déjà vu, as though he'd already done this thing. He gave himself a mental shake to rid his mind of such silly fantasies and reached toward the paleness of her slender shoulders. She gasped when he touched her and whirled toward him, wielding her pitiful weapon. He dodged and pushed gently, just hard enough to send her toppling down the stairs.

She screamed once and dropped the lamp. It shattered against the banister. Watching her, he felt detached, as if she were already dead, as if the act were so far in the past it no longer mattered.

But when she reached the bottom, he could see she wasn't dead. She was moving, moaning...alive.

With a muttered curse at his failure, he went quickly down the stairs, stepped over her still-breathing body and took a needlepoint pillow from the ridiculous little sofa in the parlor.

She looked up at him as he approached her, and he thought he saw recognition in her eyes. But that was impossible with the mask. He forced the cushion over her face, held her down until she stopped struggling. She was surprisingly strong for someone so slim.

He leaned over and picked up her limp wrist, felt for a pulse, found none and gave a sigh of relief. He had succeeded. It was over. Everything was back on track.

He replaced the pillow, then stepped over her body and hurriedly gathered up the pieces of the broken lamp. He didn't know how long he had before someone might come—that is, if anyone had heard her scream. The noise of the storm had probably covered any sounds they might have made, but he couldn't take chances. He'd have to come back later and find her illegally obtained compilations. A lot of good her clever righteousness had done her in the end.

The lamp she'd wielded against him had had no shade, so he went to her room, found it where she'd tossed it on the floor beside the bed and took it with him. As an added precaution, he moved another lamp around to the side of the bed she slept on so no one would miss or search for the broken one. He complimented himself on his thoroughness, his attention to detail.

He had to step over her again on his way down, forcing him to take one final look. It really was too bad things had come to this, but she'd brought it on herself, left him with no other way out. For a moment he felt anger at her for making him do this, but anger was a pointless emotion, and he refused to allow himself to indulge in it.

For a distressing instant, he thought he saw her breasts rise, as if she were breathing. But it had to be only a shadow. He'd verified that she was dead. He didn't make mistakes.

He turned away and left the house, locking the door behind him.

CHAPTER ONE

The face that stared at her from the hall looking glass wasn't hers!

Lightning flashed and thunder rumbled. She gasped, stepped back, looked away—away from the impossible image.

She swallowed hard, tried to reassure herself. It had to be a mistake—a portrait or a window or...something, something that made sense.

She forced herself to look again. Lightning flashed once more, invading the house, flaring in the frightened emerald eyes that watched her from the glass. Disbelief and panic surged over her, threatened to drown her. Her heart pounded as if it would push out of her chest, and fear rose in her throat.

"No," she whispered, and the strange woman's lips moved at the exact same time.

Tentatively she raised her small hand to touch the dark coil of her hair, to feel its reassuring familiarity even if she couldn't see it. The woman in the glass raised a long, slender hand and touched the pale, silvery curtain of hair that swung beside the beautiful but unknown face. She felt the length, the smooth sweep...but no tightly wound coil.

The strange eyes widened, and the woman in the mirror screamed and screamed and screamed as she slid to the floor, holding her unfamiliar hands over her unfamiliar face.

A minute or an hour later, the thunder returned, pounding at her front door. A shout sounded, followed by a thudding noise. Dimly she registered a new threat, forced herself to stop screaming, to face this latest unknown.

The front door flew open, wood splintering from the frame as the lock gave way. A man charged inside. Lightning streaked through the gray morning, briefly turning him into a hulking, featureless silhouette.

"Amanda!" he shouted, surveying the foyer, running toward her when his dark gaze fell on her as she huddled against the wall.

She felt she ought to know him, but she didn't. *He has the wrong face, just like I do,* she thought, and knew that that idea made no more sense than anything else.

"My God, what happened?" he demanded. "Are you hurt?" He reached down to her, grabbed her shoulders with powerful hands.

"No!" She struggled to break away from his grip, but he held her more tightly, hurting her.

"Amanda, it's me, Dylan. What's the matter? Why were you screaming?"

Dylan? No, that wasn't the right name. She stared up at him wordlessly, into eyes that glowed darkly from bottomless depths, eyes that, for some irrational reason, she'd expected to be bright blue, not black. He loomed over her, huge, tall, with muscles rippling under the dark, curly mat of hair that covered his naked chest and arms and disappeared into faded blue pants.

Thunder crashed and lightning streaked, flashing through the window, striking something nearby. She could smell sulfur. She cringed, moving closer to the wall, away from the fury of the storm, away from the repressed fury she sensed in the man.

"Amanda, damn it, talk to me. Are you still asleep? Are you having a bad dream? Did the storm scare you?" He rose, pulling her to her feet. "Come over here and sit down, get yourself together."

He urged her forward, but when she saw his destination—the strange parlor she'd glimpsed just before she'd looked into the glass—she balked, a whimper of fear rising from her throat.

Without hesitation he picked her up, his warm flesh touching hers where the short, thin garment she wore didn't reach. She should have flinched from his touch, but instead it evoked a delicious memory of . . . something, someone.

She blinked away the irrational thought, struggled against the man, but he held her securely, his arms like a vise, pressing her against the wall of his bare chest.

"Calm down," he ordered, his voice resonant and almost familiar, compelling her to do as he said. But she couldn't. How could she be calm when she'd seen a stranger in the mirror, when a man she didn't know broke down her door and carried her like a lifeless doll? "You're okay," he said. "Relax. Whatever happened, it's over."

Over? How could it be over when she was trapped in someone else's body? She tried to shrink into herself, away from him, from this whole nightmare that had begun minutes ago when she'd awakened at the foot of the stairs.

To add to her confusion, she was totally disoriented. She couldn't quite remember how she'd gotten there. She must have been running down the stairs to greet Papa and had stumbled. Mama was always warning her to slow down. But where was Papa? He wouldn't have left her lying there. Where was Mama? Why hadn't somebody come when she screamed?

Please, God, help me, she prayed silently as the man carried her from the foyer through the familiar arched doorway into the parlor, which had suddenly become unfamiliar.

The thunder and lightning were constant now, making the shadows writhe, the not-quite-right furniture seem to take on a life of its own.

"No," she cried, cringing as he set her on the Empire sofa. That piece of furniture rested in front of the fireplace as it had since she was a child, but the wrong carvings decorated the back, the needlepoint pillow wasn't one Mama had made and the blue upholstery had the wrong pattern. It felt solid enough beneath her—soft and smooth—and that wasn't right, either. The horsehair had always scratched.

The man stepped back, studied her from dark eyes shaded by thick brows.

Tentatively she rested her bare feet on the carpet. It was the same carpet Papa had bought two years ago, yet the pattern seemed to have faded like the petals of a plucked rose left outside in the sun and rain.

The mantel clock Papa had brought from St. Louis sat in its usual place. But the ticking sounded ominous, each beat taking her further into this unreal world, away from her comfortable, familiar life.

She could see scratch marks marring the surface of Mama's favorite lamp table, and briefly, irrationally, she worried that Mama would be upset. More importantly, though, the lamp that sat on it was painted with irises instead of roses.

The whole room looked like everything normal had disappeared and someone with a faulty memory had tried to reconstruct it.

She shivered. Her head throbbed. What in the name of all that was holy was going on?

"I'll get you something to drink." The man's voice interrupted her frenzied thoughts. "I'll be right back. Will you be okay for a minute?"

She summoned all her strength and nodded. If he left, perhaps she could find Papa and Mama, make sure they were all right, then... She couldn't think beyond that. How could she decide what to do when she didn't know what was happening?

He backed out of the room, watching her intently as though he didn't quite trust her. Was he afraid she'd escape? A bright flash of lightning lit his face, but not the depths of his eyes or the mask that seemed to cover him, hiding his real face from her.

As soon as he was gone, she forced herself to rise shakily to her feet, to gather her wits about her. First she had to get upstairs, get away from the strangeness down here, find out what had happened to her family.

Heart racing so loudly she feared the man would hear, she darted toward the stairs where this horror had begun. Taking a deep breath, she tiptoed upward, avoiding the steps that always creaked. But the seventh stair groaned alarmingly, and she almost sobbed at this continuing wrongness of things.

She reached the landing. The door to Mama and Papa's room as well as the transom above it were closed. That wasn't right, either. Even with the storm, the house was warm, and the bedrooms would be unbearably hot with no cross ventilation. She touched the glass knob, swallowed hard and forced herself to turn it, to look in.

Her hand flew to her mouth, and it took all her strength not to scream again. Her last hope of escaping the nightmare drained away, leaving her in total despair.

The four-poster bed sat where it had always sat, over by the window to catch the southerly breezes. But it wasn't the right bed. The wardrobe and chest of drawers were in their accustomed spots, and if she hadn't grown up with that furniture, she might have thought it was the same. But it wasn't.

She wrapped her arms about herself and shuddered, a sob crawling up her throat. Even Mama's ivory comb-and-brush set on the dresser were different, and their wedding picture in its silver frame was missing.

No one was there. The bed had not been slept in.

In desperation she turned and fled down the hall to her own room, only to be met with the same faulty replacements.

Her bed, however, had been slept in. In fact, the covers lay crumpled in total disarray, spilling from the bed onto the floor. She would never have left them like that.

Who had slept in her bed?

Outside, the storm raged, swirling against the house. Wind billowed the lacy curtains at her open window, bringing the first chilling drops of rain. She shivered, crossed the room tentatively as if walking on foreign soil and closed the window in an effort to shut out the storm. But it was futile. The turbulence inside battered her mind and heart with frenzied pain. She was drowning, suffocating as this unfamiliar world pressed against her. She had to fight a desire to drop to the floor and cry, to wait for Mama's reassuring arms to pick her up and comfort her.

But she had no idea where Mama was. She was alone. No one was going to rush to her rescue. She had to gather her wits and help herself. Taking a deep breath, she tried to calm her racing heart, steady her shaky legs.

Maybe the man downstairs had been right, she told herself, grabbing desperately at the possibility. Maybe she'd had a bad dream, and the image in the looking glass had been part of the dream, obscuring her own reflection. Maybe the house and furniture and even the stranger were all right after all. She was just having a hard time waking up, seeing them properly.

She forced herself to look around the room, to try to focus, to think, to get things straight. A picture on the polished walnut dresser that wasn't hers caught her gaze, and she moved across the room slowly, as if in a trance, to pick it up.

The portrait showed the blond woman from the looking glass, smiling as she stood in front of a shop with the sign Amanda's Antiques.

This time she didn't scream, didn't sob. She had no more energy. Exhausted, defeated, she sank onto the bed.

This time she could only accept the fact that she had gone quite mad.

The rain hammered incessantly on the roof, splattered against the window as though trying to force its way inside, but the thunder was losing intensity, rumbling from farther and farther away—as though it realized she was beaten. The storm had won.

"Amanda!" the man called. "Where are you?"

Amanda. That was her name, and even as she thought it, she knew it was true, knew she was Amanda...knew it as surely as she knew she was Elizabeth Dupard.

And that, of course, was impossible. She must be totally insane.

"There you are." He appeared in the doorway, filling it, invading it, dominating the room as he entered. "I thought you were going to wait downstairs. Why did you come up here?"

"I closed the window to keep out the rain," she said, forcing the words through dry, numb lips. Remembering her state of undress, she reached woodenly for the quilt and sheet, pulled them around her as much to put something between herself and the man as to cover her near-nude body. After all, she supposed, lunatics were surely excused for running around in immodest clothing.

He sat on the bed beside her and thrust a glass holding an inch of amber liquid toward her. "Drink this," he said, and she wanted to do it, felt an inexplicable urge to please him in spite of the fact that she didn't know him, didn't know what he was offering her.

"It's brandy." He pressed the glass into her hand.

Brandy! She'd never had alcohol before, but his dark gaze compelled her. Her eyes unable to leave his, she sipped, choked on the fiery beverage.

"A little more," he encouraged gently. Unable to resist, she drank again.

"That's good," he said. "One more."

And she obeyed as if from long-accustomed habit, as if she knew this person with the wrong name and eyes.

"Better now?"

She wasn't, but she nodded anyway.

Mama had been right about alcohol. She must be drunk. She yearned to lay her head on this strange man's solid shoulder and spill her confusion, as though the very strength she feared in him could help her.

His eyes weren't the black pits she'd thought, but the infinity of the midnight sky...still not the bright blue she somehow kept expecting. His tousled hair was black, though, the wild shade of a raven's wing.

He reached a hand toward her, and she jerked away, fearful though she wasn't sure of what.

"I want to look at that bump on your head," he said forcefully. She gritted her teeth and remained still while he pushed the hair off her forehead. His touch—if she closed her eyes and shut out the face, she could surely remember...

"That's a pretty nasty bruise," he said, and she flinched, more from the sudden anger in his voice than from the pain as he ran a gentle finger over her skin.

A bump on her head. That explained her headache and perhaps her confusion. Like what had happened to her cousin, Thad, when they were ten years old and he'd fallen out of the carriage. He'd kept saying things that didn't make sense, asking silly questions, calling people by the wrong names. But he'd been fine the next day. Maybe this was temporary, and everything would come clear soon.

The man muttered something under his breath, dropped her hair and lifted the quilt from her bare legs. She gasped in fear and a strange anticipation, but he made no move toward her. His searching gaze roamed over her body, returning accusingly to her face. "Amanda, what happened to you?" he demanded.

She looked down, noticed for the first time the bruises that were starting to darken on her legs and arms. She shook her head slowly. "I suppose I must have fallen down the stairs."

He raised one eyebrow, and his disbelief was obvious. "You *suppose* you must have fallen?"

She tried to focus, to remember exactly what had happened, but it all seemed jumbled. She did, however, have a vague memory of tumbling downward, a suffocating, drowning, helpless feeling.

"Amanda?"

She shook her head in an effort to dispel the frightening, irrational sensations.

"You didn't fall?" he asked, misinterpreting her gesture. His voice was ripe with anger and suspicion—of what, she had no idea. "Then where did you get those bruises?"

His words brought a dark, hurting memory swirling through the mists, tugging at her, but she pushed it away, unable to accept the pain that came with it. "I don't know. I think I remember falling."

He studied her for a moment, then nodded slowly, the action seeming to indicate a confirmation of his own thoughts rather than agreement with her comment. "Why don't I run you over to the hospital and let the doctor take a look?"

"No!" She might be insane, but she wasn't ready to die. Only dying people went to the hospital. Papa had gone and never returned.

Oh God! "Papa's dead!" The knowledge hit her with the force of a sledgehammer. How could she have forgotten that? He'd died in the winter... "What month is it?"

He scowled. "It's April. When did your father die? You didn't mention it yesterday."

"It's April? He died in January." She raised a hand to her forehead, as if she could physically wipe away the cobwebs from her brain.

He looked at her strangely, worry and concern mingling with the suspicion. "Why don't you throw on some clothes, and I'll drive you to your doctor."

She shook her head, unable to manage a stronger protest. If only he'd leave her alone for a few minutes, let her think, try to figure this out. Yet the idea of his leaving sent panic coursing through her. He was her only link to this world she no longer understood. He knew the blond woman in the mirror.

He rose abruptly, grasping her shoulders and pulling her to her feet. "You're hurt. How it happened doesn't matter. What matters is that you can't remember the month, you think your father died three months ago when he was here last week.... Obviously that head injury's worse than it looks."

His grip was so tight it was almost painful. But it was also solid, the only stability she had right now.

He released her, and she felt disappointed, fearful of losing whatever tentative touch with reality she still had. "How many fingers am I holding up?" He lifted one hand in front of her face.

"Two," she whispered, not understanding the abrupt change in subject.

"That's good. No double vision. Do you know what your name is?"

"Of course. It's . . . Amanda." That was what he'd called her, the name she'd read in the picture of the blond woman.

"Amanda what?" he asked.

A few minutes ago she'd have been able to tell him her last name without hesitation. But she was no longer certain of anything and didn't want to admit to that uncertainty. If he knew the truth, he'd surely take her to the hospital, probably to an asylum where they'd lock her behind bars forever.

She backed away from him, drew herself upright, ramrod straight. As she gathered her courage, she tried to look indignant. "I assure you, beyond a slight headache, I'm perfectly all right. I know my name. I'm fine. And now I must ask you to leave while I get dressed."

He dropped his hands to his side, but his eyes held her, forced her to look at him, to submit her soul to his inspection...dared her to look away or lie to him. "Amanda," he said, his voice grating, "what is your last name?"

For an eternity he continued to hold her with the force of his gaze. She longed to dive into those fathomless skies, find solace from this insanity, though at the same time she feared more insanity awaited her in their unknown depths.

"Dupard," she finally blurted, though she knew somehow it was the wrong answer. Her heart beat wildly against her ribs as she waited for him to do or say something, consign her to the attic or a mental asylum.

He blinked quickly, twice, gave no other outward sign. "Do you know where you are—the state and town?"

Tell me! she wanted to scream. *Tell me who I am and where I am and what's happening to me!* "Holbert, Missouri," she said, dreading his response, knowing she must be somewhere else but having no idea where.

He nodded slowly, still watching her intently, assessingly. "Yes, you're in Holbert, Missouri. But your name is Amanda Parrish, not Dupard. Do you know who I am?"

She searched her memory. He'd told her his name when he came in the front door a confusing eternity ago. "Dylan?" she asked uncertainly.

"But do you know me?"

She was almost able to catch the elusive memory, then it fled into the darkness of her mind once again. She dropped her head, looked at the quilt piled at her feet on the floor. "I'm not sure. Maybe. I can't quite remember."

"And Phillip Ryker? Can you remember him?"

She lifted her eyes to his, saw the suspicion had returned. "Phillip Ryker?" she repeated. The name stirred the mists chaotically, but no clear picture came.

"Your husband."

"My husband?" She sank back down to the bed, her legs suddenly too shaky to support her. *Husband?* A face emerged from the fog, a dark face surrounded by dark hair.

She clutched the wooden bed frame, tried to steady herself against the vortex that swirled around her, threatened to pull her under. She'd not only forgotten Papa's death, she'd forgotten her marriage...to Blake Holbert, not to someone named Phillip Ryker.

"But he's your *ex-husband* now, isn't he? The divorce became final last week." Dylan's voice came to her as if from far away.

Divorce? What horrible thing had she done to cause Blake to divorce her?

She clasped both sides of her head as a raging whirlwind roared inside her brain. She remembered Blake. She remembered marrying him after Papa died. But she couldn't remember a divorce, no matter how hard she searched. What was happening to her? Why was it happening?

Dylan crossed his arms over his chest and rocked back on his heels, moving away from her, leaving her even more alone and lost. "Are you trying to tell me you have amnesia? You're bruised and battered, and suddenly, conveniently, you get amnesia? You don't remember anything about Phillip?"

Amnesia? She turned the word over in her mind. She didn't think she'd ever heard it before, but somehow she knew he was referring to her confusion . . . to the fragments of memories that teased her, then darted away like minnows in a stream.

He watched her, his eyes narrowed, and she sensed that he was unsatisfied with her response, even though she had made none to his latest question.

She bit her lip, summoned all her determination. He wasn't going to help her. Somehow she had to get through this alone. "I'm feeling better now, but I think I'd like a cup of tea, and perhaps then we could talk. Will you wait for me downstairs?"

He hesitated, finally gave an abrupt nod. "If you're not down in ten minutes, I'll be back to make sure you're okay."

"I'll dress and be right down," she assured him.

She watched his almost-familiar back disappear as he closed the door behind him. For a moment she stood paralyzed, her mind so overloaded it couldn't function. Now ~~that she~~ was alone, she had no idea what she should do next.

Still hoping, she crossed the room slowly and stood in front of her dresser mirror. It was no use. The stranger was still there. She was taller, had to bend slightly to see her face in the mirror. She pressed her hand to her lips, held in the despondent sob that tried to escape. Her blood ran cold through the unfamiliar veins, and she wanted to turn away from the image, to hide and refuse to look. Instead she forced herself to stare directly into the eyes that were and weren't hers.

Amnesia. Loss of memory. That's what the word meant.

But she hadn't lost her memories. She just seemed to have the wrong set for this body. For herself, for Elizabeth Dupard, she had a complete set. However, she *had* momentarily forgotten about Papa and about Blake. That was proof that she was just a little askew about things, wasn't it? It would all come clear soon, just like with her cousin, Thad.

Please God, it would all come clear soon. Otherwise, she would surely go insane, was already insane, and they would have to lock her away in one of those places.

She lifted her hair off her forehead and studied the painful lump that was already turning dark, felt again the sensation of falling, of cold, wet blackness closing in.

She frowned, shook her head at the inappropriate mixture of sensations. Why should the blackness have felt cold and wet when the house was quite warm?

Alone and frightened, she moved shakily over to the wardrobe and opened the door. She wasn't even surprised to see that none of the clothes were familiar. Most of the skirts were immodestly short, but she selected one of the longer, fuller ones, a blue one from the same fabric as the man's pants. She added a white cotton waist and tried in vain to find appropriate undergarments.

Finally giving up, realizing she had to make do with what was available, she donned the skimpy, frothy articles she found in the dresser drawer.

Surprisingly, she felt quite comfortable in the completed outfit, as though she'd worn it many times before.

Trembling, but knowing she couldn't hide forever, had to try to find some answers, she made her way down the stairs.

The man who called himself Dylan waited in the kitchen. He sat in a ladder-back chair that was much too small for him at a wooden drop-leaf table almost identical to the one Mama owned. A kettle of water boiled on a cookstove that bore absolutely no resemblance to Mama's.

He looked up when she came in, his expression appraising . . . skeptical.

She joined him at the table, averting her eyes from him. Wordlessly he poured water into two cups containing paper squares, and amber tea magically appeared. Was this another secret the *amnesia* had stolen from her?

She picked up the newspaper he'd been reading, grateful for somewhere to look besides his dark, accusing gaze. But her gratitude was short-lived. While the masthead still proclaimed it to be the news for Holbert, Missouri, the print was a different style, and it was now the *Holbert Daily News* rather than *Weekly*. Something else she'd forgotten?

She took a deep breath and scanned the page. Her gaze froze on the date at the top. *Monday, April 13, 19—*

No! That was impossible! That would make her more than a hundred years old!

CHAPTER TWO

"No!"

Amanda dropped the newspaper as though it had burned her hand, then stared at it in horror.

Dylan leapt to his feet, snatched it up and scanned the front page. But he didn't see what he'd expected. A story about the new Holbert City Hall, a strike in Kansas City—nothing that should upset her...nothing that pertained to the guilty secret he knew she carried.

"Amanda? What's the matter?" She looked so genuinely distressed, he automatically laid a steadying arm across her shoulders. And she turned and collapsed against him, clinging desperately, huge sobs racking her body.

He almost staggered backward, overcome with surprise. This wasn't like Amanda. She was so self-contained, so independent. Either she was telling the truth or she was putting on a damn good act. He had to remind himself forcibly that it was most likely an act.

Something had happened yesterday afternoon. When he'd seen her yesterday morning she'd been like always...friendly but reserved—partially, he suspected, in response to his own reserved, insincere, confused friendliness. He'd been on the verge of admitting defeat, accepting that she might be as innocent as she acted. But then, yesterday evening, she'd seemed agitated, evasive and apprehensive...not to mention frightened. Possibly she'd somehow figured out who he was and what he wanted. He supposed he hadn't been very subtle in his attempts to pry information out of her.

And to his unexpected regret, her actions had pretty much confirmed his suspicions of her. He'd been right, but the knowledge brought no joy.

He'd kept a close watch on her, following her to her ex-husband's office in the middle of the night, watching her use the key she still had to get in. Now today she'd come up with this cockamamie story...and all those bruises. She was guilty. No doubt about it, and only he could see to it that she was punished.

Nevertheless, she was in his arms—something he'd fantasized about and fought against since he'd first met her. He couldn't resist wrapping his other arm around her slim body even as he told himself he shouldn't. She felt even better in the flesh than in his imagination.

"What is it? What did you see in the paper?" he asked, dragging his mind back to the issue at hand, to reality.

She pulled away, swiped at her eyes and picked up her cup of tea with trembling fingers.

A damn good act, he had to admit.

"I'm sorry," she murmured.

He slid his chair next to hers, the action making a grating noise on the hardwood floor. Her hands still shaking, she sloshed tea from her cup as she rattled it into the saucer.

He sat beside her. "Amanda, what's wrong?" he demanded. "You saw something in the paper that relates to this, didn't you?" He lifted the strands of pale, silken hair from her forehead and touched the lump gently, fighting the protective urge that came over him unexpectedly.

She looked at him, her sea green eyes wide and still shiny with tears, her expression unguarded and vulnerable.

The Amanda he'd known for two months had been friendly enough, but distant and slightly aloof, traits that had made it easier for him to lie to her...and to restrain the passion she unaccountably kindled in him. From the first time he'd met her, prepared to hate her, he'd found it necessary to remind himself regularly that what he had to do, by its nature, prohibited giving in to the attraction he felt for her.

But now he could see fear and *desire* on her features, in her eyes, as if she'd suddenly forgotten how to conceal her emotions.

The desire almost got to him. His finger on her forehead lingered, traced around the lump, over her soft eyebrows, and she just sat there watching him, her lips slightly parted, her clear eyes becoming hazy—obviously responding to his touch, though she didn't move a muscle.

To see the wanting he felt echoed in her...

She blinked. "Who *are* you?"

He dropped his hand, scooted his chair away from her. "Dylan Forrest," he lied, looking away from those translucent green depths that threatened to suck him in, swallow him, make him forget everything. "I live next door to you."

"In Rachel Waller's house?" she asked.

The previous owner. He dipped his head in a slow nod. "That's right. So you do remember some things." He waited tensely for her answer—an admission, a new ploy....

"I remember that Rachel's family takes in boarders."

She was consistent in her story. Convincingly consistent, he might have said, if not for her actions yesterday.

She looked down at her cup, drew her finger around the rim. "What's..." She hesitated, cleared her throat and started again. "What's the date?" In spite of her casual gesture, the question sounded all-important.

He told her the month, day and year. "What day did you think it was?"

She swallowed hard, her eyes lifting to his, widening even more. "I don't know exactly. Papa died in 1910, I married Blake in 1911 and that's the last I remember."

That did it, he thought, welcoming the anger that rose and covered the desire he couldn't afford to feel. It was barely possible she'd suffered a concussion, forgotten who he was, what day it was. But this nonsense of being somebody else, and now talking as though she thought she'd gone back in time...

"That's one hell of a case of amnesia." He hung onto the anger, welcomed the way it drove out everything else—his growing desire for her as well as the pain of loss that had taken over a corner of his heart.

In frustration he slapped both palms onto the tabletop. She jumped, staring at him in unmistakable fright, and in spite of his attempts to hold onto it, his anger retreated.

"Okay, okay." He raised his hands in a gesture of surrender. "You think you're Amanda Dupard and the year is 1911." There was no point in pushing her. He'd have to retreat, try another tactic.

He wasn't very good at this. Two months of failure proved that. Tom would have known how to get the job done. But Tom was dead. And because of that he wouldn't give up—*couldn't* give up.

She clenched her hands in her lap, her expression becoming so intense it was almost painful to watch...or would have been if he'd believed her. "I'm Elizabeth Dupard." The words sounded like a confession. "I only said my name was Amanda because that's what you called me. And I'm not sure about the year. It's just that I can't remember past my wedding."

"Fine. Have it your way. I'm not going to argue with you about that right now. But I am going to insist you have a doctor look at those bruises. You can tell him you fell down the stairs, that you have amnesia—I don't care. But you *will* see a doctor." Maybe her story was transparently phony, but the injuries were real. And perhaps once they'd healed, he might be able to persuade her to "regain" her memory, to give him what he needed.

She looked at him for a minute with that big-eyed, helpless, fearful stare, then straightened her back in the scared but determined way she'd done a couple of times that morning. "Very well. Perhaps a doctor can help me get everything straight. As long as you don't insist that I go to the hospital, I'll agree to see a doctor. You can go fetch him."

He leaned back, away from her, crossed his arms over his chest and smiled grimly. She was making things easier, feeding his ire, her story becoming so ridiculous he couldn't believe she'd expect him to buy into it. "*Fetch* him? Oh, I see. In 1911 doctors made house calls, didn't they? Well, they don't do that anymore. We have to go to them. I'll take you in my car. Did they have horseless carriages in 1911?"

She lifted her chin defiantly, stared straight into his distrust, and he had to fight a feeling of admiration for her courage, had to remind himself again this was all a scam.

"Automobiles?" she said. "Of course we had them. I saw two in Kansas City last summer."

"Last summer? Let's see . . . that would be some eighty years ago. Right?"

Her rigid posture dissolved, and she slumped in the chair. "Yes," she whispered. "Over eighty years ago." She looked at him, and her eyes seemed to be begging for his help.

He *didn't* believe her, didn't dare believe her.

He turned away, headed across the room to the telephone. "I suppose your doctor's name is on your list of things forgotten. Never mind. I'll call mine."

Amanda watched as he stalked away from her, crossed the room and picked up a shiny white object. Suddenly, somehow, she knew the device was a telephone, though it didn't look like any telephone she'd ever seen. As he talked to the doctor, he stood at the kitchen cabinet, his back toward her—his back that seemed, like the telephone, familiar yet totally unknown.

She touched her face, felt her cold fingers on her warm flesh. She was really here—wherever *here* was—and all this was really happening. She was trapped in a nightmare. Her heart pounded erratically, the swirling, choking mists of confusion threatened to drag her down, and she had to hold onto control tightly, not give in to panic. If she gave in for even an instant, she'd be lost forever.

The rain had stopped, but the clouds were low and gray, the air heavy with the threat of more storms when Dylan guided her outside to the street. As they walked across the wet grass, she studied the sky and shivered, wishing for the brightness of the sun, for something to illuminate whatever lay hidden in the dark corners of her mind.

At least she felt no surprise, only dismay, when the automobile he led her to bore no resemblance to any vehicle she remembered. He opened the door to the shiny black machine. "Go ahead and get in. I need to go put on a shirt. I'll just be a minute."

She shook her head. On second glance, the vehicle looked almost familiar, but the space inside was so small, and she already felt closed in by strangeness, could feel the humid air pressing against her, squeezing the breath from her lungs. "I'd rather wait outside."

He looked exasperated. "Will you stay right here? Not go anywhere?"

"Where would I go? Where would I dare to go in this unknown place?"

Though he scowled disbelievingly, he turned and loped toward Rachel's house. He was big, didn't run gracefully. In that respect he reminded her of Blake.

No, she corrected herself. He was big like Blake, yet it wasn't Blake he reminded her of. But it was someone. In spite of his obvious hostility, in spite of the fact that he didn't seem to be a close friend, in spite of the fact that she'd never seen him before this morning, she knew him. She was somehow tied to him. He evoked feelings of happiness and laughter...and fear.

The front door closed behind him, cutting off the flow of almost-memories.

She took an automatic step forward, started to follow him, to go inside and find Rachel, see her, talk to her, tell her about this insanity. But even before logic had a chance to halt her, the changes in the once-immaculate house pulled her up short. The porch had loose boards, a couple of rotten ones. The sidewalk was cracked and broken, and roots from the massive oak tree in the front yard pushed their way through—the oak tree that should be only a sapling, planted by Rachel's father to replace the one struck by lightning.

She turned slowly, fearfully, to look back at her own house, the house she'd just walked out of. In her mind's eye, she saw it light blue with darker blue and brick red trim. But even as she turned, she knew it wouldn't be.

And she was right. It was gray now with white trim.

The colors she'd always wanted it to be.

"Amanda?"

Dylan had returned. In hopeless resignation, she faced him, the only person she knew, the only person who could possibly help her, the person who frightened her with his dark, distrustful gaze and drew her to him in a way she didn't understand.

"It's true, then," she said, her voice coming to her own ears as alien and disconnected as she felt. "It's the future, and I'm not me...I'm her...I'm in somebody else's body."

He gripped her shoulders, his touch amazingly gentle for someone so big.

No, he didn't remind her of Blake at all, but his touch was so familiar....

"You're in your own body and your own time. You were here yesterday and the day before—two months before that that I personally know of." He spoke sternly, almost harshly, his words a contradiction to his touch. He opened his mouth as if to say more, but shook his head and turned away to open the car door again.

As they drove at a dizzying rate of speed along smooth ribbons of road, she clutched the dash so tightly her knuckles turned white. At first she worried that they would run over a carriage or a traveler on horseback or afoot, but they only encountered more of the strange automobiles, all speeding along as fast or faster than they were.

When she finally accepted the fact that they weren't going to crash into something, the ride became quite fascinating and astonishingly normal, as though she'd experienced it all before. Releasing her grip on the dash, she leaned back and stared out the window at the scenery flashing by.

Trees and grassy fields she'd passed while riding with Papa had been replaced by hundreds of houses—maybe thousands. Too many to count. She gaped in awe at images she'd never seen, never even dreamed of. Yet those images, after her first shock wore off, began to look "right" in an inexplicable way. Each new spectacle, startling at first glimpse, seemed to slip into and fill its own empty slot in her memory just as the telephone and automobile had.

One thing was becoming certain. The world she remembered was gone. Years she couldn't account for had passed, and she was alone in this strange place. She swallowed hard as the implications hit her. Mama must be long dead, and Aunt Hester and Cousin Thad and her best friend, Rachel—everybody she knew.

A sob caught in her throat. She couldn't lose everyone at once. If she was alive, surely they must be, too. But she knew they were gone. She'd never see them again in this lifetime. The grief of loss flooded through her, threatened to overwhelm her. She bit her lip, fighting back the tears.

"How's your head?" Dylan asked, diverting her thoughts.

"My head? Oh, I guess I'd forgotten about it. Much better, thank you. What on earth is that?" In her sorrow over her family, she hadn't been paying attention to their surroundings, hadn't noticed that they were approaching a group of tall buildings that seemed to touch the sky.

"Kansas City."

When he spoke the words, she felt the information settle into place in her memory. "Yes," she said slowly. "It is. But how did we get here so soon? It took Papa nearly half a day with our horse and buggy."

He regarded her from the corner of his eye. "Half a day. Fortunately, since I have to come here to work every day, we travel faster than that in our cars."

In his voice she heard again the disbelief, but for just an instant as he looked at her, she saw a flash of uncertainty. Before she had time to think about it, he pulled into a concrete-covered lot and stopped in the midst of a crowd of other cars.

"We're here," he said.

A couple of hours later, when they walked through the glass doors and out of the building, Amanda—she knew she had to start thinking of herself by that name—felt a great deal more relieved than when she'd gone in.

The doctor, a short, balding man with a pleasant though distracted smile, had assured her that some memory loss from a head injury was common, that her memory would likely return soon. He wouldn't have all the test results back until tomorrow, but everything looked normal so far.

Normal. What a wonderful word. If the tests said she was normal, did that mean she would soon be back to normal?

Or would the tests reveal that she'd stolen Amanda's body or that she was mad? She felt a little saner. She could accept thinking of herself as Amanda. She just couldn't stop thinking of herself as Elizabeth.

"You don't need to check on me every four hours tonight," she said as the streetlight changed from red to green and Dylan took her arm, guiding her across. He had stayed by her side every minute, even through the frightening, sometimes painful tests, but this frequent checking would be asking too much of anyone.

"You heard the doctor," he said, his gruff tone belying the compassionate way he'd been acting. "It's either that or you spend the night in the hospital, and you told him in no uncertain terms that you weren't going to do that."

She looked up at his grim expression and wondered, not for the first time, if his tenacity about never leaving her came more from concern about her welfare or from the possibility that she might get away from him. She had no idea why that should be, but she sensed that he wanted something from her.

She sighed. Since she had no idea of Amanda's life prior to this day, there could be any number of reasons for his strange behavior. In any event, whatever the explanation, she was glad he'd been there, glad he was still with her, that she wasn't totally alone in this unknown land.

Yet as they reached his automobile and he opened the door for her to get in again, as he stood so close beside her, she had to admit to another reason for being glad he was there. Even as his presence gave her a more secure feeling about this world, at the same time he made her feel insecure in an excitingly dangerous way—rather like riding the Ferris wheel at the fair in St. Louis.

Settling into the car seat beside her, he pulled out of the parking lot, into the line of cars moving down the street. She studied his ominous profile, the square, clenched jaw, the dark secrets of his gaze, and thought she was most assuredly mad.

"The doctor said you'd probably start to remember things soon," he said, his attention seemingly focused on the mechanics of operating the vehicle. But the tension in his voice told her the question was important—very important, so important it frightened her. What did he think—or fear—that she'd remember?

"I hope he's right," she said, then decided to take the plunge, see how he would react to the return of her memory. "Sometimes when I see things, like the tall buildings, or when you tell me something, I sort of get it back. But it doesn't go beyond that. When you told me this was Kansas City, I knew it was and that I'd been here, but that's all."

"You admit you're not some Victorian woman named Elizabeth Dupard." Again his voice had a peculiar edge to it, a testing.

"I know I'm Amanda Parrish," she said, choosing her words carefully. "I know I can't be Elizabeth Dupard." *But my heart still thinks I am!*

A weak sun was trying to peek through the clouds when they turned onto Amanda's street. She sat upright, gripped the dash as she noticed several cars parked in front of her house. Men in uniforms stood in the yard. Policemen. Had some crime been committed while she was gone? Or were they waiting for her? Had the doctor's tests revealed her as insane? Had he sent the police to get her?

Panic stricken, she turned to Dylan, the man whose motives she didn't understand or trust, but the only person she could turn to right now. "What's happening? What do they want?"

"You don't know?" He swung around the parked vehicles and pulled up in front of Rachel's house. "I see your ex-husband's car among the crowd." He indicated a silver vehicle.

Her ex-husband. Not Blake. She knew now he didn't mean Blake.

Did this have something to do with the divorce? Were they here to take her back to him? That thought made the world spin crazily. "I don't remember my..." She had to force the word past her numb lips. "My...ex-husband."

"Then you'd better come meet him." Dylan got out and came around for her. "Why are you trembling?" he asked as he took her hand, his gaze boring into her, trying to ferret out her secrets, her very soul.

She wanted to beg him to get back in the car and drive her far away. But she had nowhere to go. This was her home, apparently the only thing she had left. She got out, making an effort not to clench Dylan's hand too tightly, but not releasing it, either.

As they walked across the yard, one of the policemen came up to them. "Can I help you?" he asked.

"You can tell us what's going on," Dylan answered. "This is Ms. Parrish. She lives here."

Amanda waited, holding her breath, wishing she could sink into the earth or fly into the clouds, anything to escape whatever awaited her.

The officer lifted his eyebrows. ''You're Amanda Parrish?''

''Yes, she is.''

''Hey, Milton,'' he called over his shoulder, ''it's the Parrish woman!'' He turned back to her. ''We thought something had happened to you. Your husband's been worried. He came out, found the broken door but no sign of you, and called us.''

They weren't going to arrest her! ''I fell down the stairs. My neighbor took me to the doctor.''

''Amanda!''

She looked up to see a tall, slim man striding across the porch. His eyes were so light a shade of blue they almost matched his meticulous silver hair. His skin was brown as though he spent a lot of time outdoors, but his face was unlined, his clothing immaculate, not like a laborer.

''That's Phillip Ryker,'' Dylan murmured. ''Your ex.''

For a brief instant as he walked beneath the skeletal branches of the catalpa tree, his image blurred. He seemed larger, his hair and eyes darker, skin paler. *Blake?*

She clung to Dylan. ''No! I don't want to go back.'' The words came from somewhere deep inside, a place hidden even from her, for they made no sense as she uttered them.

''It's going to be all right,'' he said, dropping her hand to slide his arm tightly about her waist. ''You'll never have to go back.'' His voice was different, and it touched that hidden place. She started to call his name. . . .

But the other man rushed to her and pulled her away, into his arms. She didn't try to fight him, just let herself turn to a limp sawdust doll in his embrace.

"Thank God you're all right," he said, releasing her and stepping back to look at her. She blinked and shook her head. This was Phillip, not Blake. Not Blake. "I was so worried!" he continued. "Lottie called me when you didn't come into the shop this morning and she couldn't reach you at home. I came out and found your door broken and no sign of you! What happened?"

"She says she fell and hit her head. She's covered with bruises. She doesn't want to talk to the cops," Dylan said.

Amanda looked up at him, surprised at the hatred in his voice and in his eyes. It was apparent from his tone that he knew Phillip, had some connection with him. He couldn't have so much enmity for a stranger.

She shivered as she recalled the improper, heady feelings he evoked in her whenever he touched her. Could he be the reason for her divorce? Was that why he disliked Phillip?

Yet Phillip gave no indication that he shared the ill will. With a curt nod of agreement to Dylan, he turned to the nearest officer.

Once again Dylan touched her, taking her arm, and a nebulous, familiar world almost coalesced around her as he led her toward her house, up the steps and across the porch.

She stopped just inside the broken door. The wide staircase loomed before her at the far end of the foyer. She stared upward. That's where she'd lost her mind; if she had any chance of finding it, surely it would be there.

She walked slowly forward, stood at the bottom and looked up to the landing. A wisp of memory swirled tantalizingly just out of reach. She needed to go up there, see if she could find—

A hand grabbed her shoulder. She gasped, whirled and fought through the fog in her mind to recognize Phillip.

"I'm sorry. I didn't mean to startle you," he said, smiling. "You seemed to be in a trance. I wanted to be sure you were all right."

She nodded. "I'm fine. I was just looking. Trying to recall."

"Recall what?"

"She has amnesia," Dylan said, stepping up beside Phillip, his tone brusque, his dark eyes glowing like coals. Yes, there was definitely some animosity between them—at least on Dylan's side.

"Amnesia?" Phillip repeated quizzically.

"I can't remember...things."

"She thinks her name is Elizabeth Dupard and the year's 1911."

Amanda bit her lip, distressed that Dylan had exposed her so callously. In spite of his kindness in looking after her, she didn't think she could trust him completely. There was something going on with him that she didn't know about...but then, she didn't know about much of anything.

She looked at him and found him watching Phillip as intently as he'd watched her. Had he told about her problem deliberately, just to catch Phillip's response? Why? What was going on between the two of them?

Phillip draped a protective arm about her shoulders and smiled down at her. The only response his touch evoked in her was mild surprise that she could look almost directly into his eyes. She was only a few inches shorter than he was. The feeling of looking at a man almost on a level was new, strange and exhilarating. She'd always been so short; this sudden height gave her a feeling of power.

Appalled at the coldness of her thoughts, she lowered her gaze so he wouldn't be able to see her own callousness.

"I'm not surprised something like this would happen," Phillip said, his voice calm and reassuring.

"You're not?" She looked up at him in shock. Was she finally going to get some answers?

"It's this damned house." He waved his free arm in an encompassing gesture. "She's been acting strangely ever since she moved in here. She kept saying she felt as if she'd lived here before. She claimed to know where every piece of furniture should go. She let herself get obsessed with it. So now, a little bump on the head and she's invented a former resident for the house, taken on her name and personality—Elizabeth Dupard, a fictional woman who lived in 1911."

She listened to his words in horror. Fictional? She—Elizabeth—had never lived, was just a creation of her imagination? How was that possible?

But all the evidence told her it was.

Difficult as it might be to believe she had invented herself, it did make sense, and nothing else had so far. In fact, as Phillip had spoken, she'd found a slightly blurred memory of taking pieces of furniture from the attic, positioning them just so, replacing missing items as closely as possible.

But how could none of her life as Elizabeth have happened, when she remembered it so clearly? How could she remember a lifetime that didn't exist and forget one that did? How could her heart ache with love for people who'd never lived?

"Well," Phillip said, extending one hand to Dylan as he continued to clutch Amanda with the other, "I certainly appreciate your taking care of Amanda. Let me know how much the doctor bill was and I'll reimburse you."

Dylan was being dismissed! She didn't want him to leave. She bit her lip as that odd need for him came over her again. But, she reasoned, even though she was unsure of him, un-

comfortable with him, he had become one of the few familiar parts of this world she'd awakened into. That explained
why she didn't want him to leave. Didn't it?

One corner of Dylan's mouth quirked up as he accepted
Phillip's proffered hand and shook it once, then released it.
"That's not necessary. I have a long-standing relationship
with Dr. Wilkins. In fact, I promised him I'd check on her
every four hours until morning. That's the only reason he let
her come home rather than go to a hospital, and I wouldn't
feel right breaking my word to an old friend."

A part of her relaxed, glad that Dylan wasn't planning to
leave her alone with Phillip. But another part was becoming irritated that the two men were talking about her as if she
weren't there. Men did that, she knew, but suddenly she
didn't like it. In fact, she wasn't so sure it was proper for
men to do that in this future world she'd awakened into. It
didn't feel quite right.

Phillip tightened his arm about her. "Under the circumstances, she won't be spending the night here. We'll be going to our home in Leawood."

A vague impression of a large, rambling suburban struc-
ture began to take shape in her mind, a beautiful place where
she'd never quite felt comfortable.

She twisted out of Phillip's embrace and stood facing
both of them. "No. I don't want to go to your house. This
is my home and I'm going to stay here." She surprised herself with the firmness of her actions, but Papa had always
said she was pure pig iron beneath the flounces and ruffles.

Phillip reached for her again. She stepped backward.

"Amanda, don't be silly. My house was our home until
six months ago. It'll be a lot more convenient for everybody if you stay with me until you're completely well. You
won't have to impose on Mr. Forrest."

She didn't like what he was saying, but it made sense. She was tired and scared, and almost acquiesced, but somehow she felt she could find the answers only where she'd lost them—in her own home. And somehow she sensed that now, eighty years later, she had the right to demand that she be allowed to do that. It was a giddy, empowering feeling.

"No," she said. "I'm staying here."

Phillip's eyes blazed briefly with cold fire. She took a step backward, away from the fury she anticipated from defying her husband. Her ex-husband. But he only smiled. "Very well. Then I'll spend the night here and set my alarm clock for every four hours. We won't need to disturb your neighbor."

She relaxed, then jumped when Dylan spoke. "Since you'll be staying here, I'd better go get my tools and fix that door. I'm the one who broke it." He strode away before Phillip could protest, as she felt certain he meant to do.

When the door closed behind him, her anxiety returned in full force. That was absurd, she knew. Dylan was only Amanda's neighbor, whereas Amanda had trusted Phillip enough to marry him. Surely that counted for something. Why didn't she want to be alone with him now? He'd shown that he didn't have Blake's harsh temper.

"Let's get out of here," he said. "Your friend will be making a lot of noise with that door." His hand touched the small of her back. "We can go get a late lunch."

Why did he have to keep touching her? And why did she mind it so much when she'd clung to Dylan desperately, desired his touch?

"I'm not hungry. We stopped and had a sandwich on the way home." It was the truth, but she'd have said it even if it hadn't been. She moved away from him, headed toward the kitchen. "Would you like me to make something for you?"

"I could use a cup of coffee." If he noticed the rebuff, he gave no indication.

In the kitchen she went to the range and stood staring at it stupidly. "I don't know how to light the fire."

Phillip came up behind, reached around her and turned a knob. Flame leapt from a front burner. She gasped, jerked backward, then laughed nervously. "It's a gas range with a pilot light, isn't it?" she said, retrieving the memory. "It startled me at first, that's all."

He gave her a long, searching look, then picked up the kettle Dylan had used earlier to boil water for tea and held it under the faucet.

"Where's the coffeepot?" she asked. "I thought you wanted coffee."

"Coffeepot's over there, sweetheart." He indicated a white machine with a glass pot that didn't look anything like Mama's old battered black one. "I thought we could just have some instant right now."

Instant coffee. A picture came to mind. Bitter stuff with foam on top. "I prefer hot cocoa," she said.

Light flared deep inside Phillip's pale, penetrating eyes. Slowly he turned off the faucet. "You remembered," he said. "You're getting better fast." She realized with a start that her memory was important to him, too. He was as dubious as Dylan about her loss, as anxious to know how much she recalled. What did she know—what had Amanda known—that concerned both these men?

She sank down in one of the chairs, decided not to tell him her memories of hot cocoa came from sitting around Mama's table.

A gray sadness washed over her as she forced herself to face reality. Mama and Papa and Elizabeth had never existed, were just characters she'd created like when she was a little girl and used to play house with Rachel.

She clenched her hands in her lap, reminded herself sternly that Rachel was part of the imagined life, too. They'd never played with dolls or giggled about the way John Barker's voice was changing or whispered about her approaching marriage to Blake. She'd made it all up.

Because her life as Amanda was so horrible she wanted to forget it? She was divorced from an attractive man who turned her blood to sawdust. And somehow she was involved with Dylan; she couldn't deny that, though she had no idea about the nature or the extent of that involvement. He was a part of her life, apparently a secret part . . . and no matter how much she was drawn to him, that didn't sound good. The more she learned about Amanda, the more unsavory her life seemed. Elizabeth's life seemed much more simple and appealing—and much more real.

CHAPTER THREE

A loud pounding startled her from her reverie. Dylan, she realized. Repairing the front door. The door he'd broken down to get to her.

Phillip frowned, compressing his lips in irritation, but he made no comment as he set a steaming cup in front of her and sat down across the table. "I've been very worried about you, Amanda. I'd like to know exactly what happened." His voice was silky smooth, his expression veiled and expectant.

"I don't really know." She sipped her cocoa. It didn't taste like Mama's, but it was palatable. "I woke up at the foot of the stairs early this morning and ... didn't recognize myself in the mirror."

Phillip questioned her gently, skillfully probing. She'd been right. Like Dylan, he showed a decided interest in the recent events of her life. She couldn't answer his questions, could only keep repeating "I don't know." And she wasn't sure she would have told him—would tell him in the future—anything she did remember. Until she could figure out exactly what the two men wanted to know, how their knowing would affect her, she might be wise to keep any returning memories to herself. Their prying irritated and frightened her.

Dylan burst into the room clutching a hammer.

Amanda leapt up, shoving her chair back so fast it fell. She tripped over it, stumbled backward, and Dylan caught her, clutched her securely against him.

Panic rushed over her, and she grabbed his arms to pry them away, grateful that Phillip was there. But the adrenaline that surged through her veins seemed to give her a preternatural awareness of every inch of him that touched her—his chest against her back, his hand at her waist, his fingers on her arm. She made no further move to get away from him.

He held her, she thought, a second too long and eternities too briefly.

"You okay?" he asked, releasing her. Fortunately, he didn't wait for an answer. She wasn't sure she could have given one. "I'm finished. It's not perfect, but it'll keep the rain out." He set her chair upright, and she sank into it, her legs shaky. Again she had to ask herself what was wrong with her that she thrilled to his touch but cringed from Phillip's.

"Thanks a lot." Phillip spoke to Dylan, but his gaze was on her.

She looked down, lifting her cup to her lips in an effort to hide her face, her inappropriate feelings.

"No problem. Can I talk you out of a cup of coffee?"

From the corner of her eye, she saw Phillip's thin lips turn down in a scowl, sensed he was going to refuse. "Of course!" she exclaimed before he had a chance to speak.

Phillip glared at her, but she stood her ground. No matter what year it was, surely good manners hadn't changed that much.

Dylan went to the cupboard, took down a cup and poured in the water, then added crystals from a jar. "Amanda tells me you're a lawyer," he said, taking a seat at one end of the table.

Phillip was an attorney. A successful businessman just like Blake. A chill shivered through the room, surrounding her as a memory slid through the periphery of her mind, just out of reach.

"Oh?" Phillip raised one eyebrow at Dylan's statement. "When did she tell you that?"

Amanda recalled her earlier assumption that Phillip and Dylan knew each other. That didn't seem to be the case, yet Dylan's enmity toward Phillip was obvious, and Phillip seemed to be developing the same feeling for Dylan.

"Before the accident, of course," Dylan answered.

"How interesting. She didn't tell me anything about you."

Dylan shrugged, either ignoring or not hearing the challenge in Phillip's tone. "Not much to tell. I'm a commercial artist with a firm in Kansas City, and I live next door."

Phillip nodded. "Kansas City. So what brings you all the way up here?"

"My uncommercial art. I paint. The corner bedroom upstairs has perfect light, the house has atmosphere and the town's quiet. Suits my artistic needs. That's how I heard Amanda scream this morning. I was out on the front porch painting the approaching storm."

Phillip leaned forward, hands wrapped around his cup. "You must have moved in recently. That house was vacant when Amanda bought this one. As I recall, the owner died intestate. The estate's been tied up in probate for years."

Dylan smiled tightly. "You're absolutely correct. I'm renting from the court-appointed trustee."

Amanda averted her eyes from them, tracing the floral pattern on her cup. Was she the reason for the unexplained antagonism between the two men? If Dylan had moved in after Amanda did, had he moved to be close to her? Did he feel the same tingle at her touch that she felt at his, the almost-tangible connection between them?

The possibility was getting stronger that she'd forgotten Amanda's life because she wanted to, because she didn't want to remember. But even as the thought crossed her mind, an urgency to know filled her. However distasteful Amanda's life might have been, she *had* to remember it.

When she'd come in and stood looking up the stairs, she'd known there was something up there, something her mind had almost grasped before Phillip startled her, something important. She had to get up there and find...she wasn't sure what, but she had to find out if it was still where she'd hidden it. If it wasn't there, she'd have to—

"Amanda, what are you doing?" Phillip demanded, and she realized she was standing.

She looked at him, at Dylan, at the way they watched her every movement. She was trapped—hemmed in by the two of them and locked out of her own mind. She had to get away, be alone with her thoughts and sort through them.

"I'm very tired. I must ask you to excuse me." As she said it, she realized she was totally exhausted. The day's events had depleted her, drained her energy.

Dylan pushed back his chair and stood. "I'll be over to check on you in a couple of hours."

"There's no need for that. I'll be here." Phillip moved to stand beside her, sliding his arm about her waist—establishing his claim to her, shutting out Dylan.

Dylan nodded curtly, turned on his heel and strode from the room. They followed him to the front door, exchanged barely civil farewells, and Phillip took down the key ring from the hook beside the door where she habitually hung it and locked up behind Dylan. She stared at the closed door, distressed and relieved that her enigmatic neighbor was gone.

"He seems awfully interested in you," Phillip observed.

The idea sent a ridiculous thrill through her. But she quelled it, unsure if Dylan's interest was personal or something else—unsure whether she should be happy or frightened if it were personal. "He's been very helpful," she replied.

Wishing desperately that Phillip would leave, too, she turned and started up the stairs. He followed close behind.

"I know you never take tub baths because of your water phobia," he said, "but I think a good, hot soak might be just the thing—relax your sore muscles."

The breath froze in her lungs at the picture he painted. She tried to gasp, to breathe, couldn't. Then, as suddenly as the discomforting sensation had come, it disappeared.

How strange. Why would the idea of being in a tub of water terrify her? Of course she took baths in a tub. They weren't uncivilized people who went down to the river.

"You go change, and I'll run it for you," Phillip continued when she didn't protest.

"All right," she agreed uneasily. She went on to her bedroom, changed into a robe and returned to the bathroom, still feeling oddly disturbed at the thought of sinking into a few inches of water.

The bathroom—her mother's pride, since not everybody had one inside—looked much the same, except someone had arranged a wall display of things she normally didn't see on a wall—a paper fan, a hat, a shaving brush, a half-open straight-edged razor, a curling iron and some hairpins. Even so, the odd grouping of familiar objects had a certain appeal.

However, Phillip in his business suit looked out of place kneeling on the tile floor in front of the big, claw-footed tub. He glanced up as she approached. "What the devil is this gadget, and where's the stopper for your drain?"

She studied the contraption he indicated—coiled, flexible steel tubing on one side of the faucet leading to a round, flat object pierced with hundreds of small holes through which water was streaming.

"My shower," she said slowly as the device came clear in her mind. "I had it installed." Leaning over, she flipped a small lever. "This makes the water come out the faucet instead of the shower. And I don't have a stopper for the tub, so you can't fill it with water." Her assertion surprised her by its intensity, the relief she felt in saying it.

Phillip was right. She didn't like to take tub baths. In fact, she intensely disliked them, disliked the suffocating feeling of water around her body.

He stood, straightened his clothes. "Well, then, I'll leave you to your shower. I'll be downstairs if you need me, and I'll spend the night in the guest room." At the door he paused and looked at her quizzically. "I never did understand why you didn't take the guest room for yourself. It's bigger, next door to the bath, has a better view."

Take Mama and Papa's room? "But I've had the same room since I was born," she answered automatically, then realized what she'd said. Phillip had said she'd been in this house for only six months. "I mean . . ." She was too tired to figure out a way to cover her blunder. She bent to turn on the hot water and flip the diverter switch back to Shower.

From far away Elizabeth watched as the woman stirred, her hair spreading over the pillow like moonlight. But no moon shone through the clouds. The night was dark.

The blond woman raised her head slightly, seemed to be listening to something—perhaps the thunder that rumbled in the distance.

She turned on the lamp beside the bed and picked up the clock. The hands showed four o'clock. She switched off the light and settled into bed again.

A sound came like a whisper, a sound not of the approaching storm.

She sat upright in bed, eyes wide, head cocked to the side, listening, then slid quietly out of bed, shoving the covers to the floor in her haste.

The noise came again, closer, as if someone were on the stairs.

She yanked the lamp cord from the wall socket, tossed aside the shade and clutched the lamp around the middle, wielding its cut-crystal base as a makeshift club. Taking a deep breath, she tiptoed through her open bedroom door, down the hallway toward the stairs.

Lightning flashed, and in that instant a shadow seemed to move on the landing, but darkness immediately reclaimed the house.

Cautiously she made her way down the hall to the landing, then hesitated at the top of the stairs.

A board moaned behind her. Danger loomed suddenly, real and close. She swung the lamp up and tried to turn, to defend herself.

Cold, hard hands gripped her bare shoulders, and they were Elizabeth's shoulders. She could feel the pressure on her skin, the steel in the hands that shoved her downward. The lamp slipped from her fingers. She screamed, reached vainly for the rail.

Down and down she tumbled, over and over as her worst nightmare came true, her fear of falling abruptly known. But the cold, suffocating blackness she somehow expected didn't come, and she almost cried with relief when she hit the floor with a painful thud.

Before she could get up, he was there, a dark silhouette bending over her, shoving a pillow over her face. Panic-stricken, she fought him, flailing against him, but he held her down, pressed the softness of the pillow tightly around her nose, her mouth—and the blackness stole her breath.

Then it was over and she floated upward toward the bright light that waited, beckoning. She turned back for one last look and saw him leaning over her body, feeling for a pulse.

And she remembered everything.

Sudden anger stirred her soul. No! She would not let him get away with this.

She looked regretfully at the beckoning brilliance of the light, but made her decision.

A hand grasped her shoulder again, shook her. She struggled to rise through the darkness, through the mists that weighted down her body, glued her eyelids closed. She tried to scream, but it came out a low moan.

Straining against the hands that held her, she dragged her eyes open, saw the figure looming over her in the darkness and was finally able to scream.

"Easy, babe," Phillip soothed. "It's me. Everything's all right. You must have been having a bad dream, moaning and thrashing around in here."

She collapsed back against the pillows, let out her breath, willed her racing heart to slow down. Her gaze was drawn to the clock. Four o'clock, just like in the dream.

He sat on the edge of the bed, and took her hand. "What were you dreaming that upset you so badly?"

"I don't remember," she gasped, lying. The dream was still too close, too terrifying to discuss. She wanted him to leave, give her time to think. "I'm awfully sleepy." She lay back on the pillow and closed her eyes, remaining in that position until she felt his weight lift from the bed, heard her door close.

She stared into the darkness, replaying the dream in her mind. Every detail remained distinct and vivid. Someone had come into her house, pushed her down the stairs, smothered her—tried to kill her. Had killed her...but she'd come back, angry and determined to stop her killer.

In your dream, she reminded herself, as panic sent her heart racing, turned her skin clammy and damp. *Only in your dream.*

She sat up, turned on the bedside lamp and looked at it. Relief flooded through her. It was similar to the one in her dream, but a little different. Both had crystal bases, but the one she'd wielded and dropped on the stairs in her nightmare had been solid crystal; this one had a marble pedestal.

Only a dream.

She flicked off the light and lay back down, turned her head to the side...and even in the dark of the cloudy night, could see that the lamp on the other side of the bed was missing.

She felt again the hands on her shoulders pushing her downward, the pillow over her face suffocating her, squeezing the life from her.

Nightmare or memory? She had awakened at the foot of the stairs. Had someone pushed her? *Had someone tried to kill her?*

Of course not. Why would anyone want her dead?

She couldn't answer that question, since she couldn't remember anything about her life.

She stood and paced nervously across the room, searching desperately in the corners of her mind, willing the hidden thoughts to surface. But nothing came.

She leaned her forehead wearily against the window, and looked across the yard to the Wallers' house. She used to be able to see right into Rachel Waller's bedroom. She and Rachel had often stood in the dark and passed secret signals—signals even they didn't always understand, but the secrecy from parents was the important part, anyway.

She stepped back, wrapped her arms around her bare shoulders. *No,* she reminded herself. Dylan lived in that house. She'd invented the Wallers. She'd invented Rachel.

She straightened, lifted her head. Dylan had admitted that he lived in Rachel Waller's house.

But she slumped again. That only meant she'd heard the name of the previous owner of the house next door and used it in her fantasy.

Her breath caught in her throat as the curtain in Rachel's room moved. For an instant she thought she saw her friend standing there. Impossible, of course.

She shivered, backed across the room, gave herself a mental shake. Even if someone had been there, she wouldn't have been able to see on this overcast night. Her imagination was running away with her again.

Nevertheless, she moved slowly to the window, approaching it from the side. As though sneaking up on someone, she thought, telling herself how absurdly she was acting. She peered out cautiously, but the curtains across the way were motionless.

Still, she couldn't shake the feeling that someone had been watching her. And not just *someone.* She fancied she had felt Dylan's gaze on her, his eyes the color of the night and just as deep.

She flung herself back into bed, away from the window. But she couldn't get away from the piercing memory of Dylan's gaze or the thrilling memory of his body against hers, his hand on her arm.

Even as she recalled his touch, the dream came back to her—another feeling of strong hands. She shuddered, rebuked herself for even thinking such things. No one had tried to kill her. Certainly not Dylan. He'd helped her. His touch was gentle.

But he had shown a great deal of concern about what she did or didn't remember.

CHAPTER FOUR

In his bedroom Dylan let the curtain fall, stepped back and sank onto the edge of his bed. He drew a hand across his forehead, wiping away the damp beads of perspiration. The room was cool, but first the dream and then Amanda's presence at her window had shaken him.

It was the same nightmare he'd had all his life, and it always took him a while to recover from the horror. But this time was the worst. This time the face had changed to Amanda's at the last minute. It was Amanda who'd lifted her arms from the engulfing waves, her eyes pleading, as though he could help her. The terror, the knowledge of death and finally the look of accusation when he couldn't save her had distorted Amanda's face the way it usually did the unknown woman's.

He'd awakened, gulping for air, sweating profusely, and had vaulted to the window—to see Amanda standing at her window, staring back at him as if she somehow knew his dream, his thoughts, his plans. And possibly she did know the last.

He reached over and turned on the lamp. There was no point in going back to bed. He never slept after the dream.

Dylan headed downstairs to make some coffee. After Phillip left Amanda's house, he would go get some chocolate doughnuts, Amanda's favorite. The pastries had gained him entrance to her house on several mornings, had given him the chance to talk to her, to try to win her trust, to trap her. He'd made progress, he thought. She'd become more friendly, though a part of her had remained aloof.

Thank goodness.

He'd always suspected she felt the attraction between them as strongly as he did, but she'd never given any indication. If she had, he might well have forgotten what he was there for... and he couldn't afford to do that.

Until the events of Sunday, he'd come dangerously close to letting himself be blinded by his desire to trust her, his desire for her. The really crazy part was that, even after Sunday, even after yesterday, he wanted against all the evidence to believe she was sincere. He wanted it more than ever. Overnight she seemed to have developed a new dimension, one that called out to an unexplored dimension inside him.

The memory of her sudden openness and her demure yet blatant sensuality made him wish desperately that their circumstances were different, that he was keeping such close tabs on her for a different reason. But always the memories of Tom's charred body, of his mother screaming, of his father's agony came up to keep him focused on reality.

He peered from his living room, scanned the side of her house. All the windows were dark. There was no sign of activity. She'd gone back to bed...alone, he assumed. He'd seen a light in the spare bedroom earlier. And surely she wouldn't have been watching him from her window if Phillip had been in the same room.

Even knowing the futility of it, he couldn't stop the rise of white-hot fury that came with the thought of Phillip. He forced himself to turn away and head for the kitchen. But the picture of Phillip in his tailor-made business suit with those eyes of shiny, dirty ice pursued him. He hated the man...and he couldn't stand the thought of Amanda sleeping with him.

He snatched up the coffeepot and went to the faucet to fill it. His hands shook, and he ordered himself to get his emotions back under control. But it was tough. Before yesterday he'd seen Phillip only in pictures, from a distance as he watched his house and from the window when Phillip came to see Amanda.

Seeing him so close, being forced to shake his hand, watching him touching Amanda, suspecting that his well-manicured fists had put those bruises on her—he'd had to fight to keep from attacking Phillip on the spot and wiping that condescending smile off his face forever.

And now to think of him in the same bed as Amanda, touching her bare skin...

He wouldn't think about that. It was irrelevant, had nothing to do with the reason he was here.

He shook his head as he poured water into the coffeemaker and cursed his weakness.

As soon as Phillip left with a promise to return that evening, Amanda got up and dressed, then went downstairs. A cup of strong, sweet coffee should go a long way toward clearing the remnants of her nighttime fantasies.

When she stepped onto the landing, however, a shiver ran down her spine, so strong a sensation of doom that she actually turned around in a slow circle, making sure no threat waited in the shadows as it had in her dream.

Shaking off the eerie feeling, she continued on down to the kitchen. She found a can of real coffee, not the instant Phillip had used the night before, but she wasn't up to trying the electric machine and couldn't find a percolator. However, she could always make boiled coffee.

She turned on the fire the way she'd seen Phillip do and set on a saucepan with water and coffee. That accomplished, she relaxed, began to feel a little more normal. This house, at least, was familiar. That was a starting point. Looking around her, she determined to concentrate, to find what she'd lost.

The cabinets, the sink, the icebox, the floor—everything was different, but the room itself was the same. The back door should have a crack in the window, but it didn't, and the screen wasn't rusted. Nevertheless, it still led to the backyard.

She looked out the window, through the gray, misty morning onto a scene of large, unfamiliar trees just beginning to bud. Where her elm tree with the swing had stood were the remnants of a stump. She turned back inside, feeling as though she'd just lost an old friend.

Across the room the door that led to the narrow back stairs sat in the corner looking familiar and welcoming. She crossed to it, opened it and gazed up. The stairs were as dark, forbidding and perversely inviting as ever.

A warm feeling washed over her, and she smiled as she thought of the many times she'd climbed those stairs to the attic, to what she'd always considered her private room. After she'd discovered her own baby furniture stored up there, she'd insisted it was her dolls' room and had gone there to play in spite of the heat in summer and the cold in winter. Then she'd continued to go up there as a teenager to write in her journal. Even after she'd married, she'd left the journal there, sneaking up on her frequent visits home.

She gripped the door handle tightly, excitement surging through her. *The journal!* Would it be where she'd hidden it?

She stepped back, clenching her fists, fighting the insanity of that thought. Of course it wouldn't be there. The journal no more existed than did Elizabeth or any of the others.

But—she allowed some of the excitement to return—she had incorporated a real person, Rachel Waller, into her story. If she had created a memory of hiding something in the attic, maybe it was because Amanda really had hidden something in the attic, the "something" that had been pulling her upstairs last night. She started up, hesitated on the second floor.

Papers. That's what Amanda had hidden. But not in the attic—in the spare bedroom. She almost laughed aloud. She remembered!

She dashed down the hall and yanked open the door... stepped back, her heart sinking. The room bore no resemblance to the bedroom she remembered. It housed a baffling array of items including a big wooden desk, metal cabinets, tables, a small bookcase, strange machines. Stacks of papers covered everything. She almost backed away, confused and intimidated, but instead forced herself to enter, to sit in the chair and pick up a pile of the papers. This was a link to Amanda... her *office,* she realized.

Most of the documents seemed to deal with the antique shop she'd seen in the picture on her dresser. The antique shop she apparently owned. Many were receipts for repairs she'd had done to the house. Finally, though, she found an envelope addressed to Amanda Parrish, postmarked Tulsa, Oklahoma, from Carl and Elaine Parrish. Hesitating, feeling as if she were invading someone else's privacy, she pulled the letter from the open envelope. "Dear Amanda," it began. She flipped to the bottom of the second page. "Love, Mom and Dad."

Amanda's parents were both still alive, though they lived far away in another state.

Tears filled her eyes as she read the breezy, newsy letter, as the picture of the smiling, blond woman who'd written it took shape in her mind. She was very different from

Mama—younger, more independent, more like a friend than a mother. But Amanda adored her. For the first time, she found Amanda inside herself—a small part of Amanda, but the rest must be there somewhere. Happiness mingled with sorrow as she accepted this as the final proof that Elizabeth had never existed.

She read Amanda's letter again, searching for more pieces of her life, but none came. Finally she put it aside, sorted through more items, picked up a large brown envelope and pulled a stack of papers from it.

"In the Matter of the Marriage of Amanda Parrish Ryker, Petitioner, and Phillip Dean Ryker, Respondent." Reading the legal phrases, trying to make sense out of them, she clutched the paper so tightly it wrinkled.

She had divorced *Phillip*. The only reason given was incompatibility.

Dear God, what kind of woman was she?

A horrible, shrieking racket burst through the silence. She jumped, dropping the papers and looking frantically around her. The noise screamed on, incessant and demanding.

Heart racing, she charged down the stairs, following the intensity of the sound to its source in the kitchen, where smoke encompassed the stove.

Dylan heard Amanda's smoke detector begin to shriek as he started out his back door with the box of chocolate doughnuts.

What now?

He raced down the steps into the morning mist. Her door burst open, and she flew out holding her hands over her ears, trailed by a cloud of ugly black smoke.

"Amanda!" She looked up as he called her name, relief flooding her frightened eyes. "What's burning?"

She didn't answer, just shook her head. He thrust the doughnuts into her hands and raced past her into the house.

The smoke seemed to come from a saucepan on the stove. He yanked it off, tossed it in the sink and turned off the flame, then climbed on a chair and turned off the alarm.

From the corner of his eye, he saw her sidle tentatively back into the house. He stepped off the chair and peered into the pan holding the still-smoking remnants of something black and foul smelling. "What in heaven's name was this?" he demanded.

"Boiled coffee," she answered, her voice weak. "What was that noise?"

Boiled coffee? He studied her silently, trying to probe her mind, know what she was really thinking, what she was up to. Finally he pointed upward. "Your smoke detector."

She gave a nervous, embarrassed laugh, set the box of doughnuts on her cabinet, then sank shakily into a chair at the table. "I'd forgotten."

He let that ridiculous assertion pass. "Amanda, why would you make coffee in a saucepan?"

"I didn't feel up to figuring out that machine."

"So you put some water to boil in a pan. Were you planning to strain the grounds through your teeth as you drank it?" He wanted to tell her to give it up, that he didn't believe her, wasn't going to disappear and leave Phillip and her alone.

"You put in an eggshell to settle the grounds," she explained. "Granny taught me. Why don't you believe me?" She surprised him by the bold openness of her question.

He crossed his arms over his chest, regarded her thoughtfully, then turned away without answering. "Come over here and I'll show you how to work this 'machine.'" He wasn't sure if his offer of help was sincere or sarcastic.

She moved to the cabinet and stood beside him, gazing up at him with her heart in her eyes. And that was all part of the deception, he reminded himself sternly. He couldn't let himself be taken in.

But his body was at odds with his intellect. His body wanted to override the controls and respond to the wanting he saw on her face, felt emanating from her as she stood next to him.

He snatched up the coffeepot, leaned over the sink and filled it with water. "Pour it in the top," he said, hoping she'd mistake the gruffness in his voice for irritation with her ploy rather than the irritation he felt with himself.

Amanda had to make a determined effort to concentrate on Dylan's actions and words rather than on his closeness. He pushed out all thought, filled her mind as he filled the room. He was big—tall and muscular, dark and ominous, but something inside her was drawn to him in spite of the aura of danger about him . . . or because of it. Like the Ferris wheel. Like sitting at the top and rocking the seat.

He was talking, his voice low, but she didn't hear the words. Droplets of mist beaded on his raven's-wing hair, his jaw squared firmly below his full lips.

He reached around her to open the pantry, then suddenly stopped, frozen, his face inches from hers, one arm around her as if in an embrace. His eyes widened, then narrowed, dark wells burning from hidden depths. He didn't move, and neither did she. She couldn't. Her body seemed bonded with his.

She ordered herself to turn away, to cover her face and hide her shameful thoughts, but his gaze held her firmly in place as surely as his massive arms could hold her if he so chose. She was a bonfire in an October night, her body blazing from the touch of his body, his gaze. She felt stirrings and desires she knew she had never felt before, certainly not with Blake. Yet they were so familiar. . . .

"Were we lovers?" she whispered, needing desperately to know the answer.

Her words seemed to release him. He moved away, leaned with both hands on the counter and gazed out the window over the sink. His shoulders rose and fell as he took several deep, audible breaths.

"No," he finally said.

For a moment she didn't believe him. He'd been feeling the same things she felt. She knew he had. Yet the single word held no lies.

Still, no matter what he said, no matter what the truth seemed to be, she couldn't shake the feeling that she'd known him a long time, shared a closeness with him.

She moved away from him, from the desires she shouldn't be feeling, and sat down at the table. Primly, she scooted her chair forward as though closing that space would somehow close Dylan out of her mind. But of course it wouldn't. It didn't.

She felt his presence behind her, and knew he had been at his window watching her that morning...because she'd felt the same presence then.

"You put a filter in the basket," he said, his tone harsh. She turned to watch the movements of his big, awkward, tantalizing hands. "You spoon in the grounds, flip this switch and wait for it to brew." From the cabinet, he picked up the cardboard box he'd given her outside and tossed it onto the table in front of her. "Chocolate doughnuts. Your favorite."

With stiff fingers she opened the lid, took out one of the sugary rolls and bit into it. He knew her favorite kind of doughnut. She'd divorced her husband, and this man had moved in next door to her. He watched her bedroom window from his in the early hours of the morning. But they weren't lovers.

"So, when's hubby coming back?" He set two cups of coffee on the table and took a seat across from her.

"Hubby?"

"Excuse me." Sarcasm oozed from the words. "Your ex. Phillip."

She heard both jealousy and enmity in his words, and she was unaccountably thrilled.

"Oh," she said. "He'll be back this evening, after work." She thrust away the feeling of entrapment the idea brought to her.

She lifted her cup to her lips and drank. It was hot and sweet. He knew how she liked her coffee, too.

"Are you going back to work today?" he asked.

Going back to work? Oh, yes. Amanda worked. She owned the antique shop.

"I suppose I should. Who's been minding the shop in my absence?"

"Your assistant, Lottie Timmons, I imagine."

Phillip had mentioned calling Lottie at the shop yesterday. A picture popped into her mind. "Lottie!" she exclaimed in delight, grasping at the memory. "Short, lovely white hair, glasses she won't wear unless she absolutely has to, reads tarot cards, plots horoscopes and makes delicious chocolate fudge." She almost sobbed from happiness. She'd remembered someone, and the memory was a good one. She couldn't wait to see the kind, older woman.

Dylan nodded slowly, extracting a doughnut from the box. "So you're getting your memory back."

Again his voice held an urgent note in spite of the casualness of his actions as he chewed on the sweet roll. He still wasn't sure about her, and for some reason, he needed to be.

"Bits and pieces here and there. I think I should go to work. Maybe that will help me remember." *And I'll be with someone I can trust.*

He nodded, his eyes narrowed, studying her. "Maybe."

"Could you take me there?"

"Take you where?"

"To the shop. I'm afraid I don't know where it is."

"Take you to the shop. Sure, I can do that. I'll let you follow me there, but you'll probably want to take your car so you can come home when you want to."

"I have a car?" she asked in amazement. "I can drive an automobile?" A picture of herself herding a speeding automobile down the street with others zipping around her sent her heart racing, then, just as quickly, she relaxed. Of course she could drive. She'd driven since she was sixteen. She just couldn't quite remember how. "If you'll show me, I'm sure it'll all come back."

Again she saw a flicker of belief in the midst of his usual skepticism. "You don't believe I've forgotten how to drive or who I am, or how to operate the coffee machine," she accused. "Why would I make up something like this?" In her frustration, her voice had risen almost to a shout.

He picked up his coffee and sipped, set down his cup, raised his eyes to meet hers. She could see nothing in them. They were so black that no light reflected from their depths. "Because you're scared." His voice was no louder than a whisper, but she could have heard his words from the other room.

Because you're scared.

Of what? she wanted to shout at him. She didn't, because he was right. She was frightened and wasn't sure she wanted to know *of what.*

"I'll grab my jacket and be back to take you to your shop on my way to work," he said, sliding his chair away from the table.

"Thank you," she murmured, her energy completely drained. She stared after him as he disappeared out the door and down the steps.

Because you're scared. Of him? Of what he might do to her if he thought she remembered? Could he have pushed her down the stairs because of something she knew, something she could no longer remember? The mysterious papers she'd hidden in her office?

She closed the door behind him and leaned against it, drew in a deep breath and tried to reason with herself. Since she'd only dreamed about falling down the stairs, Dylan couldn't have pushed her. She was having enough trouble reclaiming her life. She didn't need to start making up stories about helpful neighbors pushing her downstairs, about hiding journals in her attic and important papers in her office.

Because you're scared. His words whispered through her mind. She raced upstairs as if she could run away from them.

In the safety of her room, she concentrated on selecting an appropriate outfit from the clothes in Amanda's wardrobe. A cream-colored suit and emerald green silk blouse caught her eye, and she changed into them, reminding herself that, since she couldn't find a corset, Amanda probably didn't wear one. No one probably wore them now. Like the bustle, it would be a thing of the past. And a good thing, too. Amanda's clothes were definitely more comfortable than Elizabeth's.

She started down the stairs, then paused, thinking of the attic above her and her journal. The memory was so vivid—maybe she hadn't made up that part. Maybe there really was a journal, one she'd found before. She hesitated, looking longingly upward toward the attic stairs. But Dylan would be arriving any minute. She could search when she returned from the shop.

She turned back, meaning to proceed downstairs, when a glittering on the fourth step, on the ledge outside the banister, caught her eye. She moved to the step, reached around and retrieved the item, nicking her finger in the process. It was glass—a small chunk of broken glass. Crystal, she thought, judging from the weight.

Crystal with one edge broken and the other faceted like she'd seen on the lamp in her dream. But dreams didn't leave behind real, substantial fragments.

CHAPTER FIVE

For a long moment she stared at the piece of crystal, searching its transparent depths, searching the opaque depths of her own mind. At least one part of her fantasies had a base in reality. A crystal lamp had broken on the stairs.

The need to find answers—to discover what was happening, who she was—possessed her with renewed urgency. She lifted a hand to her forehead and pressed as if she could push away the darkness. But both the crystal and her mind guarded their secrets.

A knock on the front door startled her, recalling her to the present, to the fact that Dylan was waiting to take her to her shop. What would he do if he knew what she'd discovered? She didn't dare find out, didn't dare let him know. With shaking fingers she stashed the shard in her handbag and continued downstairs on rubbery legs.

Standing on her front porch in his dark business suit, Dylan almost looked like an ordinary businessman on his way to the office, an innocent, helpful neighbor. But his bottomless eyes weren't innocent. The muscles beneath that jacket weren't innocent. She'd been lifted and carried in those arms as if she were weightless.

She shuddered as she remembered the feel of hands on her shoulders in her dream, the dream about a broken lamp. How easy it would have been for someone of his strength to push her.

"Got your keys?"

She realized he was speaking to her. "Keys?"

"To the car."

For a long moment his gaze held her, asking a thousand unspoken questions, searching for answers she didn't have. Then he blinked, breaking the nebulous contact, and reached around her. She held her breath in fear of the murderous touch from the dream, in anticipation of the thrilling touch only a few minutes before when he'd been making coffee.

But his hand remained a careful hairbreadth away as he pulled the ring of keys from the hook just inside the still-open door. Heart racing from fright and inexplicable, unforgivable desire, she stepped aside, permitting him to close and lock the door.

Without a word he turned and strode away through the mist to the white automobile sitting in the street in front of the house. She hurried to catch up.

He slid a key into the door, then motioned her inside. Tentatively she settled onto the soft seat, searching in the chaos of her mind for the memory of driving. She knew it was there somewhere, but the piece of crystal in her handbag loomed so large it obscured all else.

Dylan went around to the other side, got in and handed her back the ring of keys. His hand touched hers as she took them, and his flesh was warm. Was it the same hand that had sent her tumbling down the stairs? She couldn't stop herself from trying to compare the two, trying to determine if Dylan was her would-be murderer or lover or both.

"Amanda?"

She jumped at the sound of his voice. "What?"

"I said, put the key in the ignition."

"Uh..." She knew where the ignition was, if she could just remember, if she could just stop thinking about the lamp shattering against the stair rail, leaving a broken piece for her to find....

"Here." She gasped as his hand suddenly covered hers. With a firm but surprisingly gentle grip, he guided her hand, shoved a key into a slot beneath the steering wheel. "Turn it and give the car some gas. Put your foot on the pedal on the right."

She did as he said, twisted the key, shrieked and jumped when it made a grinding noise.

He reached over and turned the engine off, then handed her the keys. "You're in no condition to drive. I'll take you." He slid out of the car and slammed the door behind him.

She had to agree with his assessment. She wanted to remember how, knew she could, if only she could concentrate, but right now the thought of that piece of broken crystal in her handbag, of someone trying to kill her, filled her mind, pushed everything else aside.

"Come on," he said brusquely, holding her door open. She climbed out.

His car, parked in the street a few yards ahead of hers, loomed black and big and ominous...rather like Dylan, she thought. Though it was now familiar, she approached it with as much trepidation as the day before. When she was closed inside with him, she'd be entirely at his mercy. If he'd tried to kill her once, would he try it again? Her heart pounded painfully against her ribs.

Yet when he opened the door and stepped back, she slid in unresistingly, the way a prisoner might step up to the guillotine without protest, knowing there was no escape, resigned to his fate.

She stared straight ahead through the windshield as he slid into the car seat beside her. When he made **no** movement toward starting the car, she turned to look at him, expecting to meet his glowering stare. But he was regarding her curiously, the corners of his mouth tilted slightly upward in a sardonic smile.

"You seem a little more comfortable about the prospect of riding with me today than yesterday," he said. "You aren't gripping the dash, and your knuckles aren't white."

Almost against her will, certainly against her better judgment, she smiled back, a real smile, and relaxed into the soft leather seat. She didn't really know anything about this man, had reason to doubt her safety around him, but she had a horrifying suspicion that he could compel her to ride to the ends of the earth with him if he so chose.

He started the automobile and pulled away from the curb. "It must be tough, losing your memory, not knowing who you are, where you're going." Was he being sarcastic or offering an obscure apology for doubting her? Somewhere in between, she suspected.

"It's very disconcerting," she admitted, then amended, "It's terrifying."

He nodded, looking genuinely sympathetic for a moment, but then the granite mask fell into place again. "Sometimes it's harder to remember than to forget. You still don't remember how you ended up on the floor, bruised and battered?"

She clutched the edge of the seat, the tension returning. Was he asking if she recalled the broken lamp? The man in the shadows? Was he suggesting she had something she wanted to forget? Or that he himself wanted to forget something?

"No," she answered, afraid to say more for fear he'd hear the lie in her words.

His jaw clenched as if he had heard it anyway. "You don't need to be frightened. If you remember something, tell me. I'll take care of you."

She bit her lip, wanting to clutch at the words, feel secure that he could and would care for her. But she forced herself to tamp down that desire. With the anger in his voice and on his face, his promise sounded almost like a threat...though she sensed that not all the anger was directed at her.

"Amanda?"

"Yes. Yes, I'll tell you if I remember anything," she said, lying again.

He directed a quick, scrutinizing sideways look at her. "Do you still think you're some Victorian woman?"

"Victorian?" She repeated the word, examining the images it elicited.

"Women who lived around the turn of the century. They were pretty different from women today." He seemed to be talking as much to himself as to her. "More sheltered, more vulnerable, more dependent."

"Are you saying I'm different now?"

He pulled the car over to the side of the street and parked in front of a shop she recognized from the picture. Amanda's Antiques. For a moment she thought he was going to get out of the car without answering her, but he shifted in his seat and faced her.

His gaze stroked her from head to toe, stripping away her clothes, her very body down to her soul. The first layer of nakedness felt tantalizing, but the second was chilling. He lifted a hand, reached toward her as if he would touch her face, then abruptly pulled back and fumbled with the door handle instead.

"You're acting different than before," he said without looking at her. He slid from the car, away from her.

She watched his suit-clad figure as he came around to let her out. *Acting,* he'd said, unwilling to admit whoever or whatever she was could be real. His actions toward her were as contradictory and inexplicable as her feelings for him.

Climbing out, she stood beside him on the sidewalk. "What was I like before . . . before yesterday?"

He gazed at her a long time as if searching for a hidden meaning behind the question. "I didn't know you very well," he finally said. "You kept to yourself a lot. The divorce, I guess. But sometimes I thought we were . . . friends." He suddenly frowned, as if irritated with himself. "Are you ready to go inside?"

Friends? No, she didn't think so. With what she felt between them, they could be lovers or they could be enemies, but not friends.

His hand at the small of her back urged her forward.

She felt better the moment she entered the shop. The bell over the door jingled a welcome. She paused in the doorway, basking in the familiar sights and smells—the solid furniture, the lamps with crystal pendants or painted globes, the scents of wood and lemon oil, the faint floral aroma from baskets of potpourri. A blissful feeling reached her on two levels . . . the furniture that was familiar to Elizabeth as well as the shop Amanda had chosen and filled with things that appealed to her.

Lottie—Amanda recognized her instantly—bustled in from the back room. She squinted, then clapped her hands together, lips curving up in a smile.

"Amanda! I was so worried when Phillip told me you'd hurt yourself. But you look just wonderful." Lottie pulled out a high-backed wooden chair from a rectangular table with a white enamel top that sat in one corner. "Now you sit down right here. Don't exert yourself. I'll make you some nice tea. You must be Dylan, the neighbor who paints." She extended a hand toward him. "I'm Lottie Timmons, Amanda's assistant. Do you take anything in your tea? I have some lovely jam cookies. Sit right here. I'll be back in a jiffy. This won't take a minute. The water's already hot."

Amanda sank into a chair and looked up at Dylan. He blinked, then relaxed and grinned. "Is she always like that?"

"Not always but often," Amanda answered, smiling at Dylan's expression as much as at her returning memories of Lottie. This was the first time she could recall seeing him so at ease, his guard down. He was even more attractive this way, more compelling.

The older woman returned almost staggering under the weight of a tray holding a china teapot with a delicate pattern of roses, matching cups and saucers, and a plate of cookies.

"Here, let me help you," Dylan exclaimed, striding over to take the burden from her.

"Aren't you the nicest young man." She took her own seat at the table as Dylan set the tray down. "We'll let this steep for five minutes, and it'll be just perfect. It's a new blend, Amanda. Very light. I know you don't like those heavy teas. Now tell me about your accident. Are you really all right?"

Dylan sat forward, no longer relaxed. In the abrupt, unexpected silence, Amanda was acutely aware of the two intent gazes trained on her, waiting for her answer. Though Lottie's eyes were as light as Dylan's were dark, they were equally keen.

"Well, uh, I guess I...fell down the stairs." She lifted her hair off her forehead. "I got a couple of bruises, but Dylan took me to a doctor. He said I was fine." Lottie's expression didn't change. Amanda could tell she somehow knew there was more to the story.

She took a deep, fortifying breath and continued. "The bump on my head caused a little problem. I have a kind of amnesia. It's not total, at least not anymore. I just have holes in my memory. Things are coming back gradually, but..." She tried to smile, to minimize the "little problem" that changed her whole world. "But there are still parts of Amanda Parrish missing."

Lottie studied her quietly, then turned her attention to the teapot. She poured the steaming liquid into dainty cups and served the three of them. Amanda sipped her tea gratefully. Lottie was right. It was just the kind she liked—hot and light. She reached for a jam cookie. They were very similar to the kind Mama always served with tea.

Lottie sat back, sipped her own drink and shook her head. "No," she said. "That doesn't seem right. Your aura's so bright today, so dense. You have more, not less."

"More what?" Amanda whispered the words. She studied Dylan from the corner of her eye, but he only looked puzzled, his broad forehead wrinkled.

"I don't know. Just more. More life. More of you. It's almost like you have a double aura, but there's no division between the two, no war of souls going on. It's just brighter, has more light, more depth. Goodness, you must be able to feel it, something this significant." Lottie munched a cookie, as comfortable with her strange observation as if they'd been discussing the weather.

Amanda's hand trembled as she raised her cup to her lips. Lottie was talking nonsense, babbling about psychic phenomena as she was wont to do. But this time her words made a frightening kind of sense.

Amanda felt like there *was* more of her; she had two people inside her body. She felt in her heart that she was Elizabeth, but she knew in her mind that she was Amanda. Was Lottie wrong about one thing? Were there two souls warring for her body? If so, then Elizabeth was obviously the invader. She'd seen irrefutable proof that this tall, blond body belonged to Amanda.

Dylan listened to Lottie's bizarre words, watched Amanda's reactions. It was becoming harder and harder to doubt her sincerity. It was possible she really did have some amnesia, especially after the trauma of her injuries. Even so, he couldn't be sure of the degree or how long it would last. In his position, he had to assume the worst, couldn't afford to let anything slide by him. Now he even had to question Lottie's part in all this. She could be Amanda's accomplice, deliberately trying to divert him.

He decided to turn Lottie's words against her, see what she did then. "So you don't think she really has amnesia?"

"Dear me, no, I didn't say that," Lottie protested.

"Then I don't think I quite understand what you mean."

"Why, I don't know. You'll have to ask Amanda. I can only see the outside evidence of what's going on inside. Do have another cookie. I don't care what those boring people say, I think a little sugar and caffeine get one off to a good start in the morning."

He turned his attention back to Amanda and found her looking away from him, around the shop. Her gaze finally stopped on something in the opposite corner. She rose as if in a trance and moved across the room, a slim, fragile figure weaving among the dressers, tables, lamps and other items toward an old spinet piano.

Her walk, her body sway were subtly different. The contemporary suit she wore seemed out of place. In a long gown with puffed sleeves and corseted waist she'd look at home among the antiques. He had to fight an odd yearning to go to her, draw her into his arms. . . .

"It's Rachel's!" she exclaimed delightedly, plunking an out-of-tune piano key, interrupting his own strange trance. Damn! He was letting her crazy story get to him. "Where did you get Rachel's piano?" She bent to examine it more closely. "Here's the scratch on the leg where she whacked it with the broom handle. She hated to take lessons and..."

She stopped and looked over at him, then at Lottie, her expression fearful. For an instant his heart went out to her. No matter if she was lying or not, it was still possible—he wanted it to be possible—that she was a victim, caught in a web of circumstances not entirely of her own doing.

"I'm sorry," she mumbled, stumbling back to her chair. "The accident... I still get a little confused."

She looked so damned helpless, so unlike herself. He wanted to rush to her aid, lift her in his arms and soothe her, carry her away from the circumstances that had put them both in this position.

He clenched his jaw. That was illogical, emotional thinking and wouldn't get him anywhere. He had a job to do here, a mission to accomplish. She hadn't given him any reason to believe in her. Quite the contrary.

Amanda picked up a cookie, broke it in half, then broke it again. She couldn't bring herself to put the dry crumbs into her dry mouth. Damn it! She hadn't felt confused. She'd recognized the piano, remembered Rachel's tantrum quite clearly, remembered helping her friend rub the scratch with walnut meats to try to hide it.

"You seem confused about a lot of things." Dylan leaned forward, cradling the delicate cup in his big hands. If he exerted just the tiniest bit of pressure, he would surely crush the thin china.

"I don't know about the scratch on the leg, but that piano came from Rachel Waller's estate," Lottie exclaimed in defense of Amanda.

"Rachel's estate." The words hit hard, reminded Amanda that the vibrant young woman she remembered as though it were yesterday was dead. She must have known where the piano came from, woven the facts into her delusion. That was the logical explanation. "Did I know Rachel?"

"Oh, I doubt it. She died several years ago. But her house is right next door to yours. That's where you live now, isn't it, Dylan? I'm amazed they ever rented to you. So many heirs, and they can't agree on anything. She didn't leave a will, and she never married, so of course there were no children, but the cousins converged from every direction."

"Rachel never married? But she was so pretty. She had so many beaux."

No one said anything for a long moment.

Well, there, she'd dropped another conversation stopper. Was she ever going to quit doing this? She crammed the crumbled cookie into her mouth, washed it down with the now-tepid tea.

"You sound like you knew her personally," Lottie said, her voice oddly quiet and contemplative.

"You just said the woman died before Amanda moved here." Dylan turned to Amanda, his dark eyes riveting, demanding. "Unless you visited her before she died."

"Not likely," Lottie answered for her. "Rachel Waller was a recluse for most of her life. We used to talk about her when we were children. We said she must be a witch, that the only time she came outside was at night. People said you could hear her crying and moaning sometimes, but it was probably only the wind."

Happy, vivacious Rachel a recluse? Going out only at night? Crying and moaning?

"Why?" The word came out a croak. Amanda cleared her throat and tried again. "Did they say why? What happened to her?"

"There were lots of stories, of course. Some said she had a lover who left her or died. My mother always maintained she never stopped grieving for her best friend, the girl who lived in your house, Amanda. For some reason she blamed herself for her friend's death."

Amanda's breath caught in her throat. She grasped Lottie's arm. "Who was her best friend? What was her name? Who lived in my house before me?"

Lottie looked startled, blinked several times. She set her cup down and placed her hand over Amanda's. "It's been so long," she said, her voice soothing as though she recognized the urgency of Amanda's question. "I don't remember. It was a pretty name, a foreign name."

Amanda heard Dylan suck in his breath, felt his fiery gaze on her flesh.

She leaned closer to Lottie. "Dupard?" she asked, softly. "Was her name Dupard?"

"Why, yes, that's it. Elizabeth Dupard. I always thought that was a lovely name. When I was a little girl, we'd play that we were Rachel and Elizabeth—we didn't have video games then, you know—and Elizabeth always came to a tragic end. I preferred to play Elizabeth. I was sure she was as beautiful as her name, and besides, dying young sounds so romantic when you're ten years old."

"When did she die? How did she die?" Amanda realized she was squeezing Lottie's arm. She loosened her grip, clenched her hands in her lap.

"I don't know, dear," Lottie said. "Maybe an illness. They didn't have all these miracle drugs in those days, and a lot of people died young."

"But there must have been talk, like there was about Rachel. They must have wondered why Rachel blamed herself."

Lottie laced and unlaced the fingers of her small hands, obviously distressed with the intense turn the conversation had taken. "People love to gossip, of course. The theories ranged from Elizabeth being locked out in a snowstorm with

Rachel not hearing her cries and letting her freeze to death, all the way to the lurid type, like Elizabeth stealing Rachel's boyfriend and dying in childbirth. Most versions involved a man, somebody's lover."

"So you must have heard the rumors." At the sound of Dylan's voice, Amanda turned slowly to look at him. "That's where you got the information for your own story."

"Yes," she agreed reluctantly. "I must have." None of the wild conjectures Lottie related rang a bell, but she didn't argue.

"I guess that's possible," Lottie said, "but those stories died out a long time before old Rachel's death, and she's been gone six or seven years."

"Somebody probably told Amanda something when she bought the piano," Dylan suggested, his eyes remaining locked with Amanda's though he was speaking to Lottie.

Amanda would have liked to believe it, too. That would mean she was normal, just a little muddled from the fall, confusing things she'd heard with things she'd experienced.

But it didn't feel right, and Lottie was shaking her head as she poured more tea into all three cups. "The piano was part of the inventory when she bought this shop. The heirs had to sell off most of the furniture to pay Rachel's burial expenses."

Amanda's eyes misted at the sad picture Lottie painted of her former friend. *The woman she'd fantasized as her friend,* she reminded herself, but her eyes were suddenly brimming with tears anyway. She knew on a rational level that she'd never known Rachel Waller, but she *remembered* her, remembered their closeness, their laughter, their dreams.

Dropping her gaze to her hands, which were twisted around her cup, she blinked rapidly to clear the moisture from her eyes and the foolish notions from her head.

As she looked up again, she saw Dylan watching her, his features softened. He reached a hand across the table toward her, then, as though recollecting himself, changed his look to a scowl, withdrew his hand and pushed his chair back from the table.

"I'd better get on to work," he said gruffly. "Thanks for the tea. I'll pick you up about five, Amanda."

He stalked out the door. The bell jangled behind him. Through the shop window she followed his progress as he strode powerfully, purposefully through the mist to his black car with never a backward glance.

And while it made no sense, his going left an emptiness. She should have been glad to be rid of his distrust, his suspicions, his perpetual questions. But what she felt as he drove away was the loss of someone to whom she was mysteriously but undeniably tied even though she couldn't deny the possibility that he'd tried to harm her. Someone who, her heart told her, had been a part of her life through good and evil for a long time.

Even as the car vanished from sight, she knew he'd be back, knew their business wasn't finished.

If they hadn't been lovers, what had they been to each other?

CHAPTER SIX

Amanda jumped in sudden fright as she felt hands on her shoulders, but these hands were small and gentle. "What's wrong, Elizabeth? What's happening?"

"I don't know." Belatedly it hit her. Fearfully, excitedly, she looked up at Lottie. "Why did you call me Elizabeth?"

"Did I?" Lottie frowned thoughtfully. "How odd. All this talk about Rachel Waller and her friend, I suppose. You finish your tea now, and I'll tidy up. Mrs. Arnold should be in about eleven to decide which wardrobe she wants. I certainly hope she takes that big walnut one. We could use the space."

"Please," Amanda asked, "talk to me for a few more minutes. You're the first person I've felt comfortable with since all this started, the first person who doesn't seem to think I'm completely mad."

Lottie sat beside her and patted her hand. "Poor dear. Of course you're not crazy. Any time people don't understand something, instead of just accepting and believing, they have to find some way to explain it. Thinking that person is insane is a very handy method."

Amanda grinned wryly. "But I'm one of those people who think I must be mad."

"Not a bit of it. Let me brew up another pot, and you tell me all about it."

Amanda clutched the woman's arm as she started to leave. She couldn't accept Lottie's understanding without telling her everything, the worst. "Lottie, when I woke up yesterday morning, I thought I was Elizabeth Dupard." She swallowed hard. "I still think I am, even when I know better."

Lottie nodded slowly, as if Amanda had just confirmed something. "That opens up some intriguing possibilities. I'll just be a minute."

Amanda knew the only rational "possibility" for her delusions, but she sat straighter in her chair, waited hopefully for Lottie to return and offer an explanation other than insanity.

The older woman came back shortly with fresh tea and listened without comment as Amanda told of her strange tangle of memories and lack of memories. But not even to Lottie did she confide about her dream and the fragment of crystal in her handbag. She needed to think about that further, try to figure out where the dream ended and reality began.

"Phillip could be right," her assistant concluded. "You were obsessed with that old house from the minute you saw it. Harriet—your realtor—told me you were dragging furniture down from the attic the first time she showed the place to you."

Amanda nodded slowly, images settling into position like family members returning home. She'd known the minute she walked in the door exactly how the house should look.

Lottie sipped her tea, then set the cup back onto its saucer with a delicate clink. "Then you bought this shop and, oh, my, you had quite a time finding more furniture for your house. You'd get in your head exactly how a piece ought to look, then turn the countryside upside down till you found what you wanted. Do you remember that?"

Amanda nodded slowly as a collage of images flashed through her mind. "Sort of." She picked up her own cup...not so much to drink as to hold onto the solid feel of something she knew was real.

"Then again," Lottie continued, her gaze never flickering, "Phillip's theory could be all wrong. You could be Elizabeth Dupard reincarnated. That would explain how you knew so much about furnishing the house."

An invisible force punched Amanda in the stomach, jerked her upright to full attention. *Reincarnation.* The idea was absurd, of course. It ranked right up there with ghosts and seances. But...

Amanda studied the older woman intently. Lottie wasn't joking. Nor did she even appear to think the idea was a little offbeat. Her tone and expression were matter-of-fact and placid.

"Maybe being in the house where you used to live started tugging on the past, then you fell and that bump on the head scrambled the memories of two lifetimes. We only use a tiny portion of our brain. Who knows what lies hidden in the rest of it? Maybe you just accessed some of those hidden memories. Maybe you need them for some reason."

Amanda opened her mouth to protest, but somehow the words stuck in her throat. "What reason?" she asked instead, setting her cup carefully back onto the tray, no longer certain of the reality of even the smooth china.

"Well, I don't know. You'd be the one to answer that question. Elizabeth may have had some unfinished business, since she died so young. Maybe you were headed in the wrong direction and wouldn't have got things right this time, either. We have to come back again and again until we finally get it right, you know."

Amanda's logical mind rebelled at the outrageous idea. Of course she wasn't the reincarnation of Elizabeth Dupard. She'd doubtless heard bits and pieces of the life of the woman who'd lived in her house before her, and her imagination had filled in the details.

But as surely as she knew on a rational level that she wasn't Elizabeth Dupard, in her heart she still felt that she had lived as Elizabeth.

With a shiver, she remembered the first time she'd seen Phillip yesterday. As he'd walked across the yard toward her, for an instant he'd seemed to resemble Blake, one form superimposed over the other like a double image. If she were Elizabeth...

She gave herself a mental shake. She was Amanda, and Phillip was Phillip.

"Are you all right?" Lottie asked, leaning toward her.

"Yes. Yes, I'm fine." Amanda drew shaky fingers across her forehead, trying to wipe away the irrational thoughts. "Why did I divorce Phillip?" she asked.

Lottie sat back, a look of concern on her usual cheerful face. "You said you'd both changed and grown in different directions. You no longer had anything in common."

She remembered Phillip's insistence that she go home with him, his possessive attitude toward her. "Did he fight the divorce? Did he want me back?"

"If he fought the divorce, you never mentioned it. He came in here a couple of times with papers for you to sign. You were always polite to each other. To tell you the truth, I wondered why you ever got married in the first place. I didn't sense any passion, good or bad."

Amanda was reminded of the way she'd felt like a sawdust doll in his arms. "What did you think about him?"

Lottie actually looked uncomfortable for half a second. But she faced Amanda squarely. "His aura isn't clear. I can't read him. Just like Dylan. I think I like that young man, but he's hiding something. You be careful of the both of them."

Cold enveloped Amanda at Lottie's warning, the confirmation of her own nebulous fears.

The bell over the door jingled, startling her. An elderly, dignified lady made her entrance. "My lands, this weather is really nasty," she exclaimed.

"Mrs. Arnold," Lottie said in greeting. "Come over and have a cup of tea and some of my blackberry-jam cookies."

Amanda spent the rest of the day assisting customers and discovered that she possessed an astonishing knowledge of the inventory of the shop, though she wasn't sure why. Because Amanda had acquired the knowledge from others or because Elizabeth knew about the furniture from having lived with many pieces from that period?

Her memories were beginning to run together, and she couldn't determine which belonged to her fantasy of Elizabeth and which belonged to Amanda. Logically, she knew that should be comforting. She was returning to herself, to Amanda. She might very easily wake up in the morning and realize that she'd invented Elizabeth. That would solve a lot of problems, should be a real relief.

But, emotionally, she didn't want to lose Elizabeth. She didn't want to "die."

Lottie had left for the day, and Amanda was explaining the intricacies of a Victorian music box when the doorbell jingled. Every nerve in her body suddenly came alert, and she knew without looking up that Dylan had entered the shop. His force reached across the room and touched her as surely as it had the night before, when she'd stood at her window.

She concluded the sale, deliberately focusing her attention on the customer until the door closed behind the woman. Finally she turned and looked at Dylan.

He stood with arms folded across his chest, watching her. During the day she'd begun to feel at ease, safe in this one area of her life. His presence took that away and put her off balance again, made every fiber—every cell—alert, awake and expectant.

"Ready?" he asked.

She nodded, closed up the shop and followed him outside. The sun had finally emerged about noon and now shone brightly. As they walked toward his car, he touched the small of her back lightly, casually, and her breath caught in her throat. The contact didn't feel casual. It was two opposite poles connecting, a linking that allowed energy to flow between them. She heard his sharp intake of breath and knew he felt it, too. For a moment he didn't move, his hand attached to her body as if by magnetic force.

Then he turned away—angrily, it seemed—and without a word, opened the car door for her.

He wanted to avoid the attraction between them, pretend it didn't exist. Why? What did he know about her that she didn't?

Inside the automobile, with a safe space between them, he finally spoke, his tone even, conversational. "You sounded very knowledgeable, talking to that lady about the music box."

She started to tell him it was almost identical to one Papa had given Mama, so she had reason to be knowledgeable, but she swallowed the words. If she didn't understand this world, she was at least learning to survive in it.

"It's a type I know about," she replied ambiguously.

He pulled away from the curb, merged into traffic. "I guess it really is pretty easy to get wrapped up in the past when you live in one of these old houses. They do tend to kind of pull you back in time."

His statement came out of nowhere. He sounded friendly, almost apologetic. And for no sane reason, that lifted her spirits immeasurably.

"Since I moved next door," he continued when she didn't respond, "I've noticed an influence on my painting. I guess our surroundings play a part in what we think and how we feel. I can see how it would be disconcerting to wake up in that atmosphere after a scary experience like falling downstairs."

The sunlight seemed to grow brighter, to seep inside her. "What kind of an influence?" she asked, grasping at the piece of himself he'd offered, admitting to herself that she yearned to talk to him, to reach out to him, to feel him reaching for her . . . solidify that eerie bond between them.

"My paintings have taken on a more ominous tone. Even my subjects are different. I paint storms now where I used to paint sunny days. I've had the same nightmare all my life. I hate it, yet suddenly I've felt compelled to paint a gruesome picture of it."

"You think that comes from living in Rachel's house?"

For only an instant she saw a nightmare in his eyes, and she didn't think this one came while he was sleeping. Instinctively she reached to touch his arm. Then, as abruptly as it had come, the tortured look was gone, the curtained expression back. She started to draw away, unsure if her gesture of comfort would be accepted . . . and she couldn't stand for it to be rejected.

He covered her hand with one of his for a fleeting, ecstatic instant. Warmth surged upward, bringing a delighted flush to her face even as she marveled that it took so little from this man to make her happy.

But then she felt him pulling back again, and the air around them grew cooler. She snatched her hand away.

"Is Phillip coming over tonight?" he asked, his tone flat and cold. His antipathy toward Phillip filled the car, driving the sunshine out of the automobile.

"He said he would," she answered, fighting down the disappointment that rose so sharply with his sudden change.

"For an ex-husband, he certainly has a proprietary attitude toward you."

She couldn't deny that. She'd noticed it, too. "Did you know him? Before the accident, I mean," she asked, searching for some basis for the intense dislike Dylan so obviously felt for Phillip.

"I've seen him at your house a couple of times."

It didn't sound like a lie, but it didn't have the ring of total truth, either.

"You're a lucky lady," he continued in an apparent change of subject. "That's a big staircase. You could have suffered some real injuries. Did you fall all the way from the top or trip farther down?"

"From the top." The words came out of her mouth before she realized she was reporting the dream, not what she knew as fact.

The way his eyes narrowed and his jaw hardened told her immediately she'd given the wrong answer.

"So you remember now."

Had she just admitted to her would-be murderer, while trapped in a moving car with him, that she remembered his attempt on her life?

"No," she denied, answering both the question he'd asked and the one she feared he was asking. She looked away from him as she spoke, hating the breathless way the single word came out. Her heart pounded wildly as her eyes darted about the car, vainly seeking an escape.

"If you don't remember, then why did you say you fell from the top?" His voice was quiet and logical . . . and terrifying in its normalcy.

"I don't know why I said that. It just came out. I don't remember. Truly, I don't." She waited tensely for his next action. How could she have let her guard down so he could trap her like that?

"Well, I see your ex-husband is waiting for you," Dylan said, and she saw that her house was just ahead, that Phillip was leaning against her car.

Very possibly, she thought as Dylan pulled up to the curb in front of Rachel's house and stopped, this man she had divorced had just saved her life.

She opened the door and scrambled out before Dylan could come around.

Phillip's pale eyes glittered like silvery mirrors in the sunlight, following her path as she moved toward him, and she suddenly felt trapped between them. She didn't fear Phillip as she did Dylan, but his presence made her feel suffocated. She didn't want to be with him.

"I'll be over to get you in the morning." Dylan's voice came from behind her. Quiet, resonant and definite, it burned through her.

She hesitated, turning back. "Thank you for taking me," she said, laboring futilely to keep her tone polite and calm. Even to her own ears she sounded breathless . . . and she wasn't at all sure if it came from fear or the sudden surge of desire he always seemed to bring to the surface.

"My pleasure," he said, returning her politeness. But his was as strained as hers. His eyes, his voice, the way he stood, all exuded raging passion—passion to kill her or touch her? She couldn't tell. Maybe both.

At the moment, anyway, Phillip seemed the safer of the two men. She turned and ran toward him.

Her gratitude was short-lived. As soon as they were inside the house, he grabbed her arm, twisting it, forcing her to face him.

Panic surged through her as memories crowded back... but not memories of Phillip. The hand clutching her arm seemed to belong to Blake.

He shook her, and she realized he was talking.

"Where did you go with him? Did you spend the day together? Where's he taking you tomorrow? Every time I see you, he's around. What does he want from you?"

Through a haze of fear and confusion she heard the words, tried to make sense of them, tried to determine if Phillip or Blake was saying them.

She fell to her knees before him, her free hand going up to protect her face. Blake liked to hit her in the face, leave bruises so everyone would know he could control his wife.

His fingers on her arm tightened as he tried to pull her to her feet, but she slumped into a dead weight, refused to make it easy for him. She strained harder to reach the floor, to make herself into a ball. He was saying something to her, but she wouldn't answer, wouldn't give him the satisfaction. It didn't matter anyway. Whatever she said, he'd hear only what he wanted to hear.

Tears of pain and rage and fright started from her eyes, but she fought against them, refused to cry *ever again*. His power fed on her fear, her weakness.

"Amanda!" With both hands he yanked her head up to face him. She closed her eyes to keep him from seeing her terror, but the hateful tears oozed between her lids, betraying her.

Suddenly his hands were no longer hurtful, but stroked her tentatively instead. "Amanda?"

The name reached inside her. Amanda. She was Amanda. Not Elizabeth. This was Phillip, not Blake. Blake had hurt

her, beaten her, but Phillip hadn't. Trying to orient herself
to the present, she raised her face, confronted his puzzled
gaze as he knelt on the floor in front of her.

"I'm sorry." He sounded confused and oddly uncertain
as he offered her a silk handkerchief. "I don't know what
came over me. It was like I was somebody else. I didn't
mean to make you cry. You've always been so... you never
cry. I've never seen you cry."

"I'm not crying," she protested, ignoring the handkerchief, restraining herself from wiping the tears away because that would be an admission that they existed.

"I'm sorry," he repeated, decisiveness returning to his
voice. "I've been waiting for you for over an hour, wondering where you could be when your car was right here. I
was worried about you. Maybe I was jealous when I saw you
drive up with him. It seems like he's always hanging around,
more than just a neighbor."

From somewhere inside, an impulse stirred for her to rise
to her feet, tell Phillip that what she'd been doing was none
of his business. But she bit back the rush of defiance. It
wouldn't be right. He was... had been... her husband.

"I couldn't remember how to drive. Dylan took me to the
shop then picked me up. That's all." *That's all...* Except his
touch—even his gaze—set her ablaze with desires and
wantings that scorched her soul and shocked her when she
thought about it later. He frightened her and excited her,
and no matter what he said, she knew they'd been more than
friends.

Phillip rose slowly and drew her to her feet. "You
couldn't drive? You really are suffering some ill effects from
your accident, aren't you?" Again he sounded uncertain—
a rarity for him, she suspected.

"I'm doing much better," she told him as he urged her
toward the sofa in the parlor.

But he shook his head as he sat beside her and took both her hands in his. "You haven't been acting like yourself. You seem so... defenseless."

Defenseless? Well, wasn't she? What possible defense did a woman have against a man? She'd had no defense against Blake when he turned cruel after their marriage. She'd been his wife, and he'd had the right to hurt her if she displeased him. Men were bigger, stronger. Even the law was on their side.

"Let me take care of you," Phillip urged.

"I'm all right," she assured him.

His lips thinned into a half smile. "But I'm not. I miss you. And when I saw you drive up with another man... Darling, I'm so sorry. You know I'd never hurt you. I was insane with jealousy. Please come back home, and let's try again to make our marriage work. I'll do whatever it takes."

She studied him intently for a minute. After Lottie's description of their divorce, this was the last thing she would have expected. Insane jealousy? Wanting her back no matter what it took?

Still, the idea of being divorced had bothered her. Maybe Amanda could divorce her husband, but Elizabeth had a hard time accepting the idea. Whatever had happened to cause Amanda to divorce him, Phillip wanted to make it right. Whatever it was, he hadn't beaten her the way Blake had; she felt certain of that.

Lottie's peculiar idea rose to the front of her mind. She had said people reincarnated, came back to earth again and again until they "got it right." Was this what she needed to get right, what Phillip needed to get right? She hadn't been happy with Blake and now she'd divorced Phillip. Both marriages had gone wrong.

Of course, she didn't believe any of that nonsense, but if her husband wanted her back, she should go. That was her duty, wasn't it? A woman married for better or worse...forever. This man had been her husband. He cared about her, wanted to take care of her. A simple lack of feeling couldn't have been all that bad.

"No. I can't." She blinked in surprise as the words came out of her mouth. Even so, she knew she had spoken the truth. She couldn't go back to him . . . at least not yet.

Though Phillip's expression didn't really change, it seemed to harden. His grip on her hands tightened imperceptibly.

"I can't right now," she temporized. "How can we work things out when I don't remember what went wrong? Why did we get a divorce? Why do you suddenly want me back?"

He released her hands and leaned back, looking not at her but into empty space. "Yes," he agreed, "you're right. We should discuss it. I knew I had to have you back when I came out here, found the door broken down and feared that something had happened to you. I knew then how important you are to me. But I'm not sure I can tell you exactly why we got a divorce. It was for a lot of reasons. I spent too much time at work. Our interests changed. We didn't communicate enough." He refocused on her. "But that's in the past. We can work it out. Just give me a chance." His words were passionate, but his eyes were pale and distant, the reflective mirrors she'd seen earlier in the sunlight.

"Please," she said, "give me a little time. I promise to— to reconsider . . . us, our marriage."

He stood abruptly, smoothing the creases from his suit. "Okay. I guess I'll have to settle for that for right now. Where would you like to go for dinner?"

"I don't want to go to dinner," she said, bristling at the way he took her acquiescence for granted, then automatically cringing when she realized she'd defied him.

He looked at her curiously but made no move to harm her. He wasn't Blake, she reminded herself—if Blake had ever actually existed.

"Then I'll go pick up something and bring it back here," he replied.

"I'm not very hungry. There's so much going on. I'd like to stay home tonight, alone."

"Alone." He raised one eyebrow, making the word a question.

"Alone," she repeated. "I need a chance to think, to sort things out." To deal with the memories that deluged her— memories of having been abused.

Finally he left, and when he walked out the door, out of her house, relief washed over her. She'd agreed to have dinner with him the following evening, though perhaps not for the reason he seemed to want. She needed to see him. He could give her more pieces of Amanda.

She stood on her porch and waved as he drove away, then turned to go back inside. But she froze halfway. Next door Dylan sat on his own porch in front of an easel, apparently absorbed in his painting.

He'd been watching her again. She wasn't sure of many things right now, even her own identity. But she was certain of that one thing—he'd been watching her again with those eyes like deep wells that beckoned her to dive in...to drown.

She darted inside, locking the door behind her, pulling all the curtains closed. Even then she fancied she could still feel that dark gaze on her, piercing her, drawing her to him, and she had to fight an impulse to open the curtains wide and let it in.

Dylan watched the curtains closing, watched Amanda shutting him out. He laid his paints down, ceasing any pretense of work. What was she doing in there that she didn't want him to know about?

Phillip had left after a surprisingly short time, and with his going, some of the tension had eased. When he'd seen Phillip standing beside her car, when she'd run to him, he'd barely been able to restrain himself from rushing over there, from grasping Phillip's throat and squeezing until he saw the life leave those unnatural eyes.

He clenched his fist and had to resist smashing his canvas in frustration. He didn't try to stop the anger. He only marveled that he no longer seemed able to direct any of it toward Amanda. His heart insisted on believing in her innocence, if not her ignorance.

He was beginning to think she really did have amnesia, beginning to believe that fantastic story about Elizabeth Dupard. However, she had said she'd fallen from the top of the stairs as though she remembered it. If she was innocent and she did remember tumbling all the way down the stairs, that could mean... He set his jaw firmly, not wanting to face what her lying could mean. He'd come into this situation assuming she would lie. So why should he be so upset now to see possible proof that she was?

One thing was absolutely certain. He couldn't let her out of his sight . . . even though staying so close to her might be disastrous. She was too damned attractive, especially now when she seemed so vulnerable. It was becoming far too easy to slip into unguarded, unplanned conversation with her, to try to bring out her smile...and to look for ways and reasons to touch her, to lose his sanity in the feel of her slender body, her soft skin.

Even in the suits she wore to work, the blue jeans at home, she'd always been alluring. That had been something he'd had to fight from the first day he'd moved in next door to her. But yesterday, when he'd found her in that skimpy gown, seen the swell of her breasts, the darkness of her nipples through the filmy fabric, the curve of her hips and the long, sleek lines of her legs and she'd clung to him...

He picked up his paints and tried to immerse himself in the process of creation, to avoid thinking of her and the way she looked at him with undisguised desire in her eyes.

He forced himself to concentrate on the contours of her house—the ideal picture, he thought, if she should accuse him of keeping too close an eye on her. But he couldn't seem to get the lines right. It wasn't what he wanted to paint. He wanted to work on the other paintings, the ones that seemed to grow of their own volition from the fibers of his brush, the ones of her.

But he wasn't going to, didn't dare. Those pictures—especially the portrait—revealed too much, more than he could deal with.

Determinedly he studied the architecture of the graceful old house, the big tree in front of it. It would be a good painting, something he could admire when this was all over. He'd probably never be able to look at her portrait again. He ought to destroy it now.

But he couldn't concentrate on the house. His eyes strained to see through the walls, to the woman within. What was she doing now? What was she saying? To whom?

He clenched his teeth, forced himself to remain seated. He would not march across the yard, slide a credit card into that nothing lock, invade her house, make her talk to him, touch her, hold her, kiss her lush lips.... No! That was not what he was here for.

He took his materials inside, but moved his chair close to the front window, in position so he could watch her door, the side of her house, see the light in her bedroom and know when she went to bed.

A car passed, and he tensed, leaning forward, but it didn't stop. Phillip hadn't returned.

He wished Amanda hadn't pulled the curtains. But was that, he questioned himself brutally, more because he *needed* to see what she was doing—or because he *wanted* to see her?

Passing the hall mirror where she'd been so terrified of her own image, Amanda hesitated and looked again, raising a hand to touch her cheek. She felt the hand. The face belonged to her. She recognized it now. But still it seemed to be more a mask than her real face. The tale about a former resident of her house clung stubbornly.

And the journal that she'd hidden in the attic—if it existed—might very well be the source of her fantasy. If she found the history of Elizabeth Dupard recorded in a book, perhaps exposing the origins of her fabrication would shock her back to reality.

She located a flashlight and went up the stairs, determined to find the answers if they were there. But she hesitated at the door. Illogically, she felt a little sad that she might lose Elizabeth, lose a part of herself.

She forced herself to turn the knob. The door swung open easily, and she shone the beam of her light into the dimness that stretched before her.

Except for a few boxes in one corner, the attic was empty. Everything was gone—her baby furniture, the big rocker where she'd sat to write in her journal, the drop-leaf table, the trunks full of old clothes that she and Rachel had laughed at but loved to dress up in. She could visualize all of it, knew exactly where everything had been—how the rocker had wobbled slightly, the way Granny's green velvet dress had felt beneath her childish fingers, the musty smell that clung to the old clothes.

But at the same time, she could see the attic as Amanda had first seen it—dusty with a few pieces of old furniture and odds and ends, like the clock now on the mantel below. She looked down at her hands, her long, slender hands—Amanda's hands—and remembered holding the clock almost reverently, polishing it and restoring it to its proper place in the parlor.

Her gaze was drawn inexorably to the low window at one side of the room. With a thrill of excitement she crossed the floor and knelt in front of it. She'd been with Papa when he'd replaced it. A hailstorm had broken the glass, and he'd removed the entire frame to repair it.

With a child's delight, Elizabeth had exclaimed over the "hiding place" she discovered, the spaces between the attic-floor joists that had been revealed when Papa had removed the wide windowsill. He'd laughed and agreed to leave the thick board loose so she could slide it in and out, hide her treasures beneath it.

That was where, in later years, she'd kept her journal.

Excitedly she tugged on the wooden sill, but it didn't budge. The flashlight's beam revealed that several layers of paint had sealed it in place.

She sat back and examined it... and the memory returned of doing the same thing a few weeks ago. She'd still been unpacking and arranging things, and had brought up a box of Christmas decorations to store. After stashing them in the corner, she'd been inexplicably drawn to the attic window, had experienced an eerie knowledge that the sill was movable, would provide her with a much-needed hiding place.

But it hadn't moved, and she'd dismissed the odd experience.

Amanda rocked back on her heels as she considered this latest memory. Was her mind playing tricks again? Was this an instance of déjà vu or had Amanda somehow known about Elizabeth's hiding place?

How could she? Unless she'd lived Elizabeth's life, and the house had brought back memories of that life...

She shook her head to dispel the strange ideas. She had no evidence there really was a hiding place under the board. It could all be a part of her fantasy.

Going down to the kitchen, she selected two knives—one large and sturdy, the other small and pointed—and located a hammer. She could and *would* prove or disprove this particular element of her delusions. If she tore out the windowsill and found nothing, she'd have to accept that she was Amanda and only Amanda.

Returning to the attic, she positioned the flashlight so it shone on the area, kicked off her shoes and bent to her task. The paint was thick and rubbery, effectively disguising the cracks between the boards. Chipping away, she reflected that she was making quite a mess—to clean up as well as to re-paint.

Finally all the seams of the boards were exposed. She sat back and ran a hand across her forehead. Though it was by no means overly warm in the attic, she'd begun to per-spire—only partly from her exertions. If a hiding place ex-isted, what would that prove? That she had read or heard about it somewhere? But if she had found an old journal and then replaced it, such a book couldn't be hidden here; the layers of paint hadn't been disturbed in years.

Whatever the truth was, she had to know.

She slid the blade of the large knife into the crack, then smacked the handle with the hammer, driving it down, breaking through the remaining paint. A few more whacks in strategic places loosened the board.

In fear and eagerness, she grasped the windowsill and tugged. After a moment's resistance, it slid out. She pushed it aside and shone the flashlight directly into the space beneath.

It wasn't empty.

The flashlight's beam revealed a dusty, leather-bound journal.

CHAPTER SEVEN

Tentatively, she reached down to touch it, wanted to cry when she found it real and substantial. Slowly she brought it from its hiding place, cradled the thick book in her hands, gently blew away the dust.

The brown leather cover was cracked and dry, but she recognized her journal. Papa had given it to her for Christmas in 1905. He'd told her how important it was that she record the events of the rapidly changing world and the still-young century in which they lived.

Hesitantly, fearfully, joyously, she opened the cover. On the flyleaf in the familiar copperplate handwriting she'd labored so hard to learn were the words *Journal of Elizabeth Catherine Dupard. December 25, 1905.*

By the flashlight's beam she read the faded writing on the first page:

Papa says I should write about all the important things in the world, and so I shall! Surely Christmas is important, is it not? Today was wonderful. We had ever so many lovely gifts, and Mama made her ham with the delicious honey sauce.

The words flowed on, and Amanda read them and remembered the stories in vivid detail.

The winter they were snowed in for three days...

Papa says we are having the worst blizzard since he was a little boy. Truly, it sounds frightful with the wind howling and banging the tree limbs against the house. When I look out, all I can see is swirling snow. I can't even see Rachel's house.

But even though I know it's terrible outside, I feel so deliciously warm and safe sitting in front of the fire and drinking hot cocoa with Mama and Papa. I find it hard to hate the storm.

That same year they'd had an epidemic of measles, and Elizabeth had become ill.

I was home in bed for three days feeling awfully sick, but no red spots came like Rachel had. I was glad because she said they itched frightfully. But then I heard Mama and Papa talking. She said if the spots didn't break out, I'd never be well. A few minutes later Mama came to my bed and offered me a cup of something hot. I asked her what it was, and she said, "You know how much you like gingerbread? Well, this is ginger tea. Quick now, drink it all down in one big gulp."

I do love gingerbread, especially with lemon sauce. And while I didn't feel like eating or drinking anything, I did it to please Mama.

It didn't taste like gingerbread! It burned all the way down to my stomach, and before I knew it, measles were popping out all over! Mama knows such a lot about everything!

She skimmed the pages, felt a nostalgic loneliness as she read the everyday minutiae of her life.

Then in 1911 . . .

I don't know how to tell this. It's been a month, and still I can't stop crying, can't accept it.

Tears flooded her eyes as she remembered.

Dear, sweet Papa is gone. He caught a cold, like we all do every winter. But he got sicker and sicker and finally took to his bed. He didn't even go into the bank to work. He got so pale and stopped eating or even talking. All he did was cough in a way that sounded like his chest was tearing inside. When he breathed, it was loud and raspy, and I knew it must hurt him.

The doctor came and said he had pneumonia. He gave him medicine, but Papa got worse. Mama and I took turns sitting by his bed, holding his hand and trying to make him drink water a spoonful at a time. Usually he didn't even wake up. When he did open his eyes, I'm not sure he saw us.

Then the doctor came back and said we had to put him in hospital. They took him away, and he never came back.

She remembered the pain, felt it as acutely as if it had just happened . . . as if she had been there. She could see Papa's ashen face, hear his racking cough and labored breathing. She had to pause for a moment and remind herself that her father was alive and well. It was Elizabeth's father who had died.

She knew that. She just didn't believe it.

Spellbound, she read on. The next entry was only a couple of weeks later.

I thought I couldn't live with the pain of losing Papa, but now things are even worse. Mama says we don't have any money. If we can't find some boarders to take in, we'll have to sell the house and move to St. Louis to live with Uncle Otis and Aunt Martha.

How it must grieve Papa if he's looking down on us.

Even as she finished reading that page, before she turned to the next, a chill darted down her spine. She remembered what had happened next.

Surely Papa is watching over us from above! Blake Holbert has asked Mama for permission to marry me! He's come calling several times since his father died two weeks after Papa, but I never dreamed he'd offer for me. His father owned the factory, the town! And now Blake owns it all. He's a very rich man and ever so handsome. He says he'll be a good husband to me, and he'll take care of Mama. I can't believe he wants to marry me when he could have any girl in town, but of course I said I would!

Elizabeth had recorded her excitement and anxiety over the prospect of being a bride. Blake was devastatingly handsome. Every girl in town envied her. But there were secrets about marriage that Mama told her would only be revealed by her husband. Elizabeth and Rachel whispered and giggled, but really knew nothing.

The entries changed immediately after the wedding. As she read the details, Amanda relived the uncomprehending fear, the sense of weakness and vulnerability as Blake exercised the rights of a husband in 1912.

I made Blake angry again, only this time was worse than ever before. This time he didn't stop at shouting or slapping me.

When he came in from work, I could tell he was upset. I tried to be careful not to make it worse, but my gravy was lumpy. He threw the bowl at me. I ducked, and it hit the wall. Then he screamed at me for making a mess, and he grabbed me and shoved my face in it, then hit me again and again. I started to cry, and that seemed to make him even more furious, but I couldn't stop. He dragged me upstairs and into bed, and I can't tell the rest. I never knew married life was like this. Mama said there were things only my husband could tell me about, but I know Papa didn't hit Mama, and surely he never did those other things.

But I mustn't complain. Blake takes good care of Mama. He gives her money every month, a generous amount, she says.

I waited for the bruises to heal before I came home to see Mama so she and Rachel wouldn't know. The pages of this journal are the only place I dare talk about this. I must always be careful to keep it hidden in my special place here at home. If Blake becomes so enraged because I make gravy with lumps or talk too much about Papa, I shudder to think what he'd do to me if he ever found this book with all my complaining.

If only I could hide myself here as easily. If only Papa hadn't died—but he did, and I'm a married woman now.

Amanda felt the desperate anguish of being trapped, saw before her a lifetime of nothing but pain—pain that assaulted her on both physical and emotional levels. Within a matter of months, Elizabeth had changed from a sheltered, happy girl who dreamed of rainbows to a scared wife who cringed every time she heard her husband's voice.

She wanted to help that girl, have Blake thrown into jail, teach Elizabeth to stand up to him, but at the same time, she realized that neither had been a possibility in 1912.

A sudden noise from downstairs jolted Amanda back to the present. She held her breath, listened carefully. There it was again—a floorboard creaking! She was no longer alone in the house!

Heart pounding furiously, she laid down the journal and switched off the light. With a start, she realized it had grown dark while she read.

The sound came again. She hadn't imagined it.

She forced herself to control her frantic breathing. Maybe if she remained very quiet and still, the intruder would leave, wouldn't think of looking for her in the attic.

But something rose up in her. No! She'd hidden from things too long, and where had it gotten her? Blake had always found her, had continued his cruelty.

Well, Blake was gone, turned to dust, couldn't hurt her now, and if whoever was downstairs intended to try, she'd beat him to the punch. With trembling fingers, she groped in the darkness until she found the largest knife.

Someone was coming upstairs, trying to catch her unawares, just as he had in her dream. But this time she had the advantage. This time she could hide in the shadows. This time *she* could push him or stab him . . . defend herself!

Moving rapidly and soundlessly in her bare feet, she tiptoed down the attic stairs and slid along the wall until she reached the second-floor landing, the same place her attacker had stood in her dream.

A massive, hulking shadow moved stealthily up the steps. Terror rose from her chest into her throat and threatened to choke her, send her into a mindless panic. But from somewhere even deeper, anger gave her the strength to remain rational and wait.

As he reached the top and looked around, her heart seemed to stop its furious pounding and shatter into a thousand pieces. Even in the dark, she recognized Dylan's features.

Paralyzed by fear and pain, she could do nothing but watch as he turned on the landing and started down the hallway toward her room. Even with his suspicious actions, she hadn't really believed he could hurt her...hadn't *wanted* to believe it.

Obviously he could...and would.

Her great resolution of a few minutes before had come to naught. She hadn't pushed him, hadn't stabbed him... wasn't sure she could. If it had been a stranger... But it wasn't. The man stalking her, making her blood run cold with terror, was the same man who'd stayed with her through the fearful tests at the doctor's office...the same man who made her blood boil with another emotion every time he touched her.

She tore her gaze away from him, made herself face the reality of her situation. She had to get out of there before he came back and found her!

She flew down the stairs, making no effort to be quiet, only to get away. As she reached the front door, she snatched the key ring off its hook. Already she could hear footsteps behind her, pounding down the hall, on the stairs.

She raced across the yard to her car, fumbling frantically for the right key. But her fingers shook so badly she dropped the ring into the street. As she stooped to retrieve it, Dylan charged up and yanked it from her grasp.

But she still had the knife in her other hand. She focused on one spot—his throat. He wasn't a person, only a target. She drew back her arm and aimed.

He jumped backward, dodged and grabbed her arm. "Amanda! It's me!"

She kicked at his shin, her movements hampered by the narrow skirt she'd worn to work. She landed only a glancing blow, but he swore loudly. Then, with a sudden move, he locked one leg around hers, turned her and pinned the hand holding the knife behind her back.

Blind, desperate fury at her vulnerability propelled her onward. She tried to kick him again with her free leg, and they both fell to the street, Dylan landing on top.

She lay trapped beneath his weight, but unwilling to admit defeat. Struggling vainly, she searched for a weak spot.

"Damn it, stop!" he panted. "I'm sorry I frightened you. I'm not going to hurt you."

Gradually, one by one, his words penetrated, and her mania ebbed marginally. She lay still, not quite believing, but waiting her chance.

"Drop the knife, and we can both get up," he said cautiously.

"No," she gasped, unwilling to surrender something he obviously feared. "Get away from me first."

He mumbled a few more expletives as she felt his weight lessening, though he still clutched her arm. With a sudden movement, he released her completely.

She rolled away, came up in a crouch facing him. He stood a couple of feet back, both hands raised in front of him. "Now, just relax," he said, his words jerky from his own breathlessness, though he was making an effort to sound soothing. His hair tumbled in total disarray, his shirt was pulled half out of his blue jeans and he didn't look threatening at all. He looked appealing—masculine.

"What were you doing sneaking into my house?" she demanded, reminding herself he'd *acted* threatening.

"Trying to check on you, make sure you were all right. I was worried about you. Your lights never came on."

Anger replaced the fear. "What were you doing watching for my lights in the first place? Why are you *always* watching me?"

"Why? You fall down the stairs and wake up thinking you're somebody who died before you were born, and you don't consider that reason enough for me to check on you, to be concerned about you?"

"Or maybe I woke up *saying* I thought I was somebody else, *pretending* I didn't remember anything about my life or how I got down those stairs," she challenged. "Maybe you're afraid I really do remember, and maybe that's reason enough to check up on me."

He didn't answer. His stoic expression returned. "Why were you headed for your car? I thought you'd forgotten how to drive."

"I guess I forgot that I forgot. I was scared, in fear for my life. If I could have gotten into that car, somehow I'd have figured out how to drive away."

Again she had the sensation of his mind trying to probe hers, but he didn't pursue the subject. "Can we continue this discussion inside before some neighbor calls the cops on us?"

Amanda drew in a deep breath, looked around her and took notice of her surroundings, her situation, the fact that she'd ripped a seam in her skirt, still clutched a large knife in one hand and probably looked even more disheveled than he did.

"On the porch," she said, unwilling to be alone in the house with him in spite of his protestations of innocence.

He inclined his head in a brief gesture of agreement, and they walked to the porch together.

As the overpowering anger and fear left her, she began to notice the aches and pains... a scraped elbow, a battered knee and several places that would, by tomorrow, add more dark bruises to the ones she already had from her fall.

She wrapped her arms about herself, fighting off the sensation that her body had looked and felt this way before— after one of Blake's rages. But there was a difference. Her spirit wasn't broken as Elizabeth's had been.

"I really am sorry I scared you," he reiterated when they stood in front of her door. "I knocked and called your name. When you didn't answer, I tried the door and it opened. It wasn't locked. After all that's happened, I was worried."

It wasn't a good-enough explanation. "How did you know I hadn't just gone to bed early?"

He didn't reply for a long moment, but when he did, he faced her squarely, and his words held no apology. "I can see your bedroom window from mine."

A thrill of something embarrassingly akin to desire rushed through her body at the idea of a connection between their bedrooms. She shoved the absurd feeling aside, mentally assuring herself it resulted from the adrenaline still flooding her veins from her recent fright. It wasn't possible to fear a person one minute and desire him the next.

As if he could read her mind—or felt the same emotions as she—he stepped backward, crossed his arms over his chest and stood with his back against one of the porch pillars. He exuded defiance.

"In the future, you might try knocking a little louder," she said. She knew she sounded irritated and hoped he would think it was directed at him, when in fact she was equally irritated with herself for being unable to control this inappropriate attraction to him. "I was in the attic. I didn't hear you."

"In the attic?"

"Looking through some old papers I found up there."
She knew she should have told him that what she'd been
doing in the attic was none of his business, but she couldn't
resist baiting him, studying his response for any sign of interest in hidden papers.

She wasn't disappointed. Even in the dim glow from the
streetlight, she could see the dark fire blaze in his eyes.

At the same time, she *was* disappointed. Whatever she'd
hidden in the house, she didn't want it to be something she'd
had to hide from Dylan. She wanted to believe he'd only
entered her house out of concern for her safety.

"What kind of old papers?" he asked, and it was more
than an idle question.

She hesitated, but could think of no way to push her slight
deception any further, since she knew nothing else about the
papers she thought she'd hidden. In fact, she couldn't be
positive they even existed. "I found an old journal hidden
in the attic. Elizabeth Dupard's journal—a record of her
life, her father's death, her marriage to Blake Holbert. His
family founded our town, I assume."

Dylan's gaze became distant, focused somewhere beyond her. She turned automatically to see what he was staring at, but she saw only his house.

"The bastard owned the factory."

She whirled in surprise. The voice had traces of an accent, didn't sound quite like Dylan. When he'd brought her
home from the doctor and she'd first seen Phillip, he'd assured her in a similar voice that she didn't have to go back.
But tonight the strangeness was stronger—as was the familiarity she couldn't quite place.

He took a step closer to her, lifted his arms toward her.
Though he was looking at her, she wasn't sure if he really
saw her. The whole thing, especially after her recent fright,
was totally disconcerting.

"What did you just say?" she asked, snapping out the words in her bravado.

That stopped him. He dropped his arms and blinked, shook his head, and the faraway expression was gone.

"Nothing," he said in his own voice. "You were talking about the town founder. He owned a factory. That's how the town started. That's all I meant." He seemed more confused about his odd statement than she was.

"Come in and see the book," she invited impulsively. One part of her whispered that she might be putting herself in danger, asking him into her house like that. But the idea existed only on an intellectual level—didn't reach her emotions, didn't instill any fear in her. Maybe she'd been so frightened of everything lately, she'd used up her quota of fear. Or maybe she wanted to be with him more than she feared him.

He looked at her for a long moment, and she sensed some sort of battle raging behind his shuttered gaze, behind his outthrust jaw. "Thanks," he finally said, and she didn't know which side had won.

They went in, and she locked the door. Dylan had said the door was unlocked when he came in. She could have sworn she remembered locking it when Phillip left. But if she had, how had Dylan gotten in?

For that matter, if someone had pushed her down the stairs, how had he gotten inside?

"Are you okay?" Dylan asked from behind her, and she realized she'd been staring at the lock for some time.

"Yes, I'm fine." She turned her attention to him, faced him squarely. "I was just thinking that I probably need a new lock. It would be pretty easy for someone to break in here."

"A child with a library card could do it," he agreed smoothly. "You really should get a dead bolt. I've been telling you that for some time. I'll pick up one tomorrow and install it for you.''

And keep a copy of the key? she wondered, but she kept that thought to herself.

''Let's go to the kitchen,'' she suggested. ''I need to put this back.'' She indicated the knife. ''And you can put on some water for tea while I bring down the journal.''

When she opened the kitchen drawer to replace the cleaned knife, the sight of her hand wrapped around its handle brought a dawning realization. She had just been reading about Elizabeth's fear and inability to defend herself against her husband. With that knowledge fresh in her mind, plus the anger generated by the injustices done to Elizabeth, she herself had found the strength to repel someone she feared meant to harm her.

Unfinished business, Lottie had said.

She tossed the knife into the drawer and shook her head to clear the confusion.

She was Amanda Parrish, not Elizabeth Dupard. She wasn't a Victorian-era woman with no rights, tied to an abusive husband. She was an independent woman of the nineties. Because she felt sympathy for someone who'd lived and died in an unfortunate time period didn't mean she had been that person.

But she couldn't dispel the vivid picture of Blake looming over her, his breath hot on her face when he shouted, his fist hard and painful as it smacked against her face, her stomach, her arms. She couldn't dispel a feeling of victory, of freedom, of pride at being able to take care of herself— whoever she was.

Dylan watched Amanda as she stared into the drawer of knives, apparently completely absorbed in them, almost in a trance. What could she possibly be thinking about? Surely not wielding the knife against him again.

It had been stupid of him to break into her house. He'd made a grievous error, allowed himself to indulge in panic when the evening turned dark and the lights didn't come on... panic for her safety as much as—more than—panic that she'd somehow gotten away and gone to Phillip. He'd almost paid dearly for his foolish behavior. He had no doubt she'd have cut him if she could have.

But if she really had found some hidden book and he got to see it, if it was the right book with the right information, it would be well worth the risk. He didn't for a minute believe her mumbo jumbo about it being a journal of some dead woman and wasn't sure why she'd told him that, then agreed to let him see it. But he wasn't going to pass up the chance.

"Amanda?"

She looked up, eyes slightly dazed but alive with pleasure, lips curved upward in a faint smile. "Oh, yes," she said. "The journal." She closed the drawer. "I'll just run up and get it."

"I'll go with you." He told himself he'd made the offer so she wouldn't have a chance to hide the book from him. But even as he mentally uttered the excuse, he knew the real reason was much simpler... the idea of being alone with her in the dark attic sent an aching surge through him.

"All right." She agreed readily, self-confidently, her expression guileless. Whatever she'd found upstairs she saw no problem in showing to him. Which could mean it was worthless, or that she, in her current condition, didn't know what it was.

As he followed her up the wide staircase, a sudden image flashed across his mind of her tumbling downward, her slender body crumpling in a heap at the foot of the stairs. A chill darted down his spine at the idea that she could have come so close to death, that he might never have had the chance to see vulnerability and desire part the curtain of her reserve, that her crystalline gaze and soft skin could have been lost to him forever....

He set his foot down hard as he stepped onto the landing and reminded himself forcefully that his primary concern was not to let her secrets be lost to him. She might be sending his libido through the roof, she might be stirring strange protective feelings in him, but she was still Amanda Parrish—ex-wife of Phillip Ryker and still somehow, for some reason, connected to Phillip.

Seemingly unaware and innocent, she led him into the dark attic.

CHAPTER EIGHT

In the faint glow coming from downstairs through the open door, she retrieved a flashlight from the floor. "It was in there," she said, indicating with her light a hole in the floor and the paint and rubble from her efforts at exposing it.

He knew immediately this wasn't what he was looking for. This was nothing that had been hidden during the time period that concerned him...unless she'd pried loose the windowsill and set the whole thing up so she could pretend that she'd found whatever she was about to show him. Perhaps he'd be smart to reserve judgment until he knew more.

She sat on the floor and picked up the book. It appeared to be an antique, exactly what she'd told him—the journal of a dead woman. He knelt behind her and drew in her scent of flowers and woman, and had to forcibly restrain his hands from touching her, from pushing her to the dusty floor in the concealing darkness, ripping her torn skirt the rest of the way and—

He backed away from her, from his runaway desires. He was becoming aroused again, just as he had when he'd been straddling her in the street, when she'd been trying to stab him. Even that menacing action hadn't been enough to deter his out-of-control hormones.

"Listen," she said. Aiming the light onto the open pages in her lap, she began to read excerpts from the life of Elizabeth Dupard.

Oddly compelled by the diary entries of this woman he'd never met, he moved closer, straining to see the writing. It wasn't a very good idea, he knew. The journal was obviously useless to him, and sitting so close to Amanda in a dark attic wasn't the type of action that would allow him to keep his goal uppermost in his mind. He ought to at least suggest they go downstairs where the light was better, where they could sit with a table between them. But the words never came out. He sat, aroused and hard from Amanda's nearness and fascinated against his will by her and by the details of a dead woman's life.

"That's as far as I got," Amanda said, carefully turning a page, then continuing.

"It's been a week since I could come to visit Mama. I upset Blake again. I should have known better. Rachel told me the whole town's talking about the horrible things Blake has been doing, some things his father would never have tolerated. He's cut the workers' pay and makes them work longer hours. He's raised the rents on the company houses he owns, and he won't fix broken windows or repair leaks in a roof or do anything to keep their homes livable. He fires the men if they can't work because of illness, yet the long hours make many of them sick."

To Dylan's amazement, he found himself becoming outraged over Blake Holbert's treatment of his workers. It shouldn't be tolerated. Someone ought to do something. *He* ought to do something.

Ridiculous! he chastised himself. This wasn't like him to get so involved in a story—and it might as well be a fictional story. The events had happened over eighty years ago!

"I asked him about it, and he became furious. He said I should pay more attention to my needlework and stay out of the world of men. He hit me and told me we'd go to town the next day so everyone could see that he managed his wife as well as his factory. I wanted to die when he paraded me around and everybody pretended not to notice."

Anger surged through Dylan at the man's treatment of his wife.

"But they all know. Mama came to see me the next day while Blake was at work. She cried with me and hugged me and told me she was sorry. So I guess there's nothing to be done. I must learn how to keep him happy."

Amanda turned the page, the rustling loud in the silence, and Dylan blinked, startled out of complete absorption. He took a deep breath, started to excuse himself and leave, run from whatever hypnotic spell she was weaving with this ancient book.

But she read on, and he didn't move.

"Rachel's family has a guest, Shawn Fitzpatrick, the most wonderful man I've ever met. He's come from Chicago to organize a labor union here! He explained to me that means the workers all unite and force people like my husband to listen to their demands, to treat them fairly. We talked for hours, and I told him what little I know about the factory in the hopes that it would help. I barely had time to get back to Mama's before Blake came for me. I know he'd be angry if he knew about Mr. Fitzpatrick."

Elizabeth wrote effusively of the activities of the fiery labor leader, and Dylan could feel his frustration at the problems, his excitement when they gained any ground. And he could feel the love growing between Elizabeth and Shawn, the forbidden attraction that wouldn't be denied, so like what he felt for Amanda. In the darkness he found himself becoming confused, found it hard to separate the people, the years, to remember he was Dylan, not Shawn, and the woman beside him was Amanda, not Elizabeth. He wanted her as Shawn wanted Elizabeth, knew the same frustration because of the impossibility of such a thing. Elizabeth should leave Blake and go with him, let him show her what happiness could be, what love could be…what joys he could teach her about her body—such an enticing, responsive body, wasted on a man like Blake—

"Blake found out I've been talking to Shawn. He said someone told him, but I suspect he was spying on me. My mood had been so much lighter of late, he likely became suspicious. I've never seen him so angry. This time he locked me in my room for four days and instructed the housekeeper I was to have nothing to eat but bread and milk. She managed to sneak in some other foods, but I had no appetite for them. Blake says if I ever speak to Shawn again, he'll forbid me to see Mama or Rachel. I couldn't stand that. I must be very careful to avoid Shawn, but my prayers will ever be with him."

Amanda turned the page, then another and another. The final pages were blank. What had happened that Elizabeth had never written in her journal again?

"That can't be all!" Dylan snatched the book from her, flipped through the last pages so rapidly she feared he would tear them. He dropped the journal to the floor and clutched her shoulders. "I need to know what happened!" he demanded in that odd voice that wasn't quite his and yet seemed strangely right.

The beam from the flashlight she still held cast an eerie light on his face, distorting his features. *Dylan,* she reminded herself. *This is Dylan, my neighbor.*

But the image of Shawn Fitzpatrick filled her mind. She could see him as clearly as if she'd really known him. His bright blue eyes sparked with as much fire as his hair. His skin was pale, spattered with golden freckles. He was medium of height and wiry of build, not a traditionally handsome man, but he had a vitality, a charisma that drew people to him. And when he spoke in his mellow baritone with a trace of an Irish accent, people listened. The workers listened. Elizabeth listened.

He pulled her to him, and the confusion deepened. As his lips touched hers, it seemed to be Shawn kissing Elizabeth . . . and she no longer fought the sensation. It had been so long. She'd missed him so much. She drank him in greedily . . . his woodsy smell, the warmth of his body, the softness of his lips exploring hers. She could never get enough of him, not even if they were together like this for eternity.

He pulled her closer, one hand behind her neck, his fingers tangling in her hair—caressing her the same way he always did. He touched her lips with his tongue, and she parted to allow him entrance, to merge with him, to take him inside her in this prelude to the ultimate merging. She wrapped her arms around him, struggling to touch more of his body with hers. . . .

A thudding noise jolted Amanda, parting the mists of the surreal world she'd somehow fallen into, parting her from Dylan.

Dear God, what had she been doing? Who had she been kissing...and who had he been kissing? In the darkness she could hear him breathing heavily, but he said nothing.

"The flashlight," she finally managed to say, reaching to pick up the object that had disturbed them. "The flashlight fell when..." *When I reached for you.*

He cleared his throat. "The flashlight." A silence as charged as the recent thunderstorm wrapped around them. Abruptly he rose to his feet. "I'd better go home and let you get some sleep."

She nodded, though she wasn't sure he would see the motion in the near darkness. Nor was she sure she wanted him to leave.

Resolutely she stood, taking the journal in one hand and shining the beam of light ahead of them with the other. She started from the attic with Dylan following wordlessly and closely behind...so close she could feel his warm breath on her neck. So close, she reminded herself forcibly, that he could grasp her shoulders the way he'd done a few minutes ago. He could easily hold her against her will, drag her to the stairs, push her down.

She quickened her pace, almost running from the attic, down to the first floor...unsure if she ran from fear of Dylan or fear of her own desires.

When she reached the front door, she opened it with fumbling fingers, not daring to look back at him. But he laid a gentle hand on her shoulder, forcing her to acknowledge him.

He looked so troubled she thought he must be going to apologize, to explain why he'd kissed her. *Don't,* she begged silently. *Please don't say you're sorry.* Because even though she knew it was insane, she didn't regret the kiss and couldn't bear it if he did.

Conflicting emotions warred in the night sky of his eyes. He dropped his hand. "Good night, Amanda," he said, and walked out the door.

Sleep didn't come easily that night. The incredible scene in the attic played itself over and over in her mind. She'd become so mesmerized by Elizabeth's journal, she'd again let herself slip into that life. That explained why she'd kissed Dylan so eagerly . . . but what about him? Had he become caught up in the story also? He'd certainly seemed to. Was that why he'd kissed her? And did she want that to be the reason . . . or would she prefer to think he'd known who he was kissing?

Again and again she had to bring her mind back to reality. Someone might have pushed her downstairs, and that someone might have been Dylan. After all, what had he really been doing, sneaking through her house?

At the same time, she couldn't help wondering what had happened to Elizabeth after Blake forbade her to see Shawn. As if recapturing her own life weren't difficult enough, now she was also trying to find out about Elizabeth's.

She sat up, turned her pillow over and fluffed it, then stared across the room. She'd pulled the bedroom curtains tight, but a sliver of moonlight shone through. Fancifully, irrationally, it seemed as if Dylan's gaze rode in on the beam, as if she could feel him invading her room, her soul. Even more illogically, her inexplicable desire for him rose at the imagined feeling of that gaze.

She shivered and pulled the covers over her head.

Amanda awoke with a start, drenched in perspiration, heart thudding furiously. She'd been dreaming again about strong hands on her shoulders, pushing her. But this time she'd fallen straight down for a long time in suffocating, cold, wet darkness. From somewhere above, Dylan watched as she fell in slow motion. At least she sensed it was Dylan though she never actually saw him.

She looked at the clock. Five-fifteen. Too early to get up, but too late to go back to sleep. Already the crack between her curtains was lightening with dawn.

Sliding deeper under the covers, she tried once more to make sense of things.

She'd fallen down the stairs. There was nothing wet or cold about her staircase, yet she'd associated those sensations with the fall in both dreams she'd had about the experience. There must be a connection.

And how was Dylan linked to all this? Somehow he was involved in her life—if not romantically, at least in whatever was happening to her. He'd been as engrossed as she in Elizabeth's journal . . . not to mention in the kiss that had come out of nowhere. Or out of a total absorption in Elizabeth's world.

But she couldn't look to the book for an explanation of her original knowledge of Elizabeth. She couldn't have read the journal, replaced it with its layers of dust, then replaced the years of paint on the windowsill.

So maybe she'd gotten her knowledge about Elizabeth's life from another record. But what?

There were, she thought, at least two more places she could look for Elizabeth. The town library probably had old copies of the local newspaper. Judging from her diary, Elizabeth Dupard hadn't been active in local society, but at least the circumstances of her death should be chronicled. Amanda felt compelled to discover that information.

But checking through years' worth of even a weekly paper would be tedious. She needed to find out the date of Elizabeth's death. If the woman had lived in Holbert, chances were she'd be buried in the Holbert Cemetery. Her tombstone would have her date of death.

Even as the plan entered Amanda's mind, a part of her rebelled at the macabre idea. So closely did she relate to Elizabeth that she couldn't dismiss the idea she'd be viewing her own grave. But she resolutely shoved that feeling aside. She would go to the cemetery and from there to the library and... She wanted to conclude the thought with *put Elizabeth to rest* but, in spite of knowing better, she still felt that she *was* Elizabeth, a real person who didn't want to be put to rest.

She couldn't escape the feeling that learning more about Elizabeth's death would open things up rather than lay them to rest.

For the sake of comfort at the cemetery, she dressed in dark blue slacks with a pale blue jacket, despite a lingering sense of being inappropriately clad. After having a cup of coffee and a piece of toast, she took down her ring of keys and went determinedly out to her car.

Recalling what Dylan had shown her the day before, she started the engine. Fighting an irrational fear of driving—an activity as foreign to Elizabeth as wearing slacks—she scanned the vehicle and her memory.

Put it in gear. She shifted the lever to D.

Clutching the steering wheel convulsively, she gently pushed on the accelerator. The car lurched forward. In a rush of panic, she hit the brake.

Well, she thought, taking a deep breath, *this isn't so bad.* Her reflexes had kicked in when she needed to stop, and she'd found the brake. She could handle this.

But then her hopes died as she looked around her. The streets weren't the same as she remembered. She knew where the cemetery was, she knew how to get there, but the road seemed to have changed. Instead of curving off to the east, it went straight, was intersected by more streets and crowded with the houses of strangers.

She jumped, gasped, as someone tapped on the window. An unshaven, disheveled Dylan scowled in at her.

Dylan had overslept after a restless night filled with strange dreams, including the familiar nightmare with its new additions. He'd leapt from bed, filled with a sense of foreboding, and had looked out in time to see a determined Amanda striding toward her car. Yesterday she'd been unable to drive. Had her memories returned? If they had, he'd better get out there. This could be what he'd been waiting for these past two months. He threw on clothes and dashed out.

"I thought you couldn't drive," he challenged as she rolled down the car window.

"So did I. But now I think I can," she replied defiantly. Then her lost look returned. "Only...could you tell me how to get to the cemetery?"

"The cemetery? Why on earth do you want to go there?"

She flushed, then regained her composure, lifted her chin resolutely. "I want to see Elizabeth's grave."

He believed her. In fact, he realized with a start, he believed her whole crazy story—that she'd lost her memory and temporarily thought she was a dead woman. Even so, and as much as going to a cemetery again would only bring back unwanted memories, he couldn't let her go alone—not when she might remember at any moment. And not when she looked so lost and so brave at the same time.

"Unlock your passenger door," he said. "I'll show you the way."

She did as he asked without protest. He settled into the seat beside her. The light scent of wildflowers drifted over to him, surrounded him, invaded him, almost pushed from his mind exactly why he was there, what had to be done. Tom and his father had to be avenged.

"Turn left at the next street," he said. She looked over at him, her green eyes wide with surprise, and he realized he'd practically growled the direction.

"Why do you want to see Elizabeth's grave?" he asked, making a conscious effort to keep his irritation out of his voice—irritation at himself, not at her.

"To find out when she died," Amanda answered.

An eerie sensation washed over Dylan, and for the space of an instant, he wondered if he was going to pass out. No, he thought, that wasn't quite the feeling. More like he was losing touch with reality. The mention of death, probably; the thought of going to a cemetery and looking at graves, remembering Tom's closed casket waiting beside the hole in the earth, his father's only a week later. In spite of his distress—because of it—he had to regain control.

"Why?" he questioned, taking a deep breath to clear his head.

"So I can check the newspapers for information on her death."

"Why?" he asked again. Where was she going with this?

"Because I need to know," she said enigmatically.

"Why do you need to know about something that happened so long ago to someone you never met?"

He pointed her around another corner. Her driving skills were gradually progressing from shaky and erratic to fairly normal—something he felt sure she couldn't fake. Whatever she was up to, she was sincere about it.

"I'd never seen that journal before last night," she said. "That's not how I knew about those people. I need to find out where I got my information—don't ask me why, I just do. I need to find out about Elizabeth as much as I need to find out about Amanda."

Her urgency was so strong that he could feel it reaching out to him, and he knew that, no matter how hard it might be for him and no matter what had to happen when she regained her memory, he would indulge her now. And maybe, again, his motives were partially selfish. He'd been completely caught up in the contents of that old journal. His dreams had been filled with images conjured up by Elizabeth's words. The illogical, pointless idea of finding out more about those people tugged at him as it obviously tugged at her.

"There's the cemetery," he said. "Up ahead."

Amanda pulled off the road and parked. She stared at the faded letters on the weathered wooden sign over the rusty wrought-iron gates. Holbert Cemetery.

The last time I walked under that sign I was walking behind the horse-drawn hearse carrying Papa's coffin. The pain washed over her anew.

She slid from the car, walked slowly over to the gate and pushed on one side. With a creaking protest, it moved aside, permitting her entrance.

"Do you know what you're looking for?" Dylan asked, and she jumped at the sound of his voice beside her. For a moment she'd forgotten he was with her...had forgotten who or where she was.

She hesitated, then nodded in answer to his question. Against all reason, she knew exactly where she was going. Everything looked different, there were so many more graves, but she'd never forget the route to Papa's grave.

In the early morning chill not yet dissipated by the sun's weak rays, she moved unerringly among the markers. She gritted her teeth, tried to evade the morbid sadness this visit was bringing her and told herself her knowledge only proved she'd been here before...as Amanda, not as Elizabeth.

She'd never known Elizabeth's father and couldn't mourn him.

"Amanda, look." Again Dylan's voice startled her, and she whirled to find him pointing off to the side, to a large monument. She could read the names easily. The Holbert family plot. Logically, she realized, that would be where Elizabeth lay. With her husband.

She walked slowly toward it, anger and fear overpowering the sadness—anger at Blake for what he'd done to Elizabeth and irrational fear as though he might come up from the grave to attack her again. She passed the tombstone that marked the resting places of Blake's mother and father. Beside it stood a newer but similar one for Blake and Susan Holbert, husband and wife.

That wasn't possible! She stared at the carving, trying to make sense out of it. "I married him," she whispered. "The journal proved it."

"Maybe he remarried," Dylan suggested. "He lived a long time, until 1955."

"Maybe," she agreed, grateful for his words even though she could hear the doubt in them. A deceased wife would be buried in her husband's plot, even if she did later prove to be only the first.

The evidence should have made her doubt herself, but she didn't. She *knew* Elizabeth had been Blake's first wife. Maybe she'd died young, and Mama had insisted she not be near him in death after the way he'd treated her in life.

Glad to be leaving this place that held Blake's remains, she continued on her familiar route. And there it was ahead, the remembered gray stone. Gaston Dupard, Beloved Husband and Father. Born July 26, 1866. Died January 19, 1911. The carving was weathered, blurred, no longer as new and vivid as she remembered. But the pain of losing him felt new and vivid.

She forced herself to beat back the grief for someone she couldn't possibly have known, to hang on to the real world, the present world. Tearing her gaze from the stone, she looked at the one beside it. Eileen Wagoner Dupard. Born June 25, 1872. Died April 8, 1915.

Mama! She sank to her knees, grief overwhelming her, grief as real as if it had happened yesterday, as if it belonged to her and not to someone long dead. Her fingers traced the dates on the stone. Mama had died in 1915, only three years after Elizabeth's marriage to Blake. Mama hadn't had much time to enjoy her financial security.

The terseness of the carved facts suddenly hit her, the failure to award her status as a beloved mother. Elizabeth hadn't buried her mother. She couldn't remember Mama's death, hadn't been prepared to see her tombstone.

She hadn't been there when Mama died.

Involuntarily, inexorably, she felt her gaze being drawn to the other side of Papa's grave.

Elizabeth Dupard Holbert. Beloved Daughter and Wife. Born February 10, 1893. Died April 13, 1914.

CHAPTER NINE

The world began to swirl, to lose preciseness and definition. She stood slowly, stepped over to her own grave and sank again to her knees. Reality slipped away, earth and sky whirling into chaos.

She reached out, laid her hand on the ground, tried to hang on to its solidity. But the soil dissolved. Her hand sank into a cold, clinging wetness that drew her downward, sucking the breath from her lungs. She pushed upward, but she was too heavy. Leaden skirts trapped her legs. She flailed her arms in vain....

"Amanda!" The word reached her as if from far away. Strong arms pinned hers, pulled her upward, free of the grip of the suffocating cold. She felt firm solidity—a denim jacket, a cotton shirt, a wide chest. She hung on for dear life, for sanity.

Gradually the world stabilized, and she realized she was crying, had been crying for some time. Dylan held her, stroked her hair. It felt distressingly good. Just as he'd had the strength to overpower her the night before, that strength now reassured her, gave her something to hold on to.

It reminded her of...something, someone. The elusive memory flitted around the periphery of her mind, then darted away.

Reluctantly she pushed away from Dylan, left the secure shelter of his arms. "I'm sorry," she mumbled. "I don't usually cry. At least, I don't think I do." She forced a half smile at her own weak joke.

He returned the smile, handed her a handkerchief, and she dabbed at her eyes.

"I'm acting crazy, aren't I?" she asked, returning his handkerchief.

He nodded, but his expression was nonjudgmental, sympathetic, giving her permission to be crazy right now.

Gathering her courage, her sanity, and resolving to keep them, she turned back toward the graves.

April 13. The date of Elizabeth's death.

"She died on the same day you fell down the stairs." Dylan spoke quietly from behind her, echoing her thoughts.

The day she herself could have died—had died and come back, if her dream was more than a fantasy.

An eerie coincidence.

With this new information, she searched her mind for new memories that seemed to come when she heard about or discovered details of Amanda's and Elizabeth's lives.

Nothing came.

She reminded herself that the carved stones marked the resting places of people long dead—people she knew only by dint of living where they'd once lived, reading about their lives in a journal.

But Elizabeth's stone drew her gaze back for a last chilling look. Beloved Daughter and Wife. So why was she buried with her family and not with her husband? Because Mama had known how he'd treated her? But Blake could have easily overruled Mama's wishes—unless Elizabeth had done something so unforgivable that he hadn't wanted to lie beside her.

The graves guarded their secrets, and Amanda reluctantly turned to go.

Dylan waited behind her, his shirtfront wrinkled from her tears. He was staring at Elizabeth's stone as if in a trance, and in his dark eyes, she fancied she could see storms raging.

"Dylan?" she queried softly, almost afraid to disturb him.

He turned to her, his unshaven face alive with fury and anguish. She stepped backward involuntarily. The pale sunlight became even paler, almost disappeared.

He blinked, ran a hand over his jaw, and the strange expression vanished. He looked around as if to orient himself. "Are you all right?" he asked. "Let's get out of this place."

She nodded and fell into step beside him. Why, she wondered, did he seem to get so involved in her fantasy—last night when he'd grabbed the journal, when he'd kissed her . . . and now today?

"I'm sorry about your shirt," she apologized. "I'm sorry I fell apart like that. Everything just . . ."

"Seemed real to you?" he offered, and his voice was soft and deep, held no suspicion or sarcasm.

"Yes," she admitted. "It's like just last week Mama—Elizabeth's mother—was alive, and now she's dead. I don't know how to explain it. It's like I really am Elizabeth, and I miss my family." She shivered, as much from her thoughts as from the chill in the morning air.

Without a word, Dylan slid his faded denim jacket from his shoulders and settled it about hers. She started to protest that she really wasn't cold, but the faint scents of his woodsy cologne, of earth and trees, of his male strength, surrounded her. The feel of the garment, still warm with his body heat, seduced her through the thin fabric of her own jacket, reminded her of how his lips had felt on hers.

"Thank you," she said. He'd seemed so understanding ever since they'd found the graves of her family—Elizabeth's family—as though he knew how she felt. "Are your folks still living?" she asked.

She felt the anger and pain before she looked up to see them in his dark eyes. "Only my mother," he answered. "My brother and father died recently."

"I'm sorry," she murmured, afraid to question him any further, afraid of worsening the agony she'd obviously revived.

He slipped his arm about her waist as they walked, and she sensed he was taking comfort as well as giving it.

When they reached the car, he stopped. Leaning against the hood, he faced her, his eyes again opaque, bottomless oceans, the soul she'd so recently touched once again hidden from her. "So you're having problems getting rid of the notion that you really are this other woman."

She nodded, tried to answer him honestly. "I *know* I'm not Elizabeth. That's impossible, of course. I know I'm me, Amanda."

"You have your memory back." There it was again—that desperate need to know if she remembered . . . what?

"No." She shook her head. "Things keep returning a little at a time, and I have a sense of being me. But I still know more about Elizabeth than about Amanda...about me. It's like Elizabeth and I are the same, like the secrets to Amanda's life are hidden in Elizabeth's. I have to find out about her to know about myself."

His eyes narrowed intently. "Do you think you had a reason to choose her story beyond just living in the same house and having your accident on the day she died? Other parallels, maybe?"

Amanda reflected for a moment. Her feelings had been more instinctual, but what he said made sense. "Yes," she replied.

"That's why you want to find the newspaper stories about her death."

Because Elizabeth's death might somehow relate to Amanda's—or, at least, to attempts on Amanda's life. Was that the unspoken end of Dylan's sentence? Was that why he had become so fascinated with Elizabeth?

She shivered, wrapped the coat more closely about her, then remembered whose coat it was and tried to shrink away, pull inside herself. But the comforting warmth she needed held her inexorably.

Against her will, it seemed, she looked up at him and found him looking at her—caught him unawares, his barriers down. In the midnight sky of his gaze she saw eternity, and she was one with him and with the universe. The sensation of merging and bonding was so strong she gasped and staggered backward a step.

He lifted a hand to her cheek, stroked it gently. A blue jay shrieked raucously above them. Dylan dropped his hand, raised it to his eyes and stared at it curiously.

The spell was broken—for both of them. But something had been there. She'd felt it, and not for the first time. "What happened between you and me before my accident? What can't I remember?"

"Nothing happened. We were neighbors." He sounded as baffled as she felt. Without another word, he went around to the driver's door and opened it, motioning her in, his eyes fixed on a point just over her head.

She slid in and fumbled for her seat belt.

He climbed into the passenger seat beside her, his body and his presence seeming to fill the interior, expand into the empty spaces. And she was one of those empty spaces. She shivered with the same rush as the night before . . . fear or desire or both? What sort of power did this enigmatic man have over her?

"Are we off to the library now?" he asked, as if nothing unusual had happened.

We? She wasn't sure she wanted him with her, that she felt safe letting him know whatever she might find out. On the other hand, she couldn't deny that she'd been very grateful to have him today. And a part of her wanted him to be with her when she read about the details of Elizabeth's death . . . that part he'd touched when he'd given her his coat.

"I don't think I'm up to any more discoveries today," she said in compromise. "Anyway, I need to get to the shop. Lottie's expecting me. I'll have to make plans for her to open it tomorrow so I can go to the library."

"Okay," he agreed. "We'll go tomorrow."

She didn't object. She could always manage to slip away in the morning before he noticed.

Or maybe she couldn't. Did he ever stop watching her? Did he ever sleep?

She dropped Dylan at his house, assuring him she needed no assistance to get to her shop today. She fancied he would have liked to take her again, pick her up again, be certain of her whereabouts all day.

Don't be paranoid, she warned herself. But she couldn't dismiss the feeling.

When she got to the shop, Lottie was already there, waiting in the little kitchen in back of the shop with a pot of tea and fresh croissants.

"Do you come in this early every day?" Amanda asked. "Don't I ever open up and let you sleep late? And don't I ever bring breakfast?" She picked up one of the croissants and took a bite, the buttery layers melting on her tongue.

Lottie's laughter tinkled like old crystal. "I like coming in early. It's my choice. And you always insist on giving me a separate check every week to reimburse me for my little treats, though I always tell you I don't want it. I enjoy cooking. My husband, God rest his soul, weighed over two hundred fifty pounds before he got sick. He always said I was a better cook than anybody, even his mother. Of course, he never said that in front of her."

Amanda accepted a cup of tea gratefully and sank into a rickety chair at the scarred wooden table. Their best pieces of furniture didn't make it to this room.

"So tell me what's happened now," Lottie invited, joining her. "Your aura's positively vibrating this morning."

Amanda felt blood rising to her face. Could Lottie somehow discern her strange affinity to Dylan? Did she know about the way his kiss, his touch affected her? Was that what she meant by a vibrating aura?

"I found Elizabeth's journal," she said, diverting herself as well as Lottie from any thoughts either of them might have in that inexplicable direction. She told Lottie about the contents of Elizabeth's journal and of her morning visit to the Holbert and Dupard graves.

"So tomorrow morning I'd like to go to the library and read through back issues of the newspaper, if you don't mind holding down the shop alone," Amanda concluded.

"Of course, I don't mind." Lottie tapped a short fingernail against her cup thoughtfully. "We're going to have to give serious consideration to the possibility that you're the reincarnation of Elizabeth Dupard. That would explain the increased intensity of your aura and how you know so much about her life, even where she hid her journal. Living in her house and then having the accident must have jarred loose your memories. Though nothing is ever an accident, you know. There's a reason for everything. I'd guess that you need to know about Elizabeth's life to get this one right. That's usually the only reason we're allowed to remember our past lives."

Amanda was unwilling to believe Lottie's words, yet unable to disbelieve them. She poured more tea for both of them and took a sip to wet her suddenly dry mouth.

"There's a logical explanation for everything," she assured Lottie, though she hadn't found one that would take away her gut feeling of being Elizabeth. "We don't have to look to the supernatural."

Lottie eyed her over the rim of her translucent cup, returned it to the saucer. "Reincarnation isn't supernatural. It's all perfectly natural. Most of the world has always accepted it. Even the laws of physics confirm it. Nothing ever disappears, it just changes form. So our soul goes from one body to another, learning from our past mistakes, until we get it right."

"You keep saying that." Amanda ran a hand through her hair in frustration. "Get what right?"

Lottie waved her fingers vaguely. "It could be something as encompassing as transcending earthly desires, as the Tibetan lamas try to do, or something as specific as learning how to get along with your mother."

"Or my husband?" The question escaped from Amanda's mouth before she realized she was even thinking it.

"Or your husband. Why did you ask that? Do you think Phillip might have been Blake?"

"No, of course not." *But she'd confused him with Blake the first time she'd seen him and again last night when she'd feared he would hit her.*

"What about Dylan, your neighbor? Surely you realize it's no accident he's living right next door to you, in your friend's house, and he just happened to come over the morning you fell."

No, she didn't think it was an accident. But she doubted the reason for his presence in her life had anything to do with reincarnation.

"Maybe he was Blake," Lottie mused. "Are you frightened of him?"

"Yes," she admitted, then grinned wryly. "But you've got to remember, I'm frightened of everything and everyone. How would you like to wake up some eighty-odd years in the future?"

Lottie studied her for a moment, then rose decisively from the table. "We don't have many customers this early. Let's put a sign in the window that we've stepped out for half an hour, and I'll read your tarot cards."

First reincarnation and now tarot cards? This was a little too much. Of course she'd do no such thing.

"All right," she heard herself agree. What could it hurt, after all? And it would make Lottie happy.

Her assistant left the room, returning almost immediately to rummage through her voluminous bag. "Ah, here we are." She withdrew an oversize deck of cards.

"Choose the card that represents you," she said, offering Amanda a selection of four colorful drawings.

Amanda knew this was crazy, but that was nothing new. Everything had been crazy since she'd awakened at the foot of the stairs. She selected a card.

Lottie raised an eyebrow. "The Queen of Pentacles. A dark woman like Elizabeth, not fair like you." She placed the card in the middle of the table, awkwardly shuffled the remainder and asked Amanda to cut them.

"This first card covers you," Lottie said, her small hand lifting one from the deck. "It represents your general environment, your obstacles." She flipped it over, laid it across the Queen of Pentacles. From eyes as dark as midnight, the devil stared up at Amanda.

In spite of her certainty that this was all a game, she gulped and lifted her gaze to Lottie. The older woman smiled reassuringly, if a little shakily.

"It's all right. This just means you're chained to the past, and that past involves imprisonment, limitations. It's still here, I'm afraid, all around you." Her brow furrowed as she studied the card. "I'd say you can't be free in this life until you're free of your past, Elizabeth's past. You're doing the right thing, trying to find out about her."

Amanda shifted uncomfortably on the hard chair. Lottie's words were frighteningly reminiscent of what Dylan had said at the cemetery. Her life ran parallel to Elizabeth's.

"This is much better," Lottie continued, the relief in her voice obvious as she turned up another card. "This one represents the best that can be achieved." Amanda stared at the picture—of a family, a man and woman with two children contemplating a rainbow of cups with a house in the background.

"The Ten of Cups," Lottie explained. "Happiness, contentment, your dreams come true." She looked at Amanda with a misty smile. "I'm so glad. You deserve it."

Amanda found herself smiling in return.

Lottie turned over another card. "Now we see the tools you have to work with. Hmm. Yes, this is good. Justice, equity... Phillip's a lawyer, isn't he? Not that lawyers necessarily stand for those things, but there could be a connection."

She picked up the card and studied it, as if searching for a hidden message. "Maybe you have to find justice for Elizabeth and likely for yourself in order to achieve your rainbow. All these cards will pertain to the both of you, you understand. When you selected Elizabeth's card, you confirmed that you're linked."

Lottie flipped over a picture of a dark tower in a storm, of clouds rolling in and lightning flashing, striking the tower.

"Oh, dear. Well, it could be worse. This is where you're coming from, what's just passed away. It shows misery, deception, distress, ruin...all sorts of horrible things. It sounds amazingly like the last days of Elizabeth's life. Her husband was deceptive, cruel, and he caused her plenty of misery." She raised her eyes to Amanda's. "Did Phillip deceive you in some way?"

Amanda swallowed hard. "I don't know. I don't remember. He's been nothing but kind to me since my accident."

Lottie accepted the statement, lifted the next card, looked at Amanda again and reluctantly laid it out—a woman blindfolded and surrounded by swords.

"This is what's coming into being, what's directly before you. The Seven of Swords means violence, an accident, possibly a fatal one. You've already had one when you fell down the stairs, but that would be in the past. Oh, my, I'm afraid you still need to be careful. You must avert this."

Her brow creased as she hurriedly laid out four more cards in a row, muttering, "Good. Thank heavens. Yes, yes." But then she hesitated over the last one. Her hand shook, and her eyes met Amanda's beseechingly as she displayed it.

Reminding herself this was only a silly game, that these were harmless rectangles of cardboard, Amanda forced herself to look at the card.

Death.

CHAPTER TEN

The room faded to a blurred, unfocused mist. Only the stark colors on the array of cards blazed brilliantly.

Lottie's hand fluttered to her throat. "It doesn't necessarily mean a literal death," she said. "It could be the death of a relationship or a way of life or anything."

"But you think it means a literal death, don't you?" Amanda squeezed the words out past the obstruction that had suddenly risen in her throat.

"In the context of everything else, it could," Lottie admitted. "But remember, Elizabeth died many years ago. That was a literal death."

"You said our destinies are linked, that the cards pertain to both of us."

Lottie straightened, drew in a deep breath. "Yes, I did. But the cards don't dictate. They warn. They show what might happen. Look at the three that precede Death. Hope, Bravery, Wisdom . . . you couldn't ask for better tools. You have only to use them, and you can change that last card. Remember your possibility, what can be achieved." She indicated the drawing of the family looking at the rainbow.

Amanda knew the colorful layout was only a product of the random fall of cards, but there was so much that fit her circumstances, she couldn't ward off the suffocating fear that engulfed her.

"It's never easy to find the right path to follow," Lottie went on, pondering the arrangement, touching each card briefly. "You have to trust your soul to guide you."

Amanda shook her head and grinned wryly. "My soul isn't giving very clear directions here recently." It couldn't seem to figure out whether to throw her into Dylan's arms or run inside and bolt the door against him.

"Well, I know so little about your circumstances, I can only guess. But there is some evidence here that you need to work out a relationship, since your dream card—" she indicated the Ten of Cups "—shows a family. And Elizabeth's marriage didn't bring her happiness." She lifted her hands, shrugged apologetically. "The clues are all here. But I'm afraid only you can interpret them."

Work out a relationship. Of Lottie's speculations, that was the phrase that screamed at her.

If Phillip was Blake, he'd hurt her in two lifetimes, and now he seemed to be trying to make up for it. Was his soul trying to "get things right"? Did that mean she'd have to try to work things out with him? She swallowed hard, surprised at the emptiness she found at that prospect. Could she spend the rest of her life with someone whose arms made her feel hollow and cold? Could she spend the rest of her life without someone whose arms made her feel vibrant, alive— as Dylan's did?

Yet she couldn't totally dismiss Lottie's idea. Maybe her fortune-telling was nonsense, but Amanda knew in her gut—or in her soul, as Lottie would have it—that something out there had to be resolved . . . whatever the cost.

When Amanda finally arrived home, she found Phillip waiting on her porch. A quick glance to her left revealed Dylan on his own porch in front of his easel. She had a sudden urge to go over and grab that canvas, see if he really was painting or only using it as an excuse to spy on her.

Not, she realized, that she resented it so much as she just wanted to know if he was watching her. She supposed she'd become so accustomed to his always being there that she expected it—would feel sort of deserted if he weren't.

"I brought wine and steaks," Phillip said, lifting a large brown grocery sack as she approached, and she reluctantly turned her attention to him. "You just sit down and rest, and I'll have dinner prepared for you in no time at all. Medium rare, just the way you like it."

She wanted to look again at Dylan, see how he was reacting to her ex-husband's proprietary attitude, but she didn't dare for fear of what Phillip might see on her face. She smiled at him instead. "Thank you," she said. "That's very considerate of you."

He did all the right things, all the kind things. He was trying so hard to make up to her for the problems they had incurred in their marriage.

Being married to him wouldn't be horrible, she told herself as they sat on the sofa in the parlor after dinner, sipping wine and chatting quietly. He was doing most of the talking, recounting anecdotes from their marriage, feeding memories to her.

"What did I do?" Amanda suddenly asked. "I mean, I've only had the antique shop for a few months. What did I do before that?"

"What did you do?" Phillip repeated. "You were my wife. You helped me with my career. You entertained. You were the perfect hostess. Everyone loved you. And you did a wonderful job of providing a haven for me to return to after fighting the world all day."

No wonder I left him, she thought, and realized with a start how much of Amanda she'd regained. Elizabeth would have never rebelled at the idea that her identity should come through her husband. She might have been dissatisfied with it, but her world offered no alternatives.

"I never worked?" Amanda asked.

"You sold real estate when we first married, when I was still struggling to get established. But then my business improved, we didn't need the money and I did need your charm." He smiled beguilingly.

Across the screen of her mind Amanda watched the scenes he described unfold, recalled exactly how it had been. She hadn't wanted to give up her job, her independence. She'd enjoyed meeting people, finding homes for them.

But Phillip had discouraged her, had claimed the job stole time and energy that she should devote to bolstering his career. They'd rarely entertained in those early days; she hadn't participated in women's organizations.... She hadn't helped him, been his "partner." He'd made her feel so guilty, she'd finally given in.

In his own quiet, charming way, Phillip had dominated her as much as Blake had dominated Elizabeth. Even if she truly believed that fate dictated she should return to Phillip, she feared she would have a hard time going back into a relationship like that.

"Amanda," he said, breaking into her reverie, "things could be different between us. I've learned from my mistakes."

Amanda considered his words as she stared down into the bloodred depths of her wine. *He'd learned from his mistakes.* Wasn't that what Lottie said reincarnation was all about?

Nevertheless, whatever she had to do ultimately, she would not go back into a marriage she couldn't remember. She lowered her glass and faced him squarely.

"Thanks so much for dinner," she said. "I'm really exhausted. Could we call it an evening?"

"If you'll promise to let me take you out tomorrow night. We'll go to your favorite Italian place."

"Can we do it another evening? I really need some time for myself." So much was happening so fast. She had to slow down, take it all in, figure things out.

He took her hand in his cool one. "Please give me a chance," he pleaded softly. "Don't close me out. Give me an opportunity to try to show you how different it can be."

She didn't want to agree. She felt overwhelmed by his continuing presence, desperately wanted to be alone. But he was trying. Wasn't she obligated to do the same?

"All right," she finally agreed, feeling trapped, pushed by Phillip's persistence and her own uncertainty. "Dinner tomorrow," she added, lest there be any confusion about what she was consenting to.

She stood, encouraging him to leave. He rose with her, and she walked outside. He paused on the porch and turned to her, wrapping her in his arms, his thin lips descending to hers.

She wanted to push him away, but she tried to return the embrace, to respond. He was gentle and skillful, but his slim body felt strange against hers. Surely they'd shared passion at some time, but she could find no remnants of it now—not even the memory.

"Good night," she said, hands shoving against his chest, against the cool, slick silk of his shirt.

"Tomorrow," he said, then turned and walked toward his car.

She watched him drive away, lifted a hand to return his wave, then slowly faced Dylan's house. She couldn't see him on the porch, but somehow she knew he was there. She could feel his dark gaze on her as surely as she felt it when he stood before her.

She went back into the house, locking the door behind her. But as she started to draw the curtains, she felt she was not only shutting out Dylan's surveillance, but also shutting in Phillip's lingering essence, and she didn't want to do either. She left the curtains open, placed a hand on the glass as if to feel Dylan's stare, to complete the connection between them.

Absurd, she told herself. But it wasn't any more absurd than reincarnation or tarot cards or waking up in someone else's body.

She poured herself another glass of wine and sat down on the sofa, pulling her feet up under her. She ran her fingers over the soft fabric, traced the outlines of a pink cabbage rose. Not Mama's sofa, but hers. One she'd chosen carefully...because it was similar to Mama's? Because the house had called forth memories of another lifetime?

She sipped her wine, feeling its warmth radiating to all parts of her body. But it wasn't just the wine. This was her home, and she drank in the comfortable sense of belonging.

She stood, walking around the room, touching the familiar objects—the mantel clock Papa had brought from St. Louis, the lamp she'd found at an estate sale a month ago that looked so much like Mama's, the crocheted doily under it that her mother had bought for her at a craft show last week.

Everything was flowing together. She didn't really understand, didn't totally accept Lottie's theory of reincarnation, but she no longer felt she inhabited the body of a stranger. She still felt confused, sometimes expected to see Elizabeth in the mirror, but wasn't surprised to see Amanda.

Like two halves of the same person...fraternal halves rather than identical.

She strolled into the foyer and looked up the stairs. A chill ran down her spine, and she shuddered in the stillness. Perhaps her sense of identity was clearing, but nothing else was.

Slowly she walked up, searching each step for the memories she'd lost there. On the fourth step from the top, she hesitated. This was where she'd found the piece of broken crystal from the lamp in her dream. The crystal was real—sharp and jagged and substantial. It still rested in her handbag.

So what did that make her dream?

She forced her feet to move upward to the landing. She would relive the dream, stand at the top of the stairs looking down and see if that would call forth memories.

She took the last step, clinging desperately to the rail, her heart starting to pound. No one waited on the landing, she assured herself. The electric light banished the shadows. No one hid there now.

But she had to drag her hand away from its secure grip, had to force herself to turn around and stare downward.

Against all logic, she could feel ghostly hands touching her shoulders. Panic overwhelmed her, stole reason and thought, and she fled down the stairs and out the door onto the porch.

She welcomed the chilly evening air as it washed over her, restored her ability to think and chased away the mindless terror. She caught her breath, felt her heart rate slow. Could a dream cause such anxiety, such alarm? More and more she doubted it. More and more she felt certain that someone had actually tried to kill her.

On still-shaky legs she moved to the wooden glider and sat down. Leaning back, she pushed the swing to and fro. Overhead a myriad of stars rode the distant sky, their light clear and cool. The moon had not yet risen to dilute their brightness. She took a deep breath, tried to draw in some detached clarity from all around her, searched for the brief contentment she'd felt in her house.

The sound of a door opening startled her. She twisted around in the swing. In the blackness of the night the light from the open door of Dylan's house turned the form standing just outside into a menacing silhouette. For one moment she thought the specter of Death from the tarot cards stood staring at her.

Then Dylan stepped from the shadows and walked to the edge of the porch, making no pretense at anything but watching her. And she was glad to see him, wanted to run over to him, throw her arms around him, feel his hard body against hers, banish the memory of Phillip's.

She rose from the swing and walked over to lean against the rail of her porch, confronting him squarely. "It's too dark to paint," she said.

Dylan could have argued with her about that. As she stood there in the night, with only the glow from the street lamp and the window of her house illuminating her face, she made a picture that would doubtless find its way into his dreams—the good ones. Her pale hair slid softly about her shoulders, capturing and reflecting the minimal light. Her eyes shone large and luminous, almost as if they had their own source of illumination.

He forced himself to focus on other things. "The moon'll be up soon," he said, a vague reply to her comment.

"What have you been painting? Still the storm picture?"

He stepped off the porch and walked closer, then stopped as he realized what he was doing—getting closer to her wasn't the solution. He crossed his arms, putting a shield between them, between the effect she had on him and the reality of why he was here. "Actually, I'm doing a work of your house," he said, looking upward. "You have some interesting architectural details."

She looked up, too, as though she could see through the porch ceiling, through the night. "Yes, it's a true Queen Anne, with just the right amount of gingerbread to be charming, but not an excess."

"Your color scheme isn't authentic, you know."

"No, it isn't. But it looks good, right...don't you think?" She smiled, and his lips involuntarily imitated hers, moving as if they were once again on hers.

"Yeah, it looks good." She looked good, right...standing there on the old porch with her moonlight-colored hair and star-bright eyes.

"I love this house."

"The first time I saw you, when I was moving in, you were on a ladder way up by that attic window—" he pointed "—replacing a couple of those shingles—"

"Fish-scale shingles."

"Yeah. A couple of those fish-scale shingles that had blown down in a windstorm." The wind had still been blowing pretty strong, and she'd looked so fragile clinging to that ladder that, in spite of everything, he'd wanted to rush up and rescue her. That feeling hadn't changed.

With a start, he realized he'd lifted his arms to her porch rail and was leaning toward her only inches away. She had a way of making him momentarily forget his pain—his duty. That wouldn't do. He stood erect, searching for a barrier to throw up. "Relations seem to be improving with the ex," he said. That should do it.

It did. She jerked back as if he'd slapped her. "He's being supportive and kind," she said defensively. "He's been very good to me since the accident."

"Meaning he wasn't before?"

She threw up her hands. "I don't know. *I don't remember, damn it!* But if he wasn't, he's trying to make amends."

"For what?"

Amanda considered Dylan's question. Phillip had implied he regretted treating her like a possession, but there was something more. It was right there in the corner of her eye, always just out of her visual field. "I wish I knew," she murmured, speaking more to herself than to Dylan.

"What?"

"Nothing. I just told you I can't remember. You can keep asking me all night, and I still won't be able to remember."

An owl hooted eerily into the silence. Something small rustled in the dead leaves winter had left against her porch, and then all was quiet again.

"I know," Dylan said. His voice was soft, different . . . that strange-familiar voice again. The apparition of a memory teased at her then vanished.

"Who *are* you?" She didn't know she'd spoken the words aloud until he answered her.

"I'm your neighbor."

She considered his answer. If he were nothing more than her neighbor, he would have thought the question unnecessary, ridiculous. By his simplistic response, he told her that he had no intention of addressing her real question . . . and that he knew a real question existed.

"What happened to your brother and your father?" she asked, swallowing back her reluctance to bring up something she knew was painful to him. But it was the only personal part of himself he'd given her.

The night seemed to darken as if the blackness of his fury and anguish exploded from him, around him. She cringed, regretting that she'd tried to invade his soul. "It's getting colder. I think I'll go inside," she whispered, backing away, ready to leave, to spare him further agony from her prying.

"I'll be over in the morning to go to the library with you."
He turned and walked away, on to his porch and then inside, the blackness of the house engulfing him.

She remained outside for a few minutes, staring at the empty space he'd left. She'd hurt him by reminding him of his losses. She hadn't realized he had so much pain and anger bottled up.

Finally she went inside, closing the door behind her, and the staircase loomed before her again. She stood with her hand on the doorknob, unable to stop herself from wondering if Dylan's anger had exploded against her before for some reason, had sent her tumbling down the stairs.

No, that wasn't possible. He'd been too kind, taking care of her, teaching her to drive, going with her to the cemetery, taking her to the library tomorrow. Yet that could be interpreted another way. He never let her out of his sight, was obsessed with the question of her memory recovery.

But she had to admit that she looked forward to being with him tomorrow . . . to his strength that would carry her through the rough spots she might find at the library; to sitting in the car with him, her body only inches away from his; to the big hands that had rested so briefly on her porch rail touching her gently . . .

She darted upstairs, trying vainly to get away from him, away from her inexplicable, perhaps even dangerous desires.

In the light of day, which didn't penetrate to the old, musty basement of the library, Amanda was intensely grateful that Dylan had come with her. The place was creepy. She wouldn't have wanted to be there alone.

"I'm sure glad they put these old papers on microfilm," Dylan noted, taking down a tray and setting it on the long wooden table beside a viewer. He seemed completely relaxed today, with no trace of last night's distress. "Otherwise, I'm sure we'd never have been allowed to touch the sacred relics." The ancient librarian had made them sign their lives away before permitting them entrance to the storage area.

Amanda laughed nervously. The sound seemed to disappear as soon as it left her mouth, absorbed by the multitude of volumes stacked on shelves all about them.

"Here's the right year." He handed her a film. "Let's have a look at it." His fingers touched hers briefly, casually, accidentally...wonderfully.

Before he could draw back, she clutched his hand and looked up at him. "Thank you," she said. "I'm not sure why you're doing this, but I want you to know how grateful I am." She smiled weakly. "This could get tough."

A myriad of emotions—guilt, anger, concern—played across his features before he got them under control, carefully shuttered. "I'm glad I could help," he mumbled, then moved away, going back to search through more files.

I'm not sure why, she'd said. And he didn't even try to explain. She turned to the viewer, concentrating on the task immediately before her.

She found the first mention of Shawn Fitzpatrick in the *Holbert Weekly News* two months before Elizabeth's death.

Our town has a new and interesting visitor. Shawn Fitzpatrick, a radical labor leader from Chicago, has been going about harassing the good people of our town. Mr. Fitzpatrick, who immigrated to the shores of our great land from Ireland, is now betraying the country that took him in by preaching seditious Socialism.

Blake Holbert, son of the founder of our town, has had several of our citizens who work at his factory complain that Fitzpatrick is interfering with their jobs, trying to get them to organize in a labor union, to bite the generous hand that feeds them. When contacted by this paper, Mr. Holbert said, "My workers are paid a decent wage for a decent job. I treat them like my own family, and they're happy. If they aren't happy, they know they're free to leave and find employment somewhere else."

Amanda sat back, her jaw clenched. *Like his own family.* Yes, she could vouch for that.

"What did you find?" Dylan asked.

"This man was a monster," she said, indicating the viewer. "Read that. He owned the town. The newspaper would have printed whatever he wanted. So he comes out with a thinly veiled threat to fire anyone who listens to Shawn."

Dylan looked at her strangely, then leaned over to read the story, his body touching hers, warming hers. The adrenaline surged through her—from the injustices in the old news story, from Dylan's nearness, from some indefinable connection that flowed around them. She had to make a concerted effort to break that link, to scoot her chair a few inches away and give him better access to the viewer.

"The bastard," Dylan growled, then stood abruptly, backing away from the viewer. "But that's pretty much the way it was in those days. Laborers were treated badly, paid poorly, and union organizers weren't exactly welcomed with open arms."

Shawn certainly hadn't been welcomed, Amanda thought as she went back to searching through the papers.

Fights broke out at the factory. Shawn was thrown into jail, then released. The articles became more hostile.

As Amanda read the words, she could recall—or deduced from the stories, she told herself—how the atmosphere around town changed. The laborers became angry rather than depressed. They began to hope...to demand their rights.

And then without warning, she saw it, the words flashing into her field of vision.

Elizabeth Holbert Missing; Husband Fears Drowning. As she read the headline, Amanda felt again the sensation of cold suffocation. *Drowning.* Elizabeth had drowned. That would explain her lifelong fear of water, a fear so great she couldn't swim, couldn't even stand to bathe in a tub. Water pressing against her sent her into a panic.

"Amanda? Are you all right?"

She realized she had slumped in her chair, was gasping for air. "Yes," she said, the word coming out barely a whisper. She cleared her throat. "Yes, I'm fine. I found the story about my...about Elizabeth's death."

Dylan moved closer, placed his hands around her neck and massaged her tense muscles. "Relax," he said. "It's only a newspaper story. Take a deep breath."

His fingers were gentle as they caressed her skin. They felt exquisite, and she wanted to close her eyes, ignore all the crazy things going on around her, shut out the newspaper clipping about Elizabeth's death, relax as Dylan urged, escape into the pleasurable sensations he created.

But she couldn't. Somehow his touch seemed a part of the old stories, something she couldn't fully own until... She couldn't finish that thought. She only knew she had to continue reading.

Reluctantly, eagerly, she dove back into the past.

Prominent citizen Blake Holbert reported today that his wife, the former Elizabeth Dupard, is missing. He last saw her when they went to bed last night, but found her gone when he awoke this morning.

Bloodhounds were brought in from Jonas Horton's farm to track Mrs. Holbert. Her trail ended less than a mile away at the bank of the Missouri River.

"Elizabeth has been troubled of late by nightmares and sleepwalking," Holbert said. "I fear the worst."

Amanda sat back in her chair. "I wasn't sleepwalking," she whispered. "I was running away from him."

In her mind's eye Amanda could see Elizabeth dressing in the dark, feel her holding her breath for fear Blake would wake and catch her. Elizabeth's ribs still ached, and her eye was still discolored from her last infraction...and she wasn't even sure what she'd done wrong.

When her trembling fingers dropped her brush on the dresser with a loud clatter, she almost sobbed, knew for certain she'd been caught. But he lay still.

Even when she closed the front door behind her and ran into the darkness, her heart still raced with fear. She felt as if she were running through water, so slow did her progress seem. Finally, in the distance, she could see the gleam of moonlight on the river and dared to hope that she might make it.

The scene winked out, and Amanda saw nothing but the dusty library basement. The black curtain that had recently become so much a part of her settled between her and the rest of Elizabeth's life.

"Amanda? Are you still with me?" Dylan laid a hand on her shoulder. "Move over, and let me read this."

She blinked, swallowed hard. She was again having trouble distinguishing between herself and Elizabeth.

"Not yet," she whispered. "I need to find the rest."

She scanned the next edition of the paper and found it—a report that Elizabeth's drowned body had been discovered several miles downriver from Holbert.

In vain she searched her memory for details of that drowning, but her mind seemed to shy away from the incident. Perhaps, she thought, it was simply too horrifying to remember one's own death. All she knew for certain was that she had been running away from her husband and had died.

And that gave credence to Lottie's assertion that she had been reincarnated to reconcile with her husband, to make it right this time.

"Come on," Dylan ordered, crashing into her thoughts. "You're as white as a ghost. You need to get out of here for a while."

He'd watched her become totally immersed in the sepulchral atmosphere of the old library. The place had given even him the willies. When he'd read the story about Shawn Fitzpatrick, the man from Elizabeth's journal, for a moment he'd imagined he could feel the man's agony and determination. If it affected him so strongly, what must it be doing to Amanda's mental state, when she was much more susceptible than he? He shouldn't have let things go this far, but she'd seemed to need to find the end to Elizabeth's life in order to get back to her own . . . and he needed her to get back.

"Amanda? Let's go."

She nodded and went along with him unprotestingly as he led her outside and ushered her into his car. "Where are we going?" she asked as he pulled into the street, but turned in the opposite direction from which they'd come.

"I don't know. To get a cup of coffee, something to eat...something to keep you from passing out. What did the article say? What's upset you so badly?"

"That I...that Elizabeth drowned in the Missouri River. She was running away from Blake, but something went wrong. I've got to get down to the river."

Elizabeth had been running away from her husband when she died. Amanda had left her husband and survived—but she had been left with a lump on her head and bruises all over her body. Were these the parallels between Amanda's life and Elizabeth's that she'd been looking for?

He pulled up in front of a local restaurant. "We're not going anywhere until you get something to eat," he said firmly. She hadn't regained any color. Even away from the gloomy library, her fair skin was frighteningly pale. Her eyes shone with a fevered green fire, her breath came too quickly. He felt a little guilty for being a party to her distress, though he doubted if he could have stopped her.

"I can't eat right now. I have to get to the river." She spoke rapidly, her hands darting up and down, fluttering. She met his gaze, refusing to back down. He compressed his lips, equally obstinate. She needed to go home to bed, not on a wild-goose chase around the city.

"Be reasonable. You'll never be able to find the place where Elizabeth fell in."

"Yes, I will. I can find Blake's house. It may take me a little while—things are so different—but I'll find it. And then it'll be simple. I remember every inch of ground between there and the river."

"Amanda, listen to yourself." He clutched her arms, held her steady. "You're talking like you were Elizabeth. *You're not*. She's been dead for eighty years. And even if her ghost came back, she couldn't find where she fell in. The Missouri River changes courses regularly. It's not the same as it was eighty years ago."

If his words made any impression on her, he couldn't see it.

"I have to try."

"Why?" he demanded. "What more can you possibly find out about Elizabeth by locating the place of her death?"

"I can't remember. I need to remember, and then maybe I can...avoid that same fate." For a brief moment she looked frightened. He sucked in a deep breath, drew back, almost released her. Did she remember something, after all? Had he accepted her amnesia story too easily?

His fingers clutched her arms more tightly. "You can't remember Elizabeth's life because you didn't live it." His voice was grating.

He forced himself to loosen his grip, to relax. Was he trying to convince her or himself? He was no longer sure what he believed or what he was going to do with her.

"I have to understand Elizabeth before I can know what's going on with Amanda...with me. I know there's a connection."

"All right," he agreed, throwing up his hands in surrender. "We'll go to the river." She was going, with or without him. He had no doubt about that. At least he could be there with her—for whatever motive.

She accepted his acquiescence calmly, as though she'd always known it would come. "We need to go to Blake's house. That's where we have to start."

"And you know where Blake's house is?"

She blinked a couple of times, her eyes losing some of their feverish glitter as she seemed to return to a semblance of reality. "I can find it. Maybe I went there looking for antiques or something. I know where it is." She looked about her. "Sort of. I need to find a landmark. Where's the courthouse?"

"The old one?"

She smiled sadly. "Yes, it would be the old one now."

He didn't miss the meaning behind her words. In Elizabeth's time the courthouse would have been new. She was very much back in her fantasy. He had no idea where this was leading, but he knew he had to stay with her for a lot of reasons—some of which he didn't come close to understanding. Beyond the chance that she might remember everything at any time, and even beyond his crazy desire to be with her, he couldn't shake the peculiar feeling that he had to be there because he was somehow part of it all.

After they'd been driving, mostly in circles, for an hour, she finally leaned back with a sigh. "It's all changed so much. Nothing looks familiar."

"Amanda, the town hasn't changed since your accident," Dylan said firmly. He turned at the next street, heading home. She'd only been dreaming, after all. She had no knowledge of Elizabeth's world. He'd known that. Yet he felt an odd pang of disappointment.

She drew a weary hand across her forehead. "I know. I'm mixing things up again."

"It's all right," he assured her.

They passed a small church with a bell steeple, and she sat upright abruptly. "There!" she exclaimed.

Dylan slammed on the brakes. "That's not a house. That's a church."

"I know! And I could see that steeple from Blake's second-floor balcony. None of these other houses were here. There was a clear view. Blake's house is right through there." She indicated a diagonal path.

The feverish look was back in her eyes, and the green darkened, seemed more forest than ocean. Without further protest or even thought, but with an inexplicably expectant, exultant feeling, he started down the nearest street, turned at the next and made a zigzag path in the direction she'd indicated.

"There it is," she exclaimed, and he came to a stop in front of a very old, rundown house.

A hand-painted sign on the sagging front porch advertised Rooms for Rent. The house was different, Amanda realized, scarcely recognizable, but it still sent a chill through her. In that house a young girl's dreams had died cruel, violent deaths.

How fitting and just, she thought, *that the people who live in that house rent rooms, come and go and only use it. Nobody loves it enough to take care of it. There's too much hate trapped inside.*

She opened the car door and stepped out, crossed the yard between the houses. The woods and fields were gone, replaced by more houses and streets, but she had only to continue in a straight line. She circled around the chain link fence behind Blake's house, crossed to the next block, skirted the houses, ignored a barking dog, moved onward past the invasion of civilization to undeveloped land.

The trees were bigger than she remembered, but she couldn't stop to worry about that. Her heart hammered against her ribs, and her legs felt weak and shaky. She'd been lucky, unbelievably lucky, that he hadn't wakened when she'd dropped her hairbrush. But with Blake, she couldn't count on that luck to continue.

She walked faster and faster, afraid at any minute that he'd catch her, that she'd never reach the river. It seemed to take forever to get there. Please God, she hadn't taken a wrong turn in the darkness.

She broke into a run, tripped, stumbled over a fallen limb, and strong arms from behind grabbed her.

She screamed. He'd caught her! Within sight and feel of freedom, he'd caught her.

At the scream, he let her loose immediately, and she whirled to face him, already cringing away from what she knew he'd do to her.

But it wasn't Blake.

She laughed in delirious, ecstatic relief and flung herself into his arms. "Thank God it's you." She stretched up, offering her lips, herself.

CHAPTER ELEVEN

For an instant he looked surprised, didn't respond, and she almost pulled away, almost realized . . . but then his mouth came down to meet hers, the hunger matching her own. Her soul leapt with happiness as her body strained to his. The fear vanished. She was safe now.

She reveled in the familiar taste of his kiss, the softness of his lips, the special way they moved against hers. Reveled in the secure strength of his arms about her, the passion that surged in her at his touch. Until he'd come into her life, she'd had no idea a woman could feel such passion.

His hands stroked along her waist, cupped her buttocks and pulled her against him. She felt his desire for her and shivered with delighted anticipation, as though it were the first time he'd touched her this way . . . or as though he hadn't done so in a long time.

Now there'd be no more "long times" between them. They'd hold each other every night, all night, eat breakfast together in the mornings, love each other through wrinkles and gray hair and grandchildren.

As she clung to him, the fresh scents of the spring around them filled her, and she rejoiced at the rebirth of the earth, of her life. She tangled her fingers in his wiry hair and opened her mouth to him, accepting him inside her.

They should stop, she knew. They couldn't make love now. Their escape wasn't complete yet. They still had to get on the boat, get to New Orleans. But as always when she was with him, she couldn't seem to stop, didn't want to stop... not ever.

Finally it was he who pulled away, and reluctantly she let him go. Savoring the warm feel of his breath on her face, she opened her eyes and looked into his, thrilling to the way their bright blue color always darkened with desire. But something wasn't right. They were too dark, almost black...

The sound that escaped his lips was somewhere between a groan and a word. "Amanda."

Amanda. She sucked in her breath, looking into his face, into Dylan's face. She wasn't Elizabeth, and this man wasn't Shawn. Frantically she tried to clear the fog from her brain. Her mind knew who he was, who she was, but her heart didn't. She wanted to fall back into his arms, kiss him again, savor the love she'd been so long without.

This was the completion of the kiss they'd only started in the attic, and now she understood. She knew with a certainty that transcended logic that she had lived as Elizabeth, and Dylan as Shawn. She'd loved him desperately in another lifetime. She'd left her husband to meet him down by the river, to run away with him... and she'd died.

She stepped backward, away from him, away from the whirlwind that raced through her mind.

He dropped his arms. His eyes slowly cleared. As if on command, the unreadable mask he normally wore enveloped his face, hiding the blatant desire. He muttered an expletive, jammed his hands into his pockets and looked into the distance.

"Dylan," she whispered, "you have to tell me the truth. I've got to know if we were lovers before my accident."

He shook his head. "No. We have never been lovers."

He lied. Maybe they hadn't been lovers in this lifetime, but they had loved before, and the attraction between them still ran rampant. In spite of his firm assertion, she sensed that he knew he was lying. Maybe he didn't know what the truth was, but he knew he hadn't spoken it.

"You kissed me like a lover," she accused. "I know you remember. You knew it when you read Shawn's story in the attic. It was Shawn kissing Elizabeth then. And the first time I mentioned Blake, that night we were standing on my porch, you almost went into a trance. You remember when you were Shawn and I was Elizabeth, don't you?"

As he faced Amanda in the middle of the field, squared off like adversaries, Dylan's heart was still pounding, his blood still racing from that kiss . . . maybe still racing from their first kiss. He could almost believe her insane assertion that they were reincarnated lovers, so strong was his attraction to her in spite of everything. She felt so right in his arms, the passion and desire so deep, that they might have kissed a thousand times during a thousand lifetimes.

But of course they hadn't. "Stop it, Amanda! You're being irrational."

"How did you feel when you read about Shawn? Why did you call Blake a bastard?" She looked and sounded more sane, more in control than she had since her accident—maybe even before. Yet her words were insane.

"I'll admit that sometimes I get emotionally involved in the past," he said, unable to deny that he'd had the feelings she accused him of. "But that doesn't mean I lived there. I'm not Shawn, and you're not Elizabeth."

"Are you so sure?" she asked quietly, then turned and started picking her way slowly over the same ground she'd run recklessly across minutes before.

He couldn't answer her. After that mind-boggling kiss, how could he be completely sure of anything?

He followed wordlessly behind her.

She'd really lost her memory, really thought she was someone else. She hadn't been able to deal with the realities of her life and had left them behind. She'd seemed to be doing better, recovering, but now he wondered if she'd gone so far away she might never return.

Yet in spite of her doubtful sanity, in spite of her possible knowledge of if not involvement in Tom's death, in spite of what he knew he had to do, he wanted to fold her in his arms, hold her slim, vulnerable, determined body against his, kiss her until neither of them knew or cared if they were Shawn and Elizabeth or Dylan and Amanda. Until the world shifted to a place where it was okay for him to kiss her.

Amanda listened to the whisper of Dylan's footsteps behind her. She shouldn't have blurted out her realization about his identity. Now he really thought she was crazy... and with good reason. A few days ago she'd have thought the same thing if someone had told her she had lived before.

Anyway, it didn't matter, was probably for the best. She was drawn to him in this lifetime as she'd been in the last. If he returned her ardor, she might suffer the same fate as before. She'd loved Shawn, had rejected her husband for that love. And she'd died.

Elizabeth hadn't stopped seeing Shawn, as Blake had ordered. She'd believed in his cause, had wanted to help ease the agony of the people her husband oppressed. With Rachel's help, she'd continued to meet with Shawn in secret. But not just because she wanted to assist in his work.

The friendship he offered had rapidly become addictive, rapidly become more than friendship. She'd been too naive to identify the feelings at first, had only known she wanted to be with this man who was so strong and determined one minute, yet so kind and gentle with her the next.

Then, when he awakened in her the passion she hadn't even suspected she possessed, Elizabeth knew she had to be with Shawn, no matter the cost. Divorce, particularly from a man who owned the town, wasn't a viable option at that time. But when Shawn asked her to run away with him, she agreed—immediately and ecstatically.

They'd planned to catch a riverboat on the Missouri, go to St. Louis, then down the Mississippi to New Orleans. Shawn had been there before and told her wonderful stories of the carefree, colorful life in that city. As soon as they were settled, he promised, they'd send for Mama. They could all get lost in the crowd in New Orleans, and Blake would never find them.

But, Amanda reflected, Elizabeth hadn't made it to New Orleans. She'd never left Holbert. Something had gone wrong. She'd drowned, gone down into the cold, wet suffocation of the Missouri River.

Had it been an accident as the newspaper reported?

Rachel blamed herself for her best friend's death. Lottie's words came back to her. Rachel had helped her rendezvous with Shawn, had encouraged their romance. She'd delivered messages between them and come by Elizabeth's house to pick her up so Blake wouldn't be suspicious.

If Rachel blamed herself for Elizabeth's death, she must have known it had something to do with Shawn. She must have felt that her part in helping the lovers get together had contributed to Elizabeth's death.

Amanda's mind rebelled at the idea that he could have harmed her. He'd loved her! But she'd been so inexperienced then. Had she really been able to gauge the sincerity of a man's affections?

Something had happened after she met him at the river.

She shivered as she recalled the terrifying feeling of hands on her shoulders, pushing. *Her shoulders.* But had they belonged to Amanda or to Elizabeth? Or to both? How many times had she felt those hands on her shoulders?

Dylan's car loomed suddenly in her field of vision, and she realized they'd arrived back at the street, back in the reality of the present. But were the present and the past so separate, after all?

The spring air carried a chill that invaded her body, but the chill in her soul came from elsewhere.

Dylan parked in front of his house and came around to open Amanda's door. Instead of letting her out, however, he stood there, blocking her way, one hand on the door, the other on the roof. "What are you going to do now?" he asked.

"I don't know. Rest, take a nap. I promised Phillip I'd go to dinner with him tonight." She'd almost forgotten that and now wished she'd never agreed. "I need to know what he can tell me about Amanda. About my life."

Dylan's nostrils flared, his eyes darkened, losing all trace of blue. "Don't go."

Was he jealous? She felt herself blush at the pleasure that idea gave her.

He didn't appear to notice. His knuckles on the door were white, his other arm stiff as he leaned on the roof. "Why don't you take a few days off? Go stay with your parents. Get away from here for a while." His expression and tone were ominous, making his suggestions sound more threatening than concerned.

A part of her yearned to do just what he said, to stop trying so hard to find answers, let them come when and if they would. But another part whispered that that might be too late.

She shook her head. "I can't do that right now. Maybe later."

"You need to go now."

"Tell me what you know, and I'll consider it," she offered boldly.

He stepped aside and let her escape.

As she walked toward her house, she paused and turned back. He was still standing there, watching her. She stared back at him, but he didn't flinch.

She ought to resent his blatant spying. She probably ought to fear him. And sometimes she did. But mostly she wanted to give him whatever it took to erase that sorrow and rage from his heart.

But what if that meant losing her life the way Elizabeth had lost hers when she went with Shawn?

She broke the stare and went inside, closing and locking the door behind her. The day's events had left her exhausted. She needed a hot shower and a nap before she had to face Phillip. But as she passed the door to her office, she hesitated.

As much as she wanted to rest, even more she wanted to find the mysterious papers that kept nagging at the fringes of her memory, the papers her memory seemed to shy away from.

Standing in the doorway, she scanned the crowded room. The massive, old-fashioned desk held her computer and printer. A four-drawer file cabinet stood in one corner, a two-drawer one beside her desk. A telephone and answering machine with phone books sat on a utility table. A wide assortment of books filled the shelves of a small bookcase. File boxes on every surface held loose papers.

Nothing reached out to her, offered its secrets.

She began a systematic search. Pulling out the wide, shallow middle drawer of her desk, she poked through the myriad items—pens, pencils, paper clips, staple remover, rubber bands, cellophane tape....

The tape. She'd tried to secure something to the underside of the drawer.

Pulling the drawer out, she turned it over. Only a couple of pieces of torn tape remained stuck to the wood, but she could visualize the large brown envelope that had been there.

She stared at the evidence, despair washing over her. After she tried so hard to hide it, someone had found it anyway. The night he'd pushed her downstairs?

No, she thought with a surge of relief, of hope. She'd removed the envelope herself, fearful that he'd find it.

She sat straight up in the desk chair as the realization of what she'd just remembered hit her.

She'd feared that *he* might find the envelope, had felt it necessary to hide it better.

When she'd heard a noise in the night, she'd immediately taken a lamp from her bedside to defend herself. Yet she didn't think she'd known her life was in danger—at least, not from him. But there were others. . . .

She shoved the drawer hastily back into the desk, splayed a hand across her chest and tried to calm her breathing.

Who was *he*? And who were the *others*? How did Dylan fit in? Was he the man she'd hidden the papers from? Was he one of the *others*? Had someone sent him to spy on her, to harm her?

Could this have something to do with her divorce? But Phillip wouldn't harm her; he loved her, wanted her back. He was trying to make right whatever had gone wrong.

Her mind whirled like a Kansas tornado, spinning thoughts round and round, mixing them chaotically. Dylan, Phillip, Shawn, Blake, the *others*.

Damn it! Why wouldn't her memory release the answers, let her know the truth, so she could protect herself?

On the other hand, maybe she had a good reason for keeping the knowledge from herself. Maybe she didn't want to know. How could she stand it if she knew for certain that Dylan wanted to harm her?

She remembered the pain, the way her heart had shrunk inside her when she'd seen him coming up her staircase in the dark, looking for her. The bond was already so strong between them—and she knew he felt it, too, no matter how hard he tried not to. If he were guilty, he could kill her soul as well as her body.

She rose from the chair and, like a wild woman, dove into her search, desperate to find the documents that would tell her what was going on, who wanted to harm her. Yet at the same time a part of her wanted to hold back, dreaded what she might find.

She snatched the books from the shelf, flipped through the pages, then turned the shelf upside down.

Yanking open one of the file drawers, she stared in dismay at her carefully labeled folders. What should she look under? *H* for He? *M* for Murderer? The only one that seemed even a possibility was Miscellaneous, but a careful search revealed nothing enlightening.

In the small closet, she found summer clothes hanging from the rack and a large stuffed dog on the shelf. Terence.

She reached for the animal, took it down and stroked its dusty fur. The white around the black spots had become dingy. She squeezed one floppy ear and found that it still squeaked.

Phillip had won it for her at the Missouri State Fair the year before they got married. She remembered how thrilled she'd been, how impressed with his prowess. After they'd married, Terence had occupied a chair at the table and had, according to Phillip, frequently eaten his first helping of dessert so he'd had to have another.

She and Phillip had once shared a life together. How sad that things—that people—could change so drastically. As she thought of Phillip, she suddenly remembered her dinner date with him. She checked her watch, surprised to find how much time had passed.

Replacing the stuffed dog on the closet shelf with a dejected sigh, she surveyed the mess in her office. She could clean it up later. Right now she needed to change and get ready to keep her promise…to meet with one more piece in the puzzle of her life and try to determine where he fit.

She closed her office door behind her with a sense of regret that curiosity was the only emotion she could find for the man she'd once loved enough to marry.

Amanda sat across from Phillip in her favorite restaurant. Located in the Italian section of Kansas City, the place had originally been an old house and had many nooks and crannies. She and Phillip occupied a table on a second-floor loft overlooking the first floor.

"You look beautiful." Phillip raised his wineglass to her. "That's always been one of my favorite dresses."

"Thank you." Had she known that when she selected the royal blue silk with its soft neckline and swirling skirt? Had she unconsciously been trying to please Phillip, as he was so obviously trying to please her? Much as she'd like to think that, she somehow doubted it.

The waiter set a large salad with artichoke hearts, olives, Parmesan cheese and other tempting ingredients in front of her, and her attention turned to it. She hadn't eaten all day, had been so tense she really hadn't had an appetite. But now her body's demands overrode her emotions. She was starving.

"So what have you been doing?" Phillip asked. "I called the shop, and Lottie said you'd taken the day off to run some errands."

Amanda speared an olive, chewed and swallowed as she thought about how to answer him.

"I went to the library and looked through some old newspapers. I thought it might help me remember things." "Old" was a relative term. He'd likely think she meant last week, not last lifetime.

Phillip froze with his glass of wine halfway to his mouth. "And did it?" He smiled, but his eyes were frosty.

What had she said? Could he somehow know she'd been scouring through the past, that she once again believed she was Elizabeth, that she'd left him for Dylan in another life?

Of course not, she reassured herself. How could he know those things? Yet there was no denying that he was regarding her intently, waiting for an answer.

She tried to return his smile, hoped hers didn't look as phony as it felt. "Nothing significant. For the most part, the last few years of my life are still blank pages. I was hoping you might help me fill in some of them."

He relaxed, raised his wine to his lips and drank. From the time of her accident, Phillip had seemed determined to help her remember, but he appeared relieved that she hadn't. What in heaven's name did she know that no one wanted her to remember?

"Maybe we ought to get you to a psychiatrist, try hypnotherapy or something," he suggested.

She blinked, studied his cool countenance as he adroitly divided his attention between his food and her.

"I don't need to see a psychiatrist."

He reached over and squeezed her hand. "I'm just trying to help."

"I know. And you have. The things you told me last night certainly helped fill up some empty spaces."

"I'm glad," he said, smiling.

Lottie was right, she thought. With his silver hair, pale eyes and tanned, even features, he was devastatingly handsome. More handsome, really, than Dylan. Dylan had a rugged, powerful look. A dangerous look. A sensual look.

She concentrated on her salad, berated herself for the improper, traitorous thought.

"Did you go to the library alone?" Phillip asked, as though he could read her mind.

"No. My neighbor volunteered to go along and help me find the place, not to mention operate the equipment."

My neighbor. It sounded so much more innocent than *Dylan.* Just thinking his name called up his image, the feel of his lips on hers, his arms around her, his heart pounding wildly against her breast.

"Dylan Forrest," he said. "How neighborly of him."

She lowered her gaze, afraid he'd see her soul in her eyes. She stuffed an artichoke heart into her mouth, but it had turned dry and tasteless. Her appetite had disappeared again.

"Did you spend the entire day at the library?"

"No. We drove around the city." *Looking for the house I once lived in with you when we were other people, trying to find the place in the river where I drowned running away with Dylan, who was then Shawn.* If she told him that, he'd have her committed. "I wanted to go down to the river."

"You hate the river."

"Yes. I do." She cast about for a change of topic. "I was going through my office today and found Terence, the dog you won for me at the fair. Remember?"

His forehead wrinkled in a scowl. "The fair?"

"The year before we got married. The state fair in Sedalia. Now who has amnesia?" she teased.

"It seems yours is going away rapidly." She heard no happiness in his voice. But Phillip wasn't given to effusiveness.

"I wouldn't call it rapid." *I still know more about a woman who died over eighty years ago than I do about my own life.*

He lifted his wineglass. "Shall we drink to your complete recovery?"

The words and gesture, the expression of caring concern, were all exactly right. Yet his tone was cool, totally lacking in warmth.

Amanda raised her glass in return, mentally rebuking herself for being so paranoid. Was she so desperately searching for—and fearing—proof that her memory harbored a dangerous secret that she found evidence of it where none existed?

The waiter arrived a few minutes later with their entrées. He replaced Amanda's barely touched salad with a heaping plate of pasta covered in a white seafood sauce.

She twirled a large portion around her fork, determined to eat . . . if for no other reason than to escape the dizzying effect of the wine on her empty stomach. Her faculties were already severely limited; she didn't need further clouding. What she needed was illumination, information. What she needed was to know why someone would want to harm her.

"Who were our friends?" she asked. It sounded saner than asking about her enemies.

He peered at her keenly. "Mostly people from my office. Other lawyers, clients. In fact, one of them asked about you today. My client, Martin Robison. Remember him?"

"Yes. No." She winced as an arrow of pain shot through from the back of her neck to her forehead, and the memory she'd almost found fled. "No. I'm sorry. Almost."

"I've done a lot of limited partnerships for him and Michael Stevens. They're trying to buy a strip center now. I spent most of the day with them."

The pain had turned into a throbbing ache, so intense it was making her nauseous.

She stumbled to her feet, pushing her chair back clumsily. "Excuse me," she mumbled.

"Amanda, are you all right?" Phillip's words came to her through a haze.

"I need to go to the ladies' room. I don't feel so good."

He came around the table, wrapped a steadying arm about her and helped her down the stairs. As they passed under the loft, something indefinable drew her gaze to the table directly beneath where they'd been sitting.

The sole occupant sat with his back to them, face to the wall. But she couldn't mistake the black, unruly hair, the width of his shoulders or, more importantly, the magnetic field that seemed to emanate from him, drawing her to him.

What was Dylan doing here?

Phillip urged her forward, and she realized she'd been lagging. She stumbled along, trying to peer surreptitiously behind her, but Phillip blocked her view.

By the time she got to the ladies' room, her headache and nausea had virtually disappeared. Nevertheless, she went inside and splashed her face with cold water, stared at herself in the mirror and tried to read her own mind—just as Dylan always seemed to be trying to do. She could only hope she was as opaque to him as she was to herself.

Had he now taken to following her, to eavesdropping on her conversations in order to discover whatever it was he needed from her? Well, this was going too far. She'd march up to him, make sure that he knew she'd caught him, see how he handled that.

She blotted her face with a rough paper towel and went out to meet Phillip.

"Better?" he asked.

She nodded.

"Your color's coming back. You were awfully pale. What happened?"

"I haven't eaten all day. I guess the wine just got to me." But that wasn't it. She wasn't sure what the problem had been, but it was nothing as simple as wine on an empty stomach.

He put his arm protectively about her waist. "Do you want to go home?"

"No. I'm all right. Really. Let's finish dinner. I'll feel better after I eat."

As they walked past the table where she'd spotted Dylan, she saw only a white tablecloth with a candle in the middle.

Had she imagined him then? Was she so consumed with the man that she was starting to see him when he wasn't there?

She hadn't been feeling well. The raging headache had obscured her vision.

But she remembered the familiar aura he emitted. Never mind her eyesight; she'd felt him.

Dylan had been there.

CHAPTER TWELVE

After they finished eating, Phillip took her home and walked her to the door.

"Thank you for dinner," she said, immediately inserting her key in the lock, hoping to avoid another good-night kiss. The memory of Dylan's lips on hers was too new, too old, too wonderful; she didn't want it replaced or tainted.

"Are you going to invite me in?"

"Oh, well, actually I'm kind of tired. And that terrible headache . . ." She trailed off. She felt fine. There was no reason she shouldn't invite Phillip in—no reason except she didn't want to.

"I understand that you're still weak, and that's one of the things we need to talk about."

Reluctantly she opened the door and allowed him to follow her inside. At least this would give her a chance to find out more about herself. He'd been the one eliciting information at the restaurant.

"How about a cup of coffee?" he asked.

She nodded and headed toward the kitchen, but he detained her with a hand on her arm. When she looked up at him, he kissed her gently on the forehead.

"You sit down. I'll make it for you." He guided her toward the sofa in the parlor.

She sat, but bounced back up the minute he was out of sight. This was her house. She could sit where she chose. In the kitchen the light was brighter . . . and he couldn't sit beside her.

She marched in and took a seat at the table. Phillip looked up from his coffee preparations and raised an eyebrow, but made no comment.

Finally, when it was brewing, he turned to her. "Think we could invite Terence to have a cup? I haven't seen the old boy in a long time."

She'd been prepared for him to try to kiss her, to try to argue her into coming home with him—almost anything but that. She smiled softly, nostalgically for the Amanda and Phillip who'd gone to the fair together.

She stood, pushing back her chair. "I'll go get him."

He motioned for her to sit down. "You've been ill. Just tell me where he is."

"In the closet in my office." She started to sit again, then remembered the chaos she'd left in that room. "I'd better go. Things are in kind of a mess up there."

"I've seen your office in a mess before."

She caught him in the doorway. "Please. I'd really be embarrassed to have you see." And worried he'd ask what she'd been looking for.

For a long moment they stood, his stare locked with hers. A contest of wills. Then he smiled, shrugged and gave way. "I was just thinking of you, sweetheart. I didn't want you to have to go up and down those stairs an extra time tonight."

"I'm fine. Really."

She left, returning shortly with Terence in tow.

"He's a little grungy," she said, placing him upright in a chair, positioning his front paws on the table.

Phillip set down steaming mugs of coffee for each of them, including Terence. He stirred sugar into Amanda's cup, then reached over and squeaked the stuffed animal's ear.

Amanda wrapped both hands around the warmth of her coffee mug and smiled. "You remembered."

Tears misted her eyes as she wondered what had happened to the laughing young man who'd won the stuffed dog and the naive, tractable girl hanging on his arm.

Time had passed, and she'd grown into someone else. Just as time had passed and Elizabeth had grown into Amanda.

Incredible as the whole concept still seemed, she had to admit that she felt the same about her memories of Elizabeth as about her childhood memories. Had her soul exchanged one body for another? She supposed that wasn't any more amazing than exchanging the body of a baby for that of an adult.

"Amanda?"

"I'm sorry. Were you saying something? I guess my mind was wandering."

He reached over and briefly squeezed one of her hands. "I was just saying how much I miss those days when we first got married, even though we were dead broke."

She nodded, easily locating the memory. "We had that *awful* house where nothing worked, and the payments took your entire salary."

"But it was a good address."

Even in those early days status had been everything to Phillip. She chased away the disloyal thought. Everyone else at his law firm had been concerned about those things, so he'd had to be, too, if he expected to succeed.

"We thought we were out of the woods the time you had five houses scheduled to close in the same month," he said.

"Ohh!" She groaned, then laughed. "I was so proud of myself. I hadn't been in the business long enough to understand how precarious five deals could be, with four of them contingent on the sales of each other. When the fifth buyer backed out, the others collapsed like dominoes."

"We stopped looking at new cars very abruptly."

"And bought a twenty-pound bag of beans." She sipped her coffee, ruminating over the past.

We owe it to ourselves to try to recapture what we had back then."

She reached over and stroked the stuffed dog's soft ear. "All those things happened to someone else," she heard herself say. "We're different people now."

"We changed once. We can change again. We won't make the same mistakes this time."

Change. Get it right. Wasn't that what it was all about? But even though he was saying all the right words, even though her mind was going along with him, her heart resisted.

"At least let me take care of you until you're yourself again. I won't push you to make a permanent decision right now, but you need me. Tonight proved that." He stood, picked up Terence and came around to her. "Give us a second chance, Amanda. I'm trying so hard, but I can't do it if you won't let me."

She cringed inside at his words. He was trying, and she continued to reject him. That couldn't help either one of them, could it? Elizabeth had given in to her desire for another man, had left her husband and died. But Blake had been cruel to Elizabeth. She couldn't find any evidence of cruelty in Phillip. True, he'd grabbed her that evening when she'd come in with Dylan, but he hadn't really hurt her.

If she gave Phillip another chance, would they find the rainbow... and avoid the specter of death?

"Why don't you just go upstairs and pack an overnight bag?" he suggested. "We'll take this one day at a time. Stay with me tonight, and we'll renegotiate for tomorrow night."

Could she ask for more? He was being wonderfully reasonable... All he was asking was that she not close the door on their failed marriage. Against everything her treacherous heart screamed for, she forced herself to nod, to slide back her chair and rise.

Phillip's face radiated triumph.

As if in a trance, she climbed the stairs and went into her bedroom. But once inside, she froze. Try as she might, she couldn't force herself to go to the closet and take down her overnight bag.

As though she were being led, she could only move in the direction of the window. Slowly parting the curtains, she looked next door. The window was dark, the curtains closed. But she knew he was there.

As if in answer to her thoughts, he parted the barrier and stood staring at her.

And she knew, even if their relationship never went any further, never passed beyond the two kisses they'd shared, that she couldn't go home with Phillip when she felt this way about another man. Not even if it meant risking her life— and her soul.

She whirled from the window and raced downstairs, coming to a halt on the last step when she saw Phillip waiting for her in the foyer. "I can't," she said breathlessly. "I'm sorry, but I can't go home with you."

Phillip's pleased expression vanished. His face seemed to darken, only his eyes alight with pale, cold fires. "Why not?" he snapped.

She backed upward another step, cringing away from him, shaking her head helplessly.

His jaw clenched, his thin lips became compressed and he took a slow, deep breath, let it out. "Sweetheart, this constantly changing your mind is just another symptom. You've been through a lot. You're not well. I must insist that you come home with me and let me take care of you until you're better."

"Phillip, I want to do what's right, but you're going to have to give me a little more time."

"Time for what?" he demanded.

"To understand what's going on. You didn't try to stop the divorce. You only came around to get me to sign papers. Why are you pushing me so hard now?"

He stared at her a long moment, his gaze unreadable. "You're getting better fast, aren't you? Or maybe you never really had a problem in the first place."

There it was again—the obsession he and Dylan shared about whether or not she really had amnesia. She wanted to ask him why it mattered so much, but he turned and strode out the door, closing it carefully behind him.

She stared after him regretfully. She hadn't meant to make him angry. But relief that he was gone mingled with the regret, overwhelmed it.

Slowly she climbed back upstairs to her bedroom. Perhaps Phillip would be so upset he'd never come back. She searched for sadness at that idea, but found none. She was drained, she thought, too exhausted from all that had happened that day to feel any emotion.

Tomorrow, after a good night's sleep, she'd decide what to do about Phillip.

However, the instant she entered her bedroom, all thoughts of Phillip fled from her mind. Dylan was still there, still watching. She could feel him.

She went to the window and confronted him. Energy surged between them, sparked through her body. The windows, the open space, the houses, the years, the lifetimes...none of it really separated them. He was there with her and she with him.

For an infinite moment they stood, transfixed, absorbed. Then he whirled away, and she could trace his progress as surely as if there were no walls between them. Out of his bedroom, down the stairs, through the living room...his front door opened, and he appeared on the porch. For an instant he paused, looked up at her. She could almost see herself through his eyes...see the desire and need for him that must be leaping all about her. Then he was stalking across the yard.

Her blood surged through her veins, raced as her heart pumped faster and faster, thudding impatiently against her ribs. He was coming to her. For good or evil, he was coming to her, and she was waiting for him—the waiting almost at an end.

Her own front door slammed, and she heard his footsteps in the hallway, felt his presence beneath her. She'd left the door unlocked...deliberately? Had she known, somewhere deep inside, that this would happen? Planned for it to happen?

It didn't matter. All that mattered was that Dylan was coming up the stairs to join her. She turned away from the window, moved across the room to welcome him.

He charged into the room and rushed to pull her into his arms...or she threw herself into his arms. She didn't know. It didn't matter.

His fingers thrust into her hair, moving, caressing, tugging her head back until she could see the dark flames leaping in his eyes ... until he could find the matching emotions on her face.

His image blurred as his head descended toward her, his lips crushing hers, taking all of her and returning all of himself. She opened to him...needing, welcoming him inside her. His tongue slid over hers, tangling, dancing, sending impossible sensations vibrating through her. His kiss was hot and smooth and liquid. He tasted of midnight...dark and clear and free. She'd never known anything like it, yet recognized its familiarity as though they'd kissed a thousand times in a thousand lives.

His hands slid down her waist and cupped her buttocks, pressing her against him just as he'd done in the field earlier in the day. But this time she knew who touched her. He was Shawn and Dylan, and she was Elizabeth and Amanda, and they were all one and the same. Unless his soul were united with hers, she couldn't exist.

He picked her up, laid her on the softness of the patchwork quilt that covered her bed. His eyes were wild with his need for her as he loomed above her in the darkness. She stretched her arms up to invite him, though she knew he needed no invitation, could read her heart as surely as she could read his.

He sank onto the bed beside her, his hands shaking feverishly as he fumbled behind her for the zipper of her dress and drew it downward. This would be no languorous, gentle merging; they'd waited too long, their desire held in check past all endurance.

She pulled the dress over her head, unfastened her bra and tossed both articles aside, offering her breasts, her body to him. He didn't move, but gazed down at her, his eyes alight with stars on a hot summer night. "Amanda," he said, his voice deep and unsteady, "do you know what you're doing, what *we're* doing?"

She had to concentrate to make sense of his words. Her body, her heart were racing ahead, didn't need or want signals from her brain. "What we're doing?" she repeated.

"Have you thought about tomorrow? What if you regret this when you regain your memory?"

"I've waited for too many tomorrows. I don't need my memories to know I want this, I want you." She slid her hands under his knit shirt, over the hard muscles, up to tangle in the wiry mat of hair.

He groaned and pulled back, and for a moment she feared he would leave her. But he yanked the shirt over his head, then pressed his bare chest against her breasts, his lips returning to hers. Her naked flesh seemed bonded to his as if they were magnets, as if they were one person now sharing the same body.

If their lovemaking went no further, she thought as his tongue thrust into the inner recesses of her mouth, she would feel fulfilled.

But it would go further. Neither of them could stop now, not if the whole world dissolved around them. Maybe it already had; she had no way of knowing. He consumed her. Nothing else existed beyond the two of them.

His mouth and tongue devoured her throat, her shoulders, her breasts, claiming all of her for his own. She belonged to him, only to him, always to him.

Her hands roamed over his body, touching, possessing. His earthy scent of an open field in the darkness before dawn rose to her nostrils, and she drank it in, making it part of her.

As his tongue flicked across a nipple, sending unimagined ecstasy darting through her body, her head rolled back on the pillow, and she heard a moan coming from her own throat.

His impatient fingers darted beneath the elastic of her panty hose and caressed her stomach, electrifying every inch of skin he touched. She lifted her hips to help him strip away the barrier that separated them.

He stood then, his gaze never leaving hers, removed and thrust aside the rest of his clothing, the last obstacle remaining between them. She started to look away as Elizabeth had looked away from Shawn, denying her desire to capture his body in her vision, afraid to indulge so boldly.

But tonight she didn't look away. She watched his dark silhouette, let her eyes trace his wide chest, the darker shadow of hair tapering to his flat stomach... down to his blatant arousal.

Then he was beside her again, holding her again, and she could only see him with her fingertips, with her body, with her soul.

His hungry mouth darted over her, kissing her throat, flicking a nipple, caressing her stomach. Flames enveloped her, and she couldn't tell if the heat came from inside her or him. But whatever the source, it flared, scorching her. She writhed beneath him, unable to endure the separation one minute longer.

As if in an oft-rehearsed dance, he rolled over her, between her thighs, and at last she felt him inside her. She arched upward, meeting him, pulled away and rose again, their frenetic rhythm perfectly synchronized.

She closed her eyes, shutting out every sense but feeling, then opened them again as she felt his gaze on her. She understood that he needed to watch her, needed her to watch him, to join their gazes, their souls, as their bodies joined.

Waves of fire that centered in her loins blazed through her, higher and hotter with every movement. She could no longer tell if he were inside her or she were inside him, but she knew they were together, moving together.

She felt him throbbing as they exploded together. One or both of them cried out, or maybe it only sounded in her mind.

He collapsed atop her, kissed her neck gently, his lips warm and soft, then rolled beside her, taking himself from her. But it didn't matter. Their souls would be one always, even if their bodies never joined again. She curled bonelessly into his warmth. His chest expanded and contracted against her breasts in perfect rhythm with her own breathing.

He wrapped his arms about her, his big hands stroking languorously down her back. She wanted to touch him that same way, to explore and memorize at leisure every inch of him. But she was drained of energy, limp from giving and taking so much. Her eyes closed, and she drifted into a deep and dreamless sleep.

Dylan held Amanda's warm body against his, stroked her silky, sweat-damp skin, inhaled her scent of wildflowers now mingled with the musky odors of love, listened as her rapid breathing softened, became slow and even, as her hands on his back relaxed. She was asleep.

If only he could hold her like this forever, with no intrusions from the outside world. Even as the thought ran through his head, a chill seemed to creep through the room, across their bodies. They couldn't close out the rest of the world. It would have to be dealt with—especially after she regained her memory.

When that happened, would she ever lie in his arms like this again? Would he want her to?

No, that last question was stupid. Of course, he'd want her. He'd wanted her from the first minute he'd looked into those green eyes, as deep and clear as the ocean.

Maybe she'd never remember. Could they start from right here and now?

Again the answer was no. *He* remembered. He couldn't forget Tom or his father, or his mother's tormented face, which had aged twenty years and no longer smiled. People were wrong when they said the past was dead. The present was only an accumulation of all of the past.

Amanda had sensed that so strongly she'd tried to go back to the past, to escape from the present, negate the part she couldn't handle.

And he had to admit that the house where he lived, the old news stories in the library, even Amanda's insane tales, gave him an eerie sensation of actually being there. When Amanda talked of their having been lovers in another lifetime, he more than half believed her. He smiled into the dark, lifted her silvery hair and let it trickle through his fingers, savored the reality of her in this lifetime.

Well, her theory would explain why he'd been so immediately drawn to her even after her suspicious actions on

Sunday and the even more suspicious loss of her memory on Monday morning—plus her acquiring a mysterious set of bruises.

She must have figured out that he was Tom's brother. Which meant, even if she weren't directly involved, that she must have always had the information and kept it a secret. So what did that say about her? And where did the bruises come in? Had she wanted to tell him, and Phillip had beaten her to keep her quiet? But she was sticking to her story about falling down the stairs.

In her defense—and he desperately wanted to build her defense—it would appear the truth had finally become so painful, she'd been forced to lose the memory of it.

She mumbled something soft and incoherent against his chest, sighed and went on sleeping. He stroked her slender arm and had to resist the urge to crush her closer to him, so close she'd become a part of him, and they'd never have to split apart.

She moved sinuously against him, and he felt his desire for her returning. But he shouldn't give in to it again. He needed to get up quietly, without disturbing her, get away from her presence long enough to think straight and try to sort out all the complications, decide what to do now. His feelings for her—feelings he finally had to admit went beyond sexual—complicated things immeasurably.

The house creaked, and he tensed for a moment, then reminded himself that old houses did that.

Amanda awoke with a start. Had she heard something again?

Then she relaxed. She didn't have to be afraid. Dylan was beside her, holding her. She still lay curled in his arms, her head on his chest.

But Shawn hadn't been able to keep Elizabeth from harm. Holding her breath, she listened for any sound.

Dylan stirred and nuzzled her hair. His hand stroked down her back, slid along the valley of her waist and over her hip. She raised her face to his, felt his lips descend to hers. This time his kiss was teasing. Gently he nipped her upper lip, touched her lower with the tip of his tongue, explored and tasted fully.

He slid one hand between them, caressing her breast almost worshipfully. Against her stomach she could feel his desire growing even as her own rose again.

With their earlier desperation satisfied, they could indulge in slow, velvety explorations, savoring every nuance of every sensation. Finally, when she thought surely she must explode with the unbearable pressure even his gentle touches evoked, he slid into her.

Like classical music, he led her slowly, then faster and faster, building to a crescendo, from one peak to another and another and another until she was certain she had reached the outer limits of exhaustion. But then, as she felt him racing to his own pinnacle, as she felt him throbbing inside her, to her surprise she joined him, ascending to heights she hadn't known existed.

Later, as they lay in the darkness, she touched his face with her fingertips, traced his brows, his square, determined jawline, the tiny scar at the corner of one eye. She wanted to know, to claim, every inch of him.

She loved him. She'd loved him through two lifetimes, and no matter how harmful it might be, she couldn't stop loving him. Maybe she'd returned to make peace with Phillip, to give him a chance to make things right. Maybe loving Dylan was wrong, even dangerous. But she was as powerless to resist this feeling as Elizabeth had been.

Even if she had gone back to Phillip, if she never saw Dylan again in this life, she'd still love him. Elizabeth had known that the night she ran away with Shawn, the night she'd died.

No, Amanda wouldn't allow herself to think about that right now. For as long as it lasted, even if for only this one night, she wanted to revel in the glory of a consuming love that survived through the years . . . even through death.

She pressed herself as close to Dylan as possible and drifted again into sleep.

She was sinking. She flailed her arms wildly, but she couldn't swim, couldn't rise back to the surface where air would fill her lungs instead of the invading, suffocating water. The weight was too much. She couldn't fight it. She was being pulled deeper and deeper.

She could feel him watching her, see him as through a fog. His eyes shone like beacons, guiding her, compelling her to climb upward. His mouth was moving, but she couldn't hear the words, couldn't hear any sound.

The effort to reach him was too great. She wanted to turn loose, give up, sink into the dark oblivion.

But he wouldn't let her. His gaze pulled her, tugged, drew her like a magnet, and he was more irresistible than the force that drew her downward.

With an all-consuming effort, Amanda forced her eyes open. She couldn't move, didn't want to move. The quilt lay on her like a giant, leaden weight. A monster sat on her head, crushed it in viselike jaws. She gave up the fight to stay awake and closed her eyes, drifted again toward the devouring mist.

CHAPTER THIRTEEN

His stare was so strong as to be almost palpable. She tried to reach out a hand to touch him, but the mist was too strong, the weight that covered her too heavy. She wanted so badly to stop struggling, if only he'd let her.

But she dragged her eyelids open once more, trying to see what he was pulling her toward.

Nothing. Darkness still surrounded her. She started to close her eyes again, but she heard whispering...whispering that reverberated painfully inside her head.

The window the whisper came. He was outside the window. If she could get over to it, then she could stop fighting, sink into the comfortable fog and let go.

With a giant effort, she tried to get out of bed, but her body was no longer hers, didn't respond to her commands.

Harder! She had to try harder. He wouldn't leave her alone until she made it to the window.

Moaning with the exertion, summoning all her strength, she struggled to move. He seemed to be reaching to her, offering his strength, the energy that always hummed about him.

Slowly she slid out of bed. Her aching head whirled round and round. Her stomach lurched, and she toppled in a heap on the floor.

No longer sure why, she dragged herself slowly across the floor toward the window. The distance seemed infinite, every inch an agony. She didn't look up, had no real desire to see her goal, just kept pushing mindlessly forward until her hand touched the wall.

She had reached the window. She could stop.

But it wasn't enough. She had to pull herself up.

Groaning with the exertion, hanging onto the window-sill, she finally managed to haul her leaden, disconnected body from the floor, up to the translucent square of glass. She swayed precariously, her head and stomach spinning.

She could barely discern that the darkness was less intense beyond the glass, outside her room. Across the way she thought she could see his shadowy silhouette in the other window. She could still feel him all about her, pushing, urging. She had to get to him and make him stop, make him let her go.

She leaned forward, but she couldn't reach him. Weakly, again and again, she hammered against the restraining sheet of glass, the action becoming meaningless with so many repetitions. Then, as if in slow motion, her fists kept going through the window, into the lighter world outside. Shards of glass sailed away, only a few falling onto the sill and the floor beside her.

Air rushed through...crisp and bright and sweet. Of their own volition, her lungs sucked it in greedily. She coughed, swayed closer, wanting more, leaning out the hole until a spear of glass scratched her cheek, warning her back.

As she breathed in the light from the approaching dawn, she seemed to breathe out the darkness from her room, from her brain.

Gradually, breath by breath, Amanda became aware that she was standing at her bedroom window. Her head throbbed painfully, and her stomach churned with nausea. She'd been having the strangest dream...the drowning sensation again, only this time it was different. And this time she'd had the oddest sensation of Dylan being there.

She broke into another fit of coughing, then gulped in more of the fresh, cool air...air that came through her broken window! She lifted her hand to her face, saw the blood oozing from several small scratches.

She'd been walking—no, crawling—in her sleep and had broken her window!

With a gasp she turned back into the room...and smelled the sickly sweet, rotten odor of gas. For a long moment she stood, panic gripping her still-drugged mind.

Gas. It had to be coming from the space heater. Heart hammering wildly, she stumbled on shaky legs over to the stove, groped for the pliers she kept behind it and twisted the difficult handle, shutting off the flow.

She clutched her aching head with both hands, trying to think through the fuzz that clouded her mind. All she could remember was an admonition from somebody, somewhere: should she ever smell gas, get out of the house immediately.

She started toward the door across the room, then stopped. If she loosed the gas into the rest of the house, would it find a spark somewhere and explode?

She staggered across the room and opened both windows on the back wall of the house, then took several deep, steadying breaths. The nausea and headache were gradually diminishing.

The jagged hole beckoned her over to survey the damage. Through the window she could see Dylan's house. He'd been an integral part of her gas-induced hallucination. She'd struggled to reach the window because of him, because she'd thought he was watching her, calling to her.

With a start, she remembered the night before. She whirled and looked at the empty bed. Dylan had been there with her. They'd made love. She'd gone to sleep in his arms. So where was he now?

Had he seemed to be watching her in her delusions because he really had been? Had he turned on the gas, then stayed long enough to be sure she wouldn't wake up too soon?

But in her dream he'd seemed to be pulling her out of it, sending her the will to survive.

Dylan's form appeared in the window across the way just as she'd imagined it earlier...or actually seen it earlier? His eyes widened with surprise when he saw her. He blinked, then disappeared from view.

Was he surprised she was still alive? Was he coming after her to finish the job? She grabbed a robe as she dashed across the room, slid out the door and closed it behind her, then raced downstairs, yanking the key from its hook and unlocking the door, running outside.

Dylan, wearing a rumpled brown-and-beige-striped robe, was already charging across the yard toward her. She halted on her porch, looking desperately for the best avenue of escape, but he grabbed her arms before her groggy mind and body could respond.

"What's the matter? Why is your window broken?"

"Why did you leave in the middle of the night?" She tried to pull away from him, raised her hands to push him away, but he caught and held them.

"What happened to your hands? Did you break your window? Damn it, Amanda, what's going on?"

"How do you know I was the one who broke my window?" She jerked her hands from his grasp and hid them behind her back.

"You were standing in front of a broken window and you have scratches on your hands—what am I supposed to think?"

She moved away from him, around the glider, put it between the two of them. "Did you turn on the gas before you left me?'' She hadn't meant to ask him so bluntly, but the words slipped out.

''Turn on the gas?'' he exclaimed, and for a moment the mask disappeared from his face, revealing a look of horror. ''Someone turned on the gas? That's why you broke the window?''

She nodded, her insides clenching into knots, the nausea returning full force, her headache rampaging as she waited for him to do or say something that would betray his guilt.

He stood erect, looking into the distance as though searching for answers. ''Someone turned on the gas,'' he repeated—stupidly, she thought.

''I almost died,'' she stated, and he flinched. ''If you didn't do it, who did? Nobody was in my house except you and me, and you left. Why did you leave?'' Insanely, she wanted him to give her a reason, wanted him to prove to her he hadn't tried to kill her after she'd opened her body and heart to him, given him her soul and thought he'd given her his.

He took a deep breath and faced her squarely, his eyes full of pain. ''I had to get some distance, be by myself to think. Last night...us...it was all too much.''

''Too much what?''

''Too much everything. Too much emotion, too much involvement with each other.'' He raked a hand through his hair and shook his head. ''You just don't understand.''

''I know that. So why don't you tell me instead of talking in riddles?''

Again he shook his head. ''You can't really believe I'd harm you after last night. Why would I want to hurt you?''

''I don't know,'' she almost sobbed, banging her fists on the back of the swing. ''I don't know why someone would push me down the stairs or turn on the gas. If I can't remember my life, how would I know why someone wants me dead?''

His eyes and nostrils flared, and she realized she had spoken her suspicions aloud for the first time. "What makes you think someone pushed you downstairs?" he asked softly.

She didn't want to tell him about the dream or the lamp shard. "Why did you come to your window and look over at me?" she demanded instead. "Because you heard glass shattering and wanted to see if I had somehow managed to survive?"

He glared at her. "No," he said, and she snatched the word from the air, held it to her, cherished it. He had finally denied that he'd tried to kill her. She had no reason to believe him, of course—only that her heart wanted to. But was that enough?

"I was having this stupid dream," he continued. "You were drowning, and I was trying to help you." He shrugged and shook his head. "The noise of glass shattering woke me up. I guess because I was dreaming about you, I associated the noise with you. I thought you were in danger, and you were. I went to my window and there you stood, behind that broken glass."

It sounded amazingly similar to her own dream or hallucination. He'd been with her either in her dream or in her room. If he'd turned on the gas, he could have made up the dream to coincide with her reactions to the gas.

She wanted to believe him, to trust him. Maybe he was telling the truth about his dream. Maybe his soul had somehow reached out to help her. If she was going to believe their love had transcended death, it was a small leap to believe in mental telepathy.

He rubbed a hand across his face. "When I left, I made sure to lock your door behind me."

"It was still locked when I came down," she said accusingly. "No one else could have come in."

"Amanda, we've talked about this before. A child with a library card could slip through that lock."

"But why would anyone want to kill me?" She spread her arms wide, almost screaming in her frustration.

"Why would *I* want to kill you?" he asked quietly, his gaze tugging at her as it had seemed to tug her in her dream. "Maybe nobody did. Maybe it was an accident. You got cold after I left, lit the heater, and it went out."

Her heart surged with hope at the possible explanation, but she had to crush it. "The heater's very hard to light. I have to use a pair of pliers to turn the handle. I'd have remembered." Even as she spoke, she questioned herself. Would she have remembered? Hadn't she forgotten a lot of things lately?

"Then let's call the police." Dylan stood there, sturdy and real, his words cutting harshly and cleanly through the last fuzziness in her brain, making valid the possibility that someone was trying to murder her.

She wrapped her arms about herself against the chill air, rubbing the soft fabric of her robe. She couldn't say why, but the idea of calling the police filled her with foreboding, despair, guilt—

"You're cold. Let's go inside and talk about this over some hot coffee," he suggested. "I'll go upstairs and check out your bedroom to make sure it's safe."

Make sure to remove his fingerprints before she took his suggestion and called the police?

She had to stop this. She could have turned on the heater herself.

But she hadn't imagined the shard of glass on the stairs.

Unless it had been there all along, and she'd manufactured the dream around it.

She passed a shaky hand across her face and nodded, agreeing to everything—to anything. Right now she felt more confused than when she'd first awakened to see a stranger in the mirror.

"Wait here." He disappeared inside the house.

She didn't wait, following him instead. She tried to tell herself she wanted to stay close to him because she didn't trust him. She needed to see what he'd do in her bedroom. But she couldn't deny that a part of her simply wanted to be with him.

He paused in the foyer and turned to her. "This could be dangerous. You really ought to wait outside."

She shook her head, wondering if the danger he spoke of would be to her body or to her heart. As he started up the stairs, insane desire hit her unexpectedly. She'd nearly died and wasn't sure if this man had caused it, yet she couldn't take her eyes off his muscular calves protruding from the robe, stretching and flexing sensuously with each step. She knew how those legs felt; only hours before they'd been pressed against her, wrapped around her, propelling his body as he entered hers....

This was as crazy as anything that had happened to her. She mustn't think about making love when she needed to concentrate on staying alive. She forced herself to watch him closely, see if he'd react in any way as he mounted the stairs—a guilty flinch, a hasty glance in the direction where the piece of crystal had lain....

Nothing.

He opened the bedroom door, and the faint odor of gas greeted them, making her nauseous all over again though most of it had dissipated through the open windows. She waited in the doorway while he knelt by the heater and, using a handkerchief—to avoid smudging fingerprints or to stealthily wipe them off?—tried to turn the valve.

"You're right," he said. "Even I can hardly budge it. Are those the pliers you use back there?"

"Yes."

He lifted the tool, examining it as if the inanimate object might begin to speak, to tell who had been using it.

And something slid into place in her mind: the image of Dylan sitting on her floor, holding a pair of pliers and grinning.

Her hand flew to her throat, and she gasped.

He looked at her quizzically. Her legs, already shaky, were suddenly unable to support her. She slumped to the floor, half-hysterical giggles escaping her lips.

"Amanda?" He dropped the tool and came over to her. "What's the matter?"

He sat down beside her, wrapped his arms about her, and she leaned against him. "I saw you with the pliers, and I remembered."

"What?" Did she imagine it or did his arms tighten around her?

"It was so clear, you sitting there with the pliers in your hand, scowling fiercely." For an instant she'd thought she was seeing Dylan turning on the gas. Then the memory had expanded. "You came over to fix my plumbing when it started making those horrible noises, and all I could give you to work with was a hammer, a screwdriver and those things." She pressed closer to him, trembling in her relief.

"Totally useless. We sat on the floor and laughed."

"Yes," she said, letting the memory settle over her. It had been the first time she'd met him, and something very wicked inside her had started counting the days until her divorce would become final, until she could be free to pursue the spark that flared between them.

He laughed again, crinkle lines appearing at the corners of his eyes, suggesting this was something he'd done more of at some time in his past. But today, as she had that first day, she sensed something hiding behind the darkness of his eyes, something that pulled him back from the laughter they'd shared about her poor assortment of tools.

"It'll all come back soon," he assured her. Or did his voice have a warning tone?

"I'd better go put on that coffee." She stood, making an effort not to let him see how unsteady she still was. *Before his nearness and her own yearnings pulled her onto the floor with him, before she forgot caution and everything else in her desire for him.*

Dylan rose with her and stood watching as she floated down the hallway and the stairs, her silky blue robe touching and sliding over the sleek curves of her body as she moved, the bare heels of her feet peeking out from beneath. He wanted to run after her, lift her in his arms the way he'd done a few days ago and carry her to the spare bedroom, where they'd be free from the nauseating gas fumes.

When he'd lost all control and been drawn to her house, her bedroom, last night, he'd told himself that making love to her might somehow free him from this attraction that was rapidly taking over his life. It hadn't. His desire was stronger than ever—as was his need just to be with her.

The shield she'd kept between them before her accident had disappeared, and the barrier he'd deliberately erected was slipping fast. In fact, if he were truthful with himself, he had to admit that he'd taken more of her than just her body last night. He was inextricably tangled with those clear green eyes, with the vulnerable, frightened, stubborn spirit that shone through.

He'd seen the desire that matched his own in those unguarded eyes only a moment before, but she'd fought it, run away from him. What had she remembered, besides their first meeting? Why had she changed her story to being pushed down the stairs rather than falling?

They needed to talk—something they should have done in the beginning. But even then he hadn't been sure what she knew, how involved she was. Now it seemed he had more to worry about than he'd realized. *Pushed* down the stairs; almost asphyxiated in her sleep... When her memory returned, he *had* to be there.

He rose slowly to his feet and went down to the kitchen.

She stood at the cabinet, measuring coffee grounds, her long, slim fingers turning the mundane action into a graceful gesture. He had to fight a desire to scoop her into his arms, kiss away the angry red scratches on her hands, carry her far away from everything... into another land, another lifetime, where all that mattered would be their feelings for each other.

Of course, he couldn't do that. "Amanda, you've got to call the police," he said unceremoniously, slipping into one of the small, uncomfortable chairs at the table.

"No." Amanda kept measuring coffee grounds into the basket. Again she felt the inexplicable but strong aversion to his suggestion. Because she didn't want to know if Dylan had tried to kill her? She couldn't imagine why he would want her dead. He cared about her; she knew that. But Shawn had cared about Elizabeth, and there was certainly a possibility that he'd killed her.

With a start, she realized that she loved Dylan enough to risk putting herself in danger... just as Elizabeth had loved Shawn. But how could she ever endure the pain of knowing that danger came directly from him? Was that what she'd had to face as Elizabeth?

"What would I tell the police?" she asked, trying to sound logical. "That I can't remember if anyone has a reason to harm me? That I might have gotten up and turned on the gas heater? That I dreamed someone pushed me down the stairs?" She turned to watch him carefully as she uttered the last sentence.

His eyes widened, then narrowed. "What, exactly, did you dream?"

Her heart beating furiously, breath coming so rapidly she found it hard to speak, she leaned against the counter while the coffee made gurgling sounds behind her, and told him about her dream. Was she giving her would-be murderer something to speed him on? And was that causing her terror as much as the thought of the agony she would suffer should she find that Dylan had betrayed her?

When she finished speaking, he sat staring at her for an endless moment, then slowly pushed back his chair and came to her. She braced herself against the counter, wondered wildly if she'd have time to open the drawer and find the knife she'd wielded against him before.

But she made no move to follow through on that thought. As though taking on a life of their own, her arms lifted to him, encircled him as he pulled her against his hard body.

"Amanda," he murmured hoarsely, desperately. "Amanda, you don't know..."

"Then tell me!"

His lips came down and captured hers, sent her mind spinning out of control. Through the soft fabric of his robe, she could feel his desire, hard and immediate. He pulled a few inches away from her, his gaze searing. "Isn't this all we need to know right now?"

Dear God, it was. She'd risk her life to be with him, because her life was nothing without him.

His lips trailed down her throat as his hands tugged at the sash of her robe, loosening it and peeling it back to expose her naked flesh.

"You're so beautiful," he murmured, cupping one breast, igniting flames wherever he touched, while his other hand fumbled with the tie of his own robe. She looked downward, thrilled to the sight of his hardness just before he pressed himself against her stomach. He lowered his mouth to her nipple, closed his lips around it, and her head rolled back, her eyes now seeing only bright flashes of light as his lips and tongue drew electric surges from her female center to all over her body.

"Yes," she whispered. "This is all we need right now. Only this." She wouldn't think beyond the moment, even if she could. He'd stolen all thought from her, as he'd done so many years ago. Their bodies had changed, but she'd recognize that kiss, that touch, those lips on her breast, if he changed a hundred times.

He lifted her slightly to enter her, to join with her, and she didn't know or care whose body their souls were in. Together they rose though space and time, each thrust, each sensation sending them higher until they reached the sun, exploded and fused in a burst of light, together, inseparable....

Still holding him against her, inside her, Amanda drifted slowly back to earth, caught her breath, became aware of the sharp edge of the countertop against her buttocks.

Dylan traced her lips with his fingertip, then kissed them lightly. "Not a very romantic spot, I guess. But I seem to lose control around you." He eased her feet to the floor, took himself from her, breaking the physical connection. The connection of their souls could never be broken, she thought. No matter what.

He caught both sides of her robe, started to pull them together, then stopped and trailed his tongue between her breasts, down to her stomach. She arched backward at the delicious sensations he brought to her already overloaded nerves. With a smile, he drew her robe together and retied the sash.

"I think that coffee's ready," he said, grinning broadly and reaching into the cabinet behind them for cups. He poured two cups, stirred sugar into one and handed it to her, then sank to the floor. "This is as far as these legs will take me until I get some caffeine."

Laughing, she sat down beside him. Using the cabinet for a backrest, legs stretched out in front of them, they drank in companionable silence for several minutes.

He leaned over to her, brushed her hair back and kissed her forehead. "Much as I regret it, I've got to go to work sometime today."

"Mmm." She closed her eyes, savoring his touch for one more moment, then looked up at him and sighed. "I guess I do, too. As soon as I can find the energy to crawl upstairs."

He frowned. "I'd almost forgotten about your bedroom. It should be aired out by now."

"I'll just be in there long enough to grab my clothes."

With a grimace, he took her coffee cup from her, set it along with his up on the counter behind them and took her hand. She winced as he touched the scratches.

"I'm sorry," he said, bending to kiss them.

"It's okay. A little peroxide and they'll be good as new."

He nodded but took care not to touch them again. "Amanda, we need to talk about something."

She tried to tug her fingers from his grasp. She didn't want him to break the spell, to drag them back to reality. She wanted to linger in the aftermath of their lovemaking for a while longer. "We can't discuss anything serious while we're sitting in the floor in our robes," she said lightly.

"Yes, we can. Listen to me for a minute. I should have been up-front with you a long time ago. My brother didn't just die. He was murdered." He looked at her—accusingly, she thought—and a shiver threaded its way down her spine, crowding out the last of the pleasant feelings.

"I'm sorry," she whispered, unsure if she were expressing sympathy or somehow apologizing for something.

"Dad had a heart condition," he continued as if he hadn't heard her. "Tom's death killed him. Mom's aged twenty years in the past three months."

She clutched his hand with both of hers, thinking perhaps she understood some of the torment she'd always found in his gaze. "I'm sorry," she repeated, unsure why he was telling her all this now.

"Do you remember—"

The phone shrieked, interrupting his words.

He dropped her hand, and she sensed that the moment—whatever moment it was—had passed. "Let it ring," she said.

He got to his feet. "Answer it. We'll talk this evening when we have more time."

She rose, and he pulled her to him for a quick good-bye kiss.

"Don't go anywhere except to work." His dark gaze bored into hers.

"Where would I go?"

"Promise me," he demanded harshly.

"Okay."

"I'll get back as early as I can." He started from the room, then turned back. "Lock the door behind me."

She nodded and went to pick up the still-ringing phone. "Hello?"

For a moment there was silence. "Hello, sweetheart." Phillip's voice came across the wire, cheerful in a forced, taut way. The tautness wasn't surprising after her rejection of him the night before, she supposed, experiencing a rush of guilt. She hadn't rejected Dylan. Had welcomed, even encouraged, his lovemaking.

"Hello, Phillip. How are you this morning?" She wished she could take back the inane words, but didn't know what she'd replace them with in any case.

"I wanted to talk to you before you got off to work. I, uh, wanted to apologize for last night. I'm sorry if I pushed too hard. I'm just worried about you. Are you sure you're all right? You sound a little strained."

"I'm fine, really." Then, because her guilt urged her to make a propitiatory offering, she reluctantly continued, "I had quite a scare. When I woke up, my room was full of gas."

"That damned space heater! I knew something like this would happen. I told you it was dangerous. You stay right there and I'll come get you."

"No," she protested. "I'm all right."

"For how long? What'll go wrong in that crumbling mausoleum tonight? The whole place could blow up."

"There's nothing wrong with my house," she defended. "The space heater isn't defective. Somebody turned it on." The moment the words left her lips, she regretted saying them, regretted letting him goad her into revealing more than she'd intended. It seemed she'd done a lot of that this morning.

"Who?" he asked immediately.

"I don't know. It might have been me. I could have tried to light the heater in the middle of the night and didn't get the job done."

"That just proves it's not safe for you to be alone. You're not competent right now to care for yourself."

She bristled at his condescending attitude. "Or maybe it wasn't me. A child could have slipped through that lock on my door."

"Why would anyone try to kill you, Amanda?"

"I don't know." She had to back down. She had no idea why anyone would try to kill her. If only she could remember... "No reason. It was just a thought."

"Have you called the police and told them any of this?"

"No, of course not. I said it was just a thought."

"Sweetheart, you've been through a severe trauma," he said smoothly. "You've sustained a head injury, suffered amnesia, and things are bound to be a little confusing until you're well again. Trust me, nobody's trying to kill you. You got up in the middle of the night, turned on the gas, forgot what you were doing and went back to bed.''

''But—''

''After this incident,'' he continued, as though she hadn't spoken, ''I can't allow you to stay there alone. Let me take care of you, just until you're better. I'm not asking for anything beyond that, Amanda. For all the years we had, for all the mistakes I made, let me do this for you.''

Tears sprang to Amanda's eyes . . . tears for the love she'd had with Phillip, which hadn't lasted, and the love she had for Dylan, which was being crushed before it had a chance to thrive.

''I'll come by and get you around seven tonight,'' he said when she didn't respond. ''Don't you worry about a thing. I'm going to take very good care of you.''

''No,'' she whispered, but the receiver in her hand had gone dead.

CHAPTER FOURTEEN

Amanda held the telephone receiver in her hand, staring at the inanimate plastic object. Phillip had ignored her protest, was coming to get her, to take care of her. For a few days.

Maybe, a voice inside her head whispered, that's what all these accidents were pushing her toward. Lottie had said there were no "accidents." Everything happened for a reason.

If Elizabeth had died when she left her husband, and now Amanda's own life had been in danger after leaving Phillip, maybe she needed to be with him to make the accidents stop, to be safe—to get things right this time.

Her gut clenched at the idea. Maybe it was what she needed to do, but putting the thought into deed was going to be like pushing her way through quicksand. Every atom, every essence of her being rebelled against it.

Carefully she replaced the receiver in the cradle. How much of her reluctance came from an aversion to being with Phillip and how much from her desire to be with Dylan? The most charitable answer she could come up with was an equal split. And if she were totally honest, she'd have to admit that, no matter who the other man might be, she wouldn't want him if she could have Dylan instead. Just as Elizabeth had wanted Shawn.

But Elizabeth had been wrong. Elizabeth had died.

On feet that weighed a hundred pounds each, Amanda climbed the stairs to get dressed for work.

* * *

As the day wore on, Amanda had to fight the impulse to snap at customers, at Lottie, at her own thoughts. Was she having some sort of residual effects from inhaling all that gas? Maybe she should have gone to the doctor, though she had no desire to go through all the poking, prodding and questioning again.

She could tell that Lottie knew something was wrong, but she was reluctant to admit what had happened. She didn't want to hear her dear and trusted friend say that she ought to go back to Phillip. Lottie had said she had to "get it right" this time, change the direction in which she was headed. Amanda didn't want Lottie's confirmation of what her mind told her was right and her heart screamed was wrong.

However, Lottie had also told her she should let her soul lead her. And her soul wanted to be with Dylan. Her soul was bound to his, had found his again beyond death, even in another lifetime.

But Phillip had also found her again and was trying to set right what had once gone wrong.

The thoughts whirled round and round with no answer in sight.

As she started to replace a hundred-year-old, hand-painted vase after an interested customer had left, she noticed her hands were trembling. While still a couple of inches above the tabletop, the vase slipped from her shaky fingers and clinked against a lamp.

"Did it break?" Lottie asked.

She examined the vase closely. "No, but it could have. Would you mind very much if I left the shop in your hands for the rest of the day?"

"I don't mind at all. You run on home and try to get some rest. You look a little peaked. I'll take care of this place. Don't you worry, now. Everything's going to be fine."

The words were oddly reminiscent of Phillip's. But Lottie didn't sound nearly as positive as Phillip had, and Amanda was more inclined to trust Lottie.

Amanda drove home, parked in the street and got out. Before Phillip arrived, she needed to go through her office one more time and try to find those papers she'd hidden. In her mind's eye she could see them in her hand, could remember feeling disappointment, sadness and fear as she studied them, then decided to hide them. But the contents of the papers and their hiding place remained a blur.

As she started up the walk, however, the sight of Dylan's house pulled at her as strongly as the need to find her mysterious documents. She wanted to go over, knock on his door and see him, talk to him, touch him, let him hold her and make the world right, make her believe nothing else mattered for at least a little while.

But it was only three o'clock. Though he'd said he'd be home early, his big black automobile wasn't parked in its usual spot.

She left her car and went over to his house, unsure what she was doing, but unable to stay away. Walking up the sidewalk, she recalled when Rachel's father had laid the bright red bricks. Now those bricks were faded and cracked, with grass growing between them.

So far she still had Elizabeth's memories, even though Amanda's were returning. When she recaptured all of her present life, she desperately hoped Elizabeth's wouldn't leave. She no longer felt as if two people inhabited her body. Elizabeth's life was as real as Amanda's childhood—a stage that, while it might be farther in the past, was still a part of her.

She stepped onto the porch where she and Rachel had played with dolls, giggled about boys and made whispered plans for her assignations with Shawn. The boards were curled; some were rotting. The neglect, if nothing else, made her aware of how much time had passed.

Lottie's words came back to her—Rachel had lived there as a recluse, blaming herself for her friend's death, when all she'd done was help the lovers get together, encourage their love, do what her friend wanted.

Had Rachel suspected that Shawn had caused Elizabeth's death? Had he betrayed her love the night she'd run to him? Rachel must have thought that or her sense of guilt wouldn't have run so deep as to ruin her life.

Standing before the door, Amanda shivered as once more the question of Dylan's presence in her life rose to the front of her mind. Why was he here? What had he meant when he'd said, "you don't know..."? Then he'd kissed her and asked her if that wasn't all they needed to know, and it had been enough at the time. He had the ability to make her feel that, to forget everything else.

Just as Shawn had done to Elizabeth.

Even though she knew he wasn't home, she knocked loudly on his door. No one answered. No sound came from inside to suggest movement.

She started to turn away, to go to her own house and— what? Pack a few clothes to take to Phillip's? She couldn't go with him. Yet she couldn't *not* go with him. What if Lottie was right, and the only way she could escape certain death was to reconcile with Phillip?

What good was living if she couldn't be with Dylan?

She looked down the street, hoping to see Dylan's car approaching. No traffic was in sight.

As she turned back to the door, she abruptly realized that she'd stood here like this before, in this lifetime, before the accident. And been refused admittance. She'd never been inside Dylan's house. On the few occasions she'd gone over, he'd come out to join her, but he'd never invited her in.

She'd thought at the time that he was probably a lousy housekeeper and didn't want her to see the place.

But now she had to wonder. Was there something inside he didn't want her to see? Her mind raced in confused circles. She *had* to find some answers...before it was too late.

Looking about her to be sure no one was watching, she straightened her beige linen suit—as though that would make her look less like a criminal—and pulled a credit card from her wallet. Dylan had remarked that a child with a library card could get into her house, so perhaps the same was true with his. If he had come into her house like this—and she didn't know how else he could have gotten in the night she'd been in the attic—she was entitled to enter his the same way.

In spite of her justification, her fingers shook as she positioned the card between the lock and the doorsill...and noticed the shiny new dead bolt a few inches above. Almost relieved, she returned the plastic rectangle to her wallet. The decision had been taken out of her hands. She'd tried to find out about Dylan and failed.

She started to walk away, then remembered the kitchen door. When Rachel lived there, the door had never been locked. Dylan had probably put a dead bolt on it, too. But she had to check it out.

Heart hammering at her audacity, at the chance she might be caught, she walked through the side yard around to the back. The ground was still wet and spongy from the recent rains, and she almost turned back to get a sturdier pair of shoes than her flimsy heels. But that was only an excuse. Breaking into Dylan's house, ferreting out his secrets, had suddenly become a very real possibility, and she wasn't sure she was ready for what she might find.

Ready or not, she had to do it. She was tired of the unknown, of asking herself questions she didn't know the answers to. She slogged on around to the kitchen door. There was no new, shiny dead bolt, only the ancient lock.

This time her fingers shook so badly she could hardly get the card into the space. Somehow, though, she managed. It slid past the lock easily, and the door creaked open. For an instant the world spun and blurred about her, and her heart actually seemed to stop before racing on.

She dropped the card back into her purse, her fingers too numb to get it into her wallet. Raising a hand to her throat, she took a deep breath and walked into Dylan's kitchen.

Unlike the one in her house, it had not been completely modernized. With the exception of aging, the cabinets and sink were much as they had been when Rachel's family lived there. A small, old refrigerator had replaced the icebox, and a gas range stood where the old wood stove had been. A coffeemaker, toaster and microwave were the only evidence of modern living.

Tentatively, expecting every minute that someone would jump out and accuse her of breaking in, she opened a cabinet door. Paper plates and cups. Other doors revealed empty spaces.

That told her nothing. Lots of men living alone never cooked. She'd have to venture farther into the house.

Tiptoeing, holding her breath, she moved from room to room. Dylan lived very Spartanly. The dining room and back parlor were completely empty. The front parlor contained a single, rather shabby chair and a small table, both situated over by the window... the window that looked toward her house.

On the table and the floor beside the chair she saw the first real evidence that anyone inhabited the house—several empty paper cups with dark coffee stains, a couple of soft-drink cans, a book of crossword puzzles, a detective novel, an automatic pencil, a pair of binoculars and a spiral notebook.

She should have left then. She knew that. Going through his house was one thing. Reading his notes was quite another.

But the chair was positioned for a perfect view of her porch and her hall window. She had to know what he'd written in the notebook. If it didn't concern her, she'd only glance at it, then leave.

Not wanting to touch it, she leaned over the table, peering at the page that lay open, the page with yesterday's date. "Took Amanda to library—" *He was taking notes on her activities!* "—to look up stories about Elizabeth, the woman she thinks she is. She didn't get any more current than 1912. Phillip took her to Italian Taste for dinner. He mentioned Martin Robison. She didn't remember him." *Dylan had been there, had eavesdropped on her! What did he know about Phillip's business partner?*

The notes ended.

She picked up the book, flipped back a page and found the same type of notations for the day before. The data was cut-and-dried. All details of his personal involvement with her were carefully omitted from his notes.

She looked about her dazedly, her whole world falling apart. There was virtually no furniture here. This wasn't his home. He'd leased this house just to spy on her.

But why? What had she done to cause this? If only she could remember!

Something in her shriveled and crawled into a dark cave to hide. Even if he cared for her—and she believed he did—Dylan had betrayed her. He'd made love to her while keeping from her the knowledge of his spying. His notes contained no reference to any feelings for her. He kept his two lives completely separate.

Was he a stalker, obsessed with her? Would he kill her if she didn't respond to his attentions, if she tried to leave with Phillip?

Maybe he'd been hired to spy on her. If he had been, could he also have been hired to kill her? Was he one of those men she'd seen in movies and never believed existed—a man who could make love to a woman, then kill her while she lay still warm from his touch? A man to whom murder was nothing personal, just a job?

Her trembling fingers dropped the notebook. She reached down, retrieved it and, with badly shaking hands, replaced it on the table.

Slowly she mounted the stairs and walked down the familiar hallway to Rachel's bedroom.

As she grasped the cold glass knob of the door that led into the room where she knew he slept, where she'd seen him at the window, she could have sworn the knob suddenly turned hot, burning her hand. She jerked back, then reached out and touched it again. It was cold. Her own fear had deceived her.

She opened the door slowly. The first thing she saw was the unmade bed. Dylan had slept there. The body she'd caressed last night, which had seemed to belong to her, had lain there. She walked over, touched the rumpled sheets, half expecting to find them warm.

But they were cold. The only remnants of him were the faint scent of his cologne and a wispy odor of green fields and midnight that she'd come to associate with Dylan.

Across the room two open suitcases sat on the floor—further evidence that he didn't really live here. As she backed away from the bed, her gaze fell on the nightstand. Beside the lamp rested a camera with a big lens—probably telescopic, she decided.

Had he been taking pictures of her to go along with his notes? Damn him! She snatched up the camera, looking for a way to open it and remove the film.

But if she did that, he'd know she'd been here. Besides, what pictures could he possibly have of her that would harm her . . . or help anyone else?

She ground her teeth in frustration. When she didn't know what he wanted from her, how could she know what kind of pictures he might take?

She set the camera down and opened the drawer of the night stand. A big, shiny, stainless-steel gun gleamed at her.

Moving as if in a trance, she picked it up. It was heavy, much heavier than she would have thought. But Dylan had muscular arms. He could easily wield something this weighty. His big hands would have no problem holding it steady while he took aim at something . . . or someone.

She didn't know much about guns, but thought this must be an automatic. The bullets were all hidden inside—a lot of bullets, more than the revolvers in western movies, where the bad guy had only six shots. Dylan might need more than six shots.

She didn't know how to determine if the gun was loaded or not . . . but she sensed that it was.

She dropped it into the drawer, jumped when it landed with a thud.

What kind of man kept a loaded gun in his nightstand? He could very well be a hired killer. But why, in heaven's name, would anyone want her killed?

Almost afraid to breathe, she backed out of the room. She wanted to run from the house, run away, leave all this chaos, this terror, this deception. But she hesitated at the top of the stairs.

That was impossible. She couldn't do it. Elizabeth had tried to run away and hadn't made it. Instead she had to face the problem, attack it. *Hope, bravery and wisdom.* Those were the tools Lottie had said she had to work with.

She decided to check the other bedrooms. The first two were empty. In the big corner room she found his painting equipment.

A nervous burst of relieved laughter escaped her lips. He had told her the truth about one thing: he was a painter.

An easel stood facing one of the large windows. She walked around it. The unfinished oil painting of a storm was actually quite good. She could almost feel the power of the wind bending the trees and pushing the clouds, the electric sizzle of the lightning, the darkness overtaking the world.

The house on which the storm was converging was hers. The painting reminded her eerily of the tarot card showing a tower in a storm. What had it meant?

Deception, ruin.

She shivered. Certainly Dylan had deceived her.

She turned away from the painting, looking around the room. Leaning against the walls were other canvases in various stages of completion. One was a compelling picture of a tornado sweeping across the Kansas plains. The twister seemed to be moving, and she could almost hear the roar. Whatever ugly things Dylan might do with his camera and gun, he was nevertheless a very talented painter.

Three of the pictures were of her. She swallowed hard, unsure how to handle her feelings about that. One, a nude, was very sketchy, as though he drew from imagination. Had he been fantasizing about her? He'd drawn her expression as sensuous and aroused, but with a trace of wistfulness. Not the fantasy she imagined a sexual pervert would have.

Another showed her standing at her bedroom window, curtain in hand, looking outward... into his window? The face was too small to show much detail, but the figure conveyed the impression of being lost, searching for something. Or maybe Amanda was reading too much into it, since she knew how she'd felt looking out that window.

She moved across the room to inspect the third picture of her more closely. This one was a portrait. She raised an involuntary hand to her face, as if to check whether her skin was as smooth and luminous as he'd painted it.

No matter what he'd done or was going to do, she could no longer doubt that he cared about her. Maybe he didn't even know it, but he loved her. It came through in every brush stroke. He'd meticulously, carefully, recorded every detail as seen through the idealistic mist of a lover's eyes.

Her hair wasn't really that silky or shiny. He'd made her eyes seem to glow with a zest for life. Her lips were full and sensuous, ready to be kissed.

Entranced with the way he saw her, with the evidence of how he felt about her, with his incredible artistic ability, she picked up the canvas and carried it over to the window to examine it in a better light. She wanted to memorize it, drink in the sensation of being loved. Use it to ward off the horrible things that were happening all around her, reassure herself that Dylan cared for her and would never harm her.

The sound of an automobile door slamming startled her out of her trance. Had Dylan returned? What would he do if he found her in his house?

The image of the gun loomed in her mind, obscuring the portrait.

Heart hammering so loudly she fancied she could hear as well as feel it, she looked down into the street. A woman was getting out of a car parked across the way.

But it might have been Dylan, could be him at any minute. She had to get out of there!

She went to replace the picture where she'd found it and froze. Another canvas, now revealed, must have been hidden behind her portrait.

She stared in horror at a picture of Elizabeth drowning.

CHAPTER FIFTEEN

Elizabeth was sinking into the wetness of death, one hand reaching vainly upward, ebony hair floating on midnight waters, her face a study in terror and grief.

The world seemed to close in about Amanda, to crush the breath from her body the way the dark water was stealing the life from Elizabeth. She felt again the sense of betrayal, of love lost.

Hands on her shoulders had pushed her downward, over the rail of the boat into the dark, terrifying depths of the river. The river that should have taken her to a new life, a life of joy with the one she loved, was stealing her life from her, taking away forever her chance at happiness.

Amanda gasped, tearing her eyes away from the painting before the waters overwhelmed her, drowned her even as she stood in a second-floor bedroom.

It wasn't just the realism in Dylan's painting. She could *remember* how it had felt to drown, how she'd felt at the instant that was captured on canvas... cold, wet, suffocating and *betrayed*. Pushed to her death from the boat she'd thought would be her way to salvation.

The painting was done from the perspective of someone above, someone on the boat. She lifted her gaze toward the ceiling, as if she could see the man watching her, the one who'd done this painting.

Shawn had bribed the riverboat captain to stop and pick them up in the middle of the night. They'd boarded the vessel and stood together at the rail, watching Holbert disappear behind them....

Then she'd felt hands on her shoulders, and the next instant, she'd plunged downward into the chilling depths of inky water. Startled, unbelieving, she'd reached upward, toward Shawn on the deck, begging him to save her, just as she was reaching in the picture.

Oh, God! Shawn had killed her. And somehow Dylan knew that. Dylan had painted her death. His memories might not be as complete as hers, he might deny them, but they were there!

Elizabeth had loved Shawn, had run away with him, and he'd shoved her overboard. Because he'd changed his mind? Because he feared Blake? She couldn't begin to imagine why he'd done it, but obviously he had.

She loved Dylan, and for some reason she couldn't begin to imagine he was trying to kill her. He had pushed her down the stairs. He had risen from their bed of love and turned on the gas.

Her head reeled with the pain. He'd held her, touched her, spoken words of love—just as Shawn had so many years before.... If only she could remember more about this present life, maybe she'd know why Dylan would want to get rid of her. Maybe it wasn't even something she'd done in this lifetime. Maybe Shawn's feelings were as strong to Dylan as Elizabeth's were to her, and he felt compelled to repeat what he'd done before.

She turned her head to the side, as if she could avoid looking at the image in her mind—in her heart.

Was there any reason to fear him now? She was dead inside already. Dylan—and Shawn—had awakened in her emotions she hadn't even known she possessed, then murdered them as surely as he had destroyed her body and was trying to destroy it again.

Whatever his reason—because he was obsessed, because he was hired by someone, because he was overwhelmed with Shawn's feelings and needs—he could kill her even while he loved her.

With hands that trembled from the pain as well as the remembered cold of the water and the fear of death, she tried to put back the portrait of herself exactly where she'd found it. She needed to reposition it precisely so he wouldn't know she'd been here. But more than that, she needed the terror on Elizabeth's face, the pain of love betrayed, to be hidden again from her and from Elizabeth's murderer.

She stumbled from the room on rubbery legs that threatened to give way. As in a nightmare, she moved in slow motion down the stairs, each step taking an eternity. She feared she might have to crawl once she reached the first floor and could no longer hold on to the rail, but somehow she managed to move through the empty rooms, to get outside into the open air, onto the wet grass.

But the yard between the houses stretched endlessly before her. She knew she'd sink to the muddy ground and never make it. A part of her—the dead part—wanted to give up, lie down on the grass and wait for her body to join her heart.

But she kept going. Halfway across, once again on her own domain, she cast a frightened glance back to be certain no one followed.

Neither Dylan nor the devil himself dogged her footsteps . . . but she had left his kitchen door gaping open. She hesitated only briefly, then turned again for the haven of her own home. She couldn't go back, didn't have the strength, emotional or physical.

She reached her back steps and suddenly realized she'd left her purse and keys inside Dylan's house, on the table where she'd stopped to read his notebook.

She had no choice. She had to return. The bag would leave no doubt she'd been inside. But, more importantly, without her keys, she couldn't get into the safety of her home. A brief, hysterical laugh escaped her lips. She didn't even have a credit card to break into her own place.

She started across the yard again and discovered that the initial shock of seeing Elizabeth—herself—in her last moments of life, of knowing her lover had betrayed her in two lifetimes, had lost some of its numbing grip. Her legs carried her back to Dylan's more easily than when she'd left. Still, entering the house filled with his essence was agony.

The rooms, devoid of furniture, of humanity, crowded in on her as if they'd trap her, swallow her up as surely as the river had. She saw her purse lying incriminatingly on the little table, next to the notebook. She approached, snatched it up and started to flee.

But something—*someone,* she corrected, even before she focused on the object—stopped her in midstride, drawing her attention to the window. She recognized that feeling, that attraction. Dylan's car was coming down the street.

She turned, reaching the open kitchen door her only thought. As she ran, the empty house echoed her footsteps, made it sound as if someone were following close on her heels. She ran faster, terror overwhelming her, though she knew on a rational level that Dylan couldn't be inside yet.

She made it to the back step, then forced herself to stop and close the door behind her. As she did so, as her mind fought with the haze of panic, she realized she couldn't move yet.

If he were getting out of the car, coming up the walk, he'd see her crossing the side yard. She *had* to wait, listen for the sound of the front door opening before she dared flee to the sanctuary of her home.

Leaning against the screen, frozen in place, she strained to hear over the roar of her own blood as her heart sent it racing. She was sure she'd never be able to hear Dylan. He was probably already inside, striding toward her. Any second he'd descend on her, the fires of hell blazing in his midnight eyes.

But she did hear him with a crystal clarity, heard every sound as he mounted the steps, crossed the porch and turned his key in the lock. When the front door creaked open, she ran as if suddenly released from captivity... ran home, fumbled with her keys, dropped them, finally connected with the lock and stumbled inside.

She wanted to sink to the floor, through the floor into oblivion, away from the painful knowledge of Dylan's deceit. But she didn't have time for that self-indulgence.

If she'd sensed him coming down the street, surely he'd sensed her in his house. The strange link between them worked both ways.

She closed the kitchen door, but knew the puny lock wouldn't keep him out. Dragging over a kitchen chair, she wedged it between the knob and the floor. Taking another chair, she repeated the procedure in the front hall.

The phone rang shrilly, demanding her attention, and she knew it was him. Was he calling to accuse her of being in his house, to threaten her? Not wanting to hear anything he had to say and fearful that the sound of his voice might be enough to rob her totally of her senses, she ignored it.

As she checked the windows, made sure they were locked, drew the curtains, the ringing went on and on, screaming at her, demanding her attention. It frayed her nerves even more than they already were, reminding her of the love she'd had so briefly—beautiful, consuming, deceitful love.

She raced up the stairs and checked all the windows on the second level. The broken window! She ran to the basement, returning with a piece of plywood she frantically nailed over the jagged hole... as though he could have charged straight through from his bedroom to hers.

Finally she was barricaded in her house, and still she feared he'd get to her. Insane, irrational, yes; but the feeling of the omnipotence of their connection wouldn't leave her.

She had to relax. She'd let herself get totally out of control.

She went back downstairs to the kitchen and forced herself to make a cup of hot chocolate, to calm down and try to figure out what she needed to do next. Finding the papers she'd hidden would seem to be a priority now. That was the only clue she had at the moment.

Just as she sat down at the table and raised the steaming beverage to her lips, a loud knocking sounded from the front door. She jumped, splashing hot liquid onto her hand.

It could be anyone, she told herself.

But she knew it was Dylan.

Rising, moving as if in a trance, she went through to the foyer. The pounding came again, halting her as though she'd run into a wall.

"Amanda?" he shouted.

She gulped back an answer. Even now, knowing what she knew—having seen the gun, the notebook, the painting—even now his voice called to her on a level she found difficult to resist.

"Amanda, are you all right?" The frame shook from his pounding. "I know you're in there. If you don't answer me, I'm going to break down this door."

"Go away," she whispered, then said it again, louder. "Go away!"

For a long moment there was silence. Finally his voice came again, softer, relieved...because he knew she was still within his reach? "Thank God you're all right. It's me, Dylan. Let me in. We have to talk about this."

She moved closer, felt his resonance through the wood and backed away, needing the distance for the sake of control. "I can hear you just fine. Go ahead. I'm listening."

"This isn't something I want to stand on your front porch and shout for all the neighbors to hear."

She'd just bet it wasn't. "I'm...not dressed." *As though that made a difference after last night and this morning.* "I was resting. I don't feel well." The last part, at least, was the truth.

"Well, get dressed." His tone was becoming irritated. "I'll wait. This is important."

Why? she screamed inside her head. What had she done that he would want her dead?

"Go back home, and I'll come over in a little while," she offered. See how he liked that option.

He paused for scarcely a heartbeat. "All right," he said. "Come on over." A longer pause. "You can have the chair in the living room. I'll take the floor."

She heard his footsteps leaving her porch.

He knew! Somehow he knew she'd been snooping, knew she'd discovered the truth and was letting her know he knew. Did her knowledge make her immediate death necessary?

Surely he couldn't really expect her to return, to close herself in with him alone...just him and her, that shiny gun and the picture of Elizabeth. She moved to the window and watched him walk away, stride across the yard. He didn't bother with the steps, merely lunged onto the porch then went into the house without a backward glance.

And why wouldn't he think she'd be there if he asked? Elizabeth had followed Shawn unquestioningly. This man had beguiled her totally in one lifetime, *almost* in another.

Almost, but not quite.

She wouldn't repeat Elizabeth's mistake. She wouldn't run from the arms of her former husband to the treacherous arms of a lover who promised the world and delivered death.

Again Lottie's words about "getting things right" filled her mind. She didn't want to go home with Phillip tonight, didn't think she could ever be a real wife to him again. But she didn't want to die, either. She loved Dylan, but she had no future with him. At least Phillip would take her away from that picture of Elizabeth, from the cold notes in Dylan's notebook, from the strong hands that could caress her so tenderly yet send her tumbling downstairs to her death.

Phillip was coming to pick her up at seven o'clock, but that wasn't soon enough. She needed him here before Dylan did something crazy—before *she* did something crazy. Even now she found herself searching for an explanation of Dylan's behavior, of the picture—anything that would allow her to run to his arms.

She rushed to the phone and dialed Phillip's number, counted the rings, willed him to answer.

"Hello."

"Phillip, thank goodness—"

"You've reached the residence of Phillip Ryker. No one is available to take your call right now. Please leave a message at the tone."

She slammed down the receiver, checked her watch.

Four-thirty. Her exploration of hell had taken only a little over an hour, not an eternity, after all. Phillip would still be at his office.

Becoming more frantic with each moment that passed, she dialed that number and reached his secretary.

"Dorothy, this is Amanda. I need to speak to Phillip."

"Amanda! I haven't talked to you in ages. How are you doing? I heard about your little accident."

"I'm fine, thank you. Please, I've got to get hold of Phillip immediately."

"He's in a meeting with Robison and Stevens. The big three, you know."

At Dorothy's words, something stirred, trying to surface through the fog. Something painful—so painful her head actually started to ache. No! She couldn't bear any more pain right now. She shoved the almost-memory away.

"I'll have him call you as soon as he's free," Dorothy continued.

"No, I can't wait that long. I have to speak to him *immediately*."

"You want me to interrupt him?" Dorothy asked, sounding a little peeved as well as puzzled at Amanda's insistence.

"Yes. I want you to interrupt him."

"Very well. Hold on." She was definitely peeved.

Amanda waited, pacing back and forth as far as the phone cord would allow, too tense to sit even though her leg muscles ached from all the tension.

Finally Dorothy returned. "He asked me to take a message," she said primly. "He can't come to the phone right now. He'll call you back as soon as they're finished."

Amanda bit her lower lip, forcing herself to remain calm. "Tell him I need for him to get over here as soon as possible. Tell him it's very important. He doesn't have to call me unless he can't do that. And if he calls, he should let the phone ring once, then hang up and call back."

"I'll be sure he gets the message." Dorothy's voice took on an almost-haughty tone, as though she found the idea of delivering such a strange message beneath her.

"Please tell him *now*, Dorothy."

Dorothy's only response was an indignant grunt. Well, if Phillip's secretary thought she was crazy, it couldn't be helped. Better crazy than dead.

She started upstairs to her bedroom to pack, but the ringing of the phone stopped her. One ring, silence, then it started again. Phillip.

The receiver seemed oddly heavy as she lifted it. She knew she was doing the right thing, but every cell in her body protested.

"Amanda, what's going on? Dorothy interrupted our meeting to give me your message."

"Nothing. Everything. I'll tell you when you get here. Please, come immediately. I need to get out of here right now."

"Calm down. I'm on my way. I'll get there as fast as I can. Promise me you won't do anything until I can get there."

Don't do anything? What did he think she was going to do? "I'll have my bag packed and ready to go. Please hurry."

"I'll do eighty all the way. Just swear to me, Amanda, that you won't do anything foolish before I get there."

Anything foolish? Did he somehow know about Dylan? "I promise," she said wearily.

Puzzling over Phillip's odd admonitions, she went upstairs to her bedroom, took a bag from the closet and began trying to pack. She had to force herself to concentrate on the mundane details of which items she'd need in the next couple of days.

Folding a nightgown, she felt her heart dissolving. Would Phillip's eyes be the ones to see her in the silky white garment? Would he expect to touch her the way Dylan had touched her?

She threw the gown back into the drawer and sank onto the bed, head in her hands, tears escaping from her eyes onto her fingers. Why, now that she knew the truth about Dylan, did she still love him, feel that she'd be a hollow shell without him? Maybe living to a ripe old age wasn't such a wonderful option after all if your soul was already dead.

Damn! What was the matter with her? She hated herself for feeling that way, but she couldn't help it. A part of her wanted to go to Dylan, throw herself in his arms and beg him to somehow explain everything away, to make it all right, to hold her forever.

But that would be suicide. Forever wouldn't last very long.

Determinedly ignoring her heart, she set about packing her bag.

Finally she brought down two suitcases and placed them in the foyer. They were probably missing half the things she was going to need; she hadn't been able to concentrate on articles of clothing and toiletry items when her thoughts kept running to oil paintings of Elizabeth drowning and of her own face glowing—and to Dylan's face above hers as they'd joined the first time.

The phone had rung again as she was packing, but she'd ignored it. If it was Dylan, he'd probably be back on her front porch before long, and somehow she'd have to keep him out there.

She tested the chair at the door, made sure it would hold, then went over to the window and looked out at his house. As though he knew she was watching, he stepped out.

She almost shriveled from her post as he stared directly at her. But she couldn't afford to give in to her fears. She had to know what he was going to do.

He took two giant strides across the porch, but stopped on the edge. As his gaze turned toward the street, the darkness of a thousand stormy midnights erupted in his eyes and hardened on his face. She stepped back involuntarily.

A car door slammed outside. Phillip! Her mind told her she was glad Phillip had arrived, perhaps just in time. What might Dylan have done? Broken down her door and forced his way in? Now he had a witness and would have to re-strain himself.

But against all common sense, she wasn't ready to see Phillip, to leave with him.

"Good afternoon, Mr. Forrest," she heard Phillip say.

She reminded herself that she should be grateful he'd come. He'd kept his word—left the meeting with Robison and Stevens and broken every speed limit on his way over. She could count on him. It showed his devotion, that he would walk out on his two best clients, his partners....

Those names... That same feeling of pain, physical as well as emotional, had come when Phillip had mentioned them at dinner at the restaurant, and again when Dorothy referred to them only a few minutes ago. Amanda put her hands to her head, fighting the ache while she tried to trap the hazy memory inside until she could focus on it.

A knock sounded, scattering the fragments before they could coalesce.

Dragging back the chair, she opened the door. Phillip stood on her porch—tall, slim, immaculate and smiling. She should be happy to see him there. She should feel safe now.

To her chagrin, she had to force herself to respond to his smile, to his sterile embrace.

"Ready, sweetheart?" he asked, releasing her and lean-ing down to pick up one of her bags. "What's this?" He indicated the ladder-back chair lying on its side.

"I'll tell you all about it on the way," she said, gathering up her handbag and an all-weather coat.

But the sight of the chair halted her, sent her mind spin-ning. When she left, she wouldn't be able to put it in place under the knob. She wouldn't be able to keep *him* out. He could slip in and go through everything, take his time and eventually find it—the envelope, the papers.

Her gaze darted up the stairs, to her office. She had to find the list she'd hidden. She could almost see it, in a file. In the middle of a file; the wrong file...

"Come on, Amanda," Phillip urged. "Let's go."

She dropped her purse and coat and started up the stairs.

"Where are you going? I thought you were ready."

"Five minutes, Phillip," she called over her shoulder. "I think I can remember where I put it. Maybe this will give me some answers, tell me why Dylan wants to kill me."

"Why Dylan wants to kill you? Amanda, what on earth are you babbling about? Nobody wants to kill you, and you're not Elizabeth somebody. That fall did more damage than we realized. Come back down here and let's go home."

But she was already inside her office. "In a minute. I have to find this."

She yanked open the top drawer of the file cabinet, scanned the designations on the tabs. They were all personal; that wasn't it.

The second drawer. The files from the shop. Her mind felt like a kaleidoscope, with the pieces slowly falling into place but not yet forming a recognizable pattern.

Addresses. Computer. Customers. She looked toward the back. Suppliers.

She jerked out the fat folder and thumbed through the papers, the lists of companies... and there it was. She'd taken the pages out of the envelope she'd originally taped to her desk drawer in order to more effectively disguise them among her other lists.

She stared at the photocopies, the names of corporations... umbrella groups that hid the real owner so none of the fires could be connected, could be traced back to...

"Phillip," she whispered.

"Right here, sweetheart."

She hadn't heard him come up, but he was standing at her elbow, his breath hot on her cheek. The dark fires she'd seen in Dylan's eyes weren't so horrible after all, she decided. Phillip's eyes were glacial, almost colorless and totally devoid of emotion.

And suddenly it came flooding back, the memory too painful to face.

"You used your clients," she said, the words tumbling out as the memories returned. "You and Robison and Stevens. You bought distressed properties from your clients through phony corporations, then burned them down and collected the insurance."

"And you lived very comfortably on the proceeds."

She shook her head as the pain and guilt encompassed her. "But I didn't know. Not until last week...Sunday. I was going through my records of last year for income-tax purposes and I found some of yours mixed in." She shivered as she recalled every agonizing detail. "I called you for an explanation. I wanted to believe it wasn't what it looked like."

Phillip's hand closed over her arm. "And I told you my clients were glad to get rid of those properties, to recoup any portion of their investment. The insurance companies have plenty of money. Nobody got hurt. But that wasn't good enough for you. You got all self-righteous on me. You actually threatened me!"

She tried to back away from him as the final pieces tumbled into place in her mind. But he held her firmly in his cold, impersonal grip. She had told him she would go to the police. Phillip had laughed at her, saying that what she had would never stand up in court.

So she'd gone to his office that night, letting herself in with the key she'd neglected to give back to him, and had made copies of his computer files, enough to prove what he was doing.

"The security guard phoned to tell me you'd been in my office," he said, as if reading the progression of her returning memory. "So I went down and checked. You can't hide your tracks when everything's computerized. Everything but my personal files, at least, and I knew where every piece of paper ought to be. You weren't very careful."

She swallowed hard, flinching from the horror of the memory. "In your personal files. That's where I found it. Three months ago you killed a man!"

"Tom Hunter was an insurance investigator about to cause problems. Not that I had anything to worry about legally. I'm a lawyer, after all. But Martin and Robison..." For an instant she thought she saw fear in his glacial gaze. "Do you have any idea what it means to be involved with them? They have connections. They're powerful men."

"And they'd have killed you before they took the chance of letting you betray them to the law," she guessed. "So you murdered a man and burned his body in your next fire to hide the evidence."

Phillip smiled, and the ice in his eyes pierced her chest, settled around her heart. "I couldn't let him ruin everything. Burning down useless buildings is just the beginning. I'm on my way up, and I had hoped you'd come with me. You're very beautiful and quite entertaining. Robison and Stevens were most taken with you. I really am sorry, sweetheart, but I can't let you ruin things, either."

Amanda's blood froze as the implications of his words hit her. "You..."

"Pushed you down the stairs? Yes. And turned on the gas. I knew your amnesia, if it ever existed, wouldn't last forever. But it would have been so much easier for both of us if you'd come home with me. You could have taken too many sleeping pills or something else painless. Now..." He shrugged, lifting one shoulder of his gray suit jacket. "For all our years together, I'll do the best I can."

Amanda's mind reeled as her world shifted around her. *Phillip* had tried to kill her. Phillip was *going* to kill her. Not—

"Dylan?" she asked. "Is he working for you?"

"Dylan? Your lover?" He jerked her arm painfully at that, and his eyes turned even colder, something she hadn't thought possible. "I saw him leave last night. I've suspected something was going on for some time, but you kept insisting you were just friends. Last night finally proved I was right." He jerked her arm again. "How long? Was he the real reason you left me?"

She tried to pull free of him, but his grip was like steel. "I left you because you're cold and uncaring. I needed more than money, but you didn't have more to give. Your recent actions proved that."

Suddenly she had to get away from him. Even more than fearing for her life, she didn't want him to touch her, not ever again. She kicked at his shin, felt her foot connect, heard him curse. She got her balance, drew back to kick again, but the small pistol appearing in his hand stopped her.

"I said I'd try to make this as easy on you as possible, but if you force me, it can be nasty. I really don't owe you anything after your activities with Dylan last night." He yanked her toward him. "Come on. Into the bathroom."

Now that she was face-to-face with imminent, real danger, Amanda found herself remarkably calm and lucid. She allowed him to lead her down the hall. "Why the bathroom? I don't have any sleeping pills in there."

"I know, but thanks to your penchant for antiques, you have a mint-condition, very sharp, straight-edged razor. I noticed it the night I tried to run your bath." He shoved her into the small room. "Fill the tub with water. You're going to slash your wrists. It won't hurt at all. You'll just drift away, out of my life and my business."

She backed against the tub, watching Phillip take the razor down from the collection of bric-a-brac mounted on the bathroom wall. "Slash my wrists? Commit suicide?"

He extended the blade fully from its decorative half-open position. "You're suffering from a traumatic concussion. We have the doctor's records for that. My secretary will testify that you were distraught when you called and that she then heard me begging you not to harm yourself. I came over here to take you home, protect you from yourself, but you went upstairs to the bathroom and never came back." He waved the gun at her. "Fill the tub with water, Amanda. Please don't be difficult. Don't make me have to shoot you. That's messy and painful."

Amanda turned her back to him and twisted on the faucets. Her heart and mind were both racing. How could she get out of this? Why wasn't Dylan here? Why did he choose this, of all times, *not* to be nosy.

She had to stall for time, figure out something.

"I don't have a stopper. I always take showers."

"Use a rolled washcloth."

Taking a cloth from the wicker shelf, she complied, moving as slowly as possible. But finally it was in the drain, and the water started to fill the tub.

The water. Always the water. The water surrounding her, pulling her down as she looked up at Shawn on the deck of the boat, called to him for help. He shouted her name, prepared to dive in after her. She couldn't swim, but she'd heard him brag that he'd swum across the Missouri River. He'd save her.

He was climbing over the rail. But the dark figure beside him grabbed him with one large hand, lifted a club with the other and smashed it against his head, then tipped him into the ebony waters to join her in death.

Blake stood alone on deck, his silhouette the last thing she saw before the darkness settled around her.

CHAPTER SIXTEEN

"Blake?" Phillip asked. She realized she'd turned toward him, spoken the name aloud. "Who the devil is Blake?"

She shook her head, twisting back around to stare at the hated water rising in the tub. A blinding fury possessed her. Damn it, he wasn't going to do it to her again! It wasn't the water that had killed her; it was *him*. The water was neutral, an instrument, nothing to fear. It belonged to her as much as to him.

"I think that's full enough," he said. "Stand up and take off your clothes."

She plunged a hand into the water. "It's too cold. Please, I need a little more warm."

She turned the cold tap all the way off, watching the steam rise from the hot water as it poured into the tub. With one hand she grabbed the flexible shower hose and with the other twisted the diverter, sending the entire flow through the hose. Then she whirled and sprayed the scalding water in Phillip's face.

He stumbled backward, dropping the razor as he raised his hands to protect his eyes. But he continued to clutch the gun.

Amanda rose to a crouch from her kneeling position, trying to keep the spray on him as she groped blindly for the razor. He stumbled, slipping on the water, and fell to the floor.

Her chance! If she could only get out of there before he got to his feet, she might be able to escape. Gasping for breath, she pushed herself upright, dropped the hose, which was losing its effect as the water became merely warm, and tried to run past him. The room was small, the door only two strides away. But he grabbed her ankle, and she plummeted painfully to the wet tile floor.

"Ungrateful bitch," he snarled, struggling to his feet.

"Murderer!"

She wanted to turn on him, scratch him, hurt him, punish him for all he'd done to her, to Shawn, to the insurance investigator. But she couldn't allow her rage to overwhelm her, to steal her control. She didn't want to die. She didn't want Phillip to have the satisfaction of killing her again. She didn't want to lose the second chance she'd been given with Dylan. If she had any possibility of getting away, she had to force herself to remain calm enough to find it, to take it.

The gun, small and black and deadly, suddenly appeared in her face. He grasped her shoulder, pulling her to a sitting position. She felt the cold steel touch her temple.

In a desperate move, knowing it might be her last, she kicked upward into his groin and shoved as hard as she could.

He fell backward with a loud grunt, and the gun exploded. A slight sting touched her cheek, but she was still alive, still moving. She rolled away from him, staggered to her feet and lunged through the open door, her wet shoes slipping precariously as she ran down the polished hardwood hallway.

"Amanda!"

Did he really think she'd stop just because he called to her?

She hit the stairs, taking two at a time, clutching the rail for balance as she charged downward. But just as she reached halfway, she felt familiar hands on her shoulders, pushing, and this time one of those hands pressed the cold metal of a gun against her. She stumbled, hanging on to the bannister desperately, refusing to let him do it to her again.

A thud sounded at the front door, which came crashing open. "Let her go!"

Dylan! Her heart surged. This time would be different. This time they'd make it.

Phillip's grip changed, but he didn't let go. One arm wrapped around her shoulder, pressing the barrel of the gun against her neck. His other hand caught her elbow. She clutched the rail more tightly, prepared to hang on for dear life, but this time he steadied her, helped her regain her balance.

"I'm certainly glad you're here. I could use some help with her," he said.

She looked down to see Dylan at the foot of the stairs, his big, silvery gun pointed in Phillip's direction. He moved slowly upward, glowering from beneath storm-cloud brows, his eyes dark, raging maelstroms. "Give me the gun, Ryker."

"I had to take it away from her," Phillip said, his voice oily. "She was trying to kill herself. If you'll put down *your* gun and help me restrain her, I'll get her in my car and take her to the hospital."

Amanda tried to jerk away from Phillip's grasp, but he tightened his hold. "Take your filthy hands off me," she gasped, struggling against him.

"Calm down, sweetheart. Everything's going to be all right." His tone was soothing, condescending.

Dylan was only two steps below them now. The hurricane barely contained in his eyes seemed to gain in fury. "It won't wash, Ryker. I know all about your activities. My name isn't Forrest, it's Hunter. Tom Hunter was my brother.

I've been trying to find the proof of what he told me about you ever since his death. Now turn Amanda loose and hand me the gun, real slow—with two fingers, just like in the movies.''

Amanda was so shocked by Dylan's revelation that she almost missed the fact that Phillip must be equally distracted. Taking advantage of the situation, she kicked backward and felt her foot connect with his knee, heard him curse. His grasp loosened as he stumbled, and she twisted away, shoving him this time, sending him tumbling—against Dylan. Both men toppled downward.

Amanda scrambled to her feet, reaching for Phillip's gun, which had fallen on the stairs.

The two men landed at the bottom, Phillip scrambling to his feet, Dylan sprawled on his back. Amanda grasped the gun and aimed, her finger tightening on the trigger. She could and would shoot this man who threatened her life and Dylan's, who had already destroyed their happiness in another lifetime.

But Dylan unwittingly saved Phillip's life when he rolled over and grabbed both his legs, dragging him to the floor.

She watched helplessly as the two men fought, but it soon became apparent that Phillip's sleek body, which looked so good in business suits, was no match for Dylan's muscles. After scuffling briefly, Dylan rolled Phillip onto his back and planted a knee in his chest, smashed a fist into his jaw and drew back to do it again.

Amanda was torn between wanting Dylan to punish Phillip and fearing that he would kill him, then go to jail himself.

The scream of a siren pulled Dylan up short, and he staggered to his feet, jerking a semiconscious Phillip up with him. Amanda hurried down the stairs to stand beside him, to touch him and know they were both still alive. Through the open door she could see uniformed officers piling out of two squad cars parked in the street.

"I called when I heard the shot," Dylan panted in explanation. "I may not have proof of what he did to my brother, but surely we can get him for your attempted murder." He let out a long sigh, as if he'd been holding his breath for months.

"I've got proof of everything," she said quietly. "That's why he tried to kill me. He'll pay for Tom's murder, too."

She looked up to see a sad smile spread over Dylan's face. Some of the darkness had left his eyes.

Amanda walked across her porch and opened her front door, examining the splintered wood in the pale light from the moon. "This is getting to be a habit," she teased, smiling up at Dylan as they entered the house. "Breaking down my door, I mean."

"You could give me a key." He smiled his first smile of the evening.

She arched an eyebrow. "Or you could use your credit card like you did the other night."

He drew her into his arms and grinned sheepishly. "Ouch. Can we discuss this over a cup of coffee, preferably one with a liberal shot of brandy in it? This has been a long, grueling day." He touched the bandage on the side of her face, where Phillip's bullet had grazed her temple. "For both of us."

"Caffeine and alcohol sound pretty good to me," she admitted, reluctantly leaving his embrace to lead him to the kitchen. "While the coffee's brewing, you can explain about this coincidence of your being next door to the former wife of your brother's murderer. And if I like your explanation, you can stay to drink the coffee."

She took the pot to the sink and turned on the water.

He ran a hand through his dark hair, tousling it even more than it already was, then pulled out a chair and sat down at the table. "That's a tough one. I'm not sure you're going to like the answer."

She turned off the faucet and looked at him in surprise. Since she knew Shawn had been innocent in his actions toward Elizabeth, she had assumed Dylan would be the same.

"Go ahead," she said, suddenly as serious as he.

"Tom and I were very close," he began, speaking quietly. "He was only a year younger. He told me everything, including his suspicions about the warehouse fires. He was a good investigator. He was getting close to Phillip, close to finding proof. Then he ended up dead. The police said it was an accident. They couldn't find any evidence to the contrary. But I knew better."

He paused and looked at her, and his eyes were no longer masked, but dark pools of infinite pain. She sat at the table beside him and took his hand.

"Dad had a bad heart. The news of Tom's death and the way the police handled it killed him. As you can imagine, Mom isn't taking this too well. She's pretty close to a nervous breakdown. I had to do something."

"So you moved next door to me."

He nodded. "That vacant house seemed like an omen. I assumed because you'd been married to him that you were guilty by association...that you at least knew everything and were keeping quiet about it. I thought you would be easier to get information from than he would be."

Amanda's heart clenched at his distrust of her. She stood and moved away, went to check the coffeemaker. "You thought I would be a party to murder?"

"My head told me you must be, that you had to know. But as soon as I met you, I couldn't believe you were guilty. At least, I didn't want to believe it."

His voice entreated her, but she kept her attention focused on the rising level in the coffeepot. Though she understood what he must have felt, his doubts about her hurt. "I had no idea until Sunday," she said. "I found some documents of his mixed in with mine. I still had to go to his office to find enough proof to take to the authorities."

"That's when I began to get really suspicious," Dylan confessed. "I followed you there because you'd been acting so guilty and evasive Sunday afternoon. I watched you get into his office with your own key, then the next day you woke up claiming amnesia. I thought at first that Phillip had beaten you to keep you quiet."

"Close enough." Amanda took down two cups and poured in coffee, then generous slugs of brandy, and returned to the table. "He tried to kill me to keep me quiet. Even knowing he was a murderer, I just couldn't imagine that he'd hurt me." She took a sip of her scalding drink.

When she looked at Dylan again, he was gazing at her, and she wondered why she'd ever thought his eyes were dark. They held the light from all the stars.

"I was so scared when I heard you scream that morning," he said. "Something woke me up about an hour before that—the approaching storm, I guess."

Or that crazy mental link I have with you, she thought.

"I knew something was wrong. I have to admit, I panicked when I came through that door and saw you huddled on the floor. I guess I was already half in love with you. If I believed in such things, I'd say it was love at first sight."

"Or second lifetime."

He grinned, arching an eyebrow quizzically. "Back to the reincarnation stuff?"

"I can see you're still not convinced. Dylan," she said, "Phillip killed me. In this lifetime. After he pushed me down the stairs, he held a pillow over my face and I died. I had a near-death experience." She heard his sharp intake of breath as he reached for her hand and gripped it tightly. "It was just like you read about—the bright tunnel of light, the overwhelming peace. But with it came knowledge. That's when I got back Elizabeth's memories. And I became angry. It wasn't fair that he should do it to me—to us—in two lifetimes. I came back."

Dylan was silent for a long moment. "You're saying you died?"

"Yes."

"And came back another person?"

"No. I just came back a little confused, with the wrong set of memories. Or maybe it was the right set, what I needed to work things out."

"And you really believe you were this Elizabeth Dupard and I was Shawn Fitzpatrick."

"We were, and we are. Our bodies changed, but not our souls. We were meant to be together, but we didn't make it last time. Something happened. Somehow Blake must have found out." Suddenly an idea hit her. "Your house. Rachel had a hiding place, too. After Papa made mine, she had to have one, so she loosened a board in the corner of her bedroom. Maybe she left a journal, too, or at least some notes."

For a moment she thought he would argue with her, tell her she was being ridiculous, but he only shrugged. "Let's go look. You won't be happy until we do." He might not completely believe her, but he didn't disbelieve, either, she decided.

As they crossed the yard from one kitchen door to the other, Dylan wrapped his arm about her waist and held her close. She felt warm and comfortable against his body and marveled at how different this trip was from the one she'd made only a few hours before.

"How did you know I broke into your house?" she asked.

"I don't know. It was like I could sense your recent presence. I caught a faint whiff of your scent. I seem to have a sixth sense where you're concerned."

At least he'd admitted that much.

In his bedroom—Rachel's former bedroom—she went straight to the far corner and, with very little effort and Dylan's screwdriver, raised the floorboard. In the revealed space lay a letter. It was addressed to Elizabeth in a handwriting shaky with age but recognizable to her as Rachel's.

Dylan leaned over her shoulder. "This gets eerier all the time," he admitted.

Tears filled Amanda's eyes as she retrieved the last communication from her dear friend. With trembling fingers, she opened it and pulled out a single sheet of paper.

My dear Elizabeth,
I know you're dead, and I'm not quite sure why I'm writing this. Maybe I've gotten dotty with age. Everyone says I have. But somehow I feel you're going to read it. Maybe the angels will take it to you. I should be able to tell you in person, soon, and I do so look forward to that. At least I look forward to leaving this life. I'm ashamed to face you and can only hope you'll be able to forgive me.

Elizabeth, believe me when I say no one ever loved a friend more than I loved you, and I would never have done anything to hurt you. But I did. The night you ran away with Shawn, Blake came here. He'd woken up and found you'd left. Then he came here and demanded to know where you'd gone.

He was furious! Mama and Papa left me alone with him because he was your husband, and a rich and powerful man. He hit me and threatened to kill my parents and me. He hit me until the pain was so bad the words came out and I told him.

Elizabeth, I'm so sorry! I could have bitten off my tongue when I realized what I'd done. If only I'd bitten it off before I betrayed you!

Even so, I had no idea he'd kill you and Shawn, but when they found your body, I knew that's what had happened. I went to the sheriff, but it was no use. Blake owns him, too. He just laughed at me. For all the years of my life I've lived with this secret and never forgiven myself. I only hope that when I pass through to the other side, you'll be able to do what I haven't and forgive me.

A tear dropped onto the paper, blurring part of Rachel's signature. "It's okay," Amanda whispered. "Everything's okay, Rachel. Oh, Dylan, why did she have to die blaming herself?"

He wrapped his arms about her and pulled her to him. "You know, if I believed in all this stuff, I'd say she'd probably pop up as one of our kids."

His determinedly frivolous tone and the implication that they'd be having children together brought a smile to her lips. She leaned back in his arms to look at him. "How can you not believe after all this?" she challenged. "What about that picture of me you painted?"

"Which picture? I've seen your face enough to do the portrait, and the nude . . . well, I confess, I fantasized about you. A lot." He ran a hand over the curves of her breasts, down her waist, then clasped her bottom. "But the reality's even better."

"Not those paintings. The one of the woman with dark hair who's drowning."

He shifted uncomfortably, looking away and clearing his throat. "Oh, that one. Actually, that's from a dream I've had all my life. A nightmare, really. Strange thing about it— after you lost your memory, that woman kept turning into you in the dream."

"The woman is Elizabeth. That's the face I expected to see when I looked in the mirror after falling down the stairs. That scene, from just that angle, is the last thing Shawn saw before he died."

His eyes clouded over, and he walked away from her, over to the bed, where he sat down. "You make a pretty strong case, lady."

She went to sit beside him. "I don't see how it could get any stronger."

"If it's true, that would explain why I was so drawn to you the first time I saw you, in spite of the fact that I thought you were involved in my brother's death."

"And the way you sometimes break into speech patterns that aren't quite yours. You have almost an Irish brogue at times."

"I know one thing." He wrapped his arms about her again, his face only inches from hers. "I love you, Amanda or Elizabeth or whoever you are today."

"And I love you, Shawn and Dylan and whoever you may be in your next lifetime."

His lips touched hers, and she responded, allowing herself to become lost in the exquisite sensations of his body against hers. She lifted her arms and wrapped them around his neck. It felt so right. It *was* right. She could have— should have— trusted her instincts—the voice of her soul— all along.

She could feel his heart rate increasing, hear his breath coming faster and faster as he pulled her down to the bed with him. His lips were still soft, but the kiss had become more demanding . . . demanding what she was only too willing to give—her body, her heart, all of her.

His mouth left hers, reluctantly it seemed, with a soft kiss to ease the parting, and he drew back a couple of inches, just enough that she could focus on his face, read the question in his eyes. He must have seen the answer in hers, because slowly, as though they had all the time in the world—and didn't they?—he began unbuttoning her blouse, his lips claiming the territory exposed by his fingers. She moaned, already moving shamelessly in her need for him.

By the time he'd removed the last piece of clothing and covered every inch of her flesh with his tantalizing mouth, she was starved for him. She reached for him, touched him, but with a groan he pulled away, his eyes roving over her body in the light from the bedside lamp.

"I want to memorize every detail of you," he said huskily. "I need you so badly I'm greedy for you, as if I'd been searching forever and just now found you. As if we'd been separated for years."

"You did. We have," she murmured, knowing he wouldn't believe, but saying it anyway. She lifted her arms to him. "We've been apart for a lifetime. Please don't make me wait any longer."

When he finally joined himself with her, Amanda locked her long legs around him and held him tightly for an instant before they began moving in the dance of love. She felt as if they weren't really two souls at all, but each an incomplete half now made whole.

At first slowly, then more rapidly, they raced to a crashing crescendo, for a few seconds soaring into infinity together, returning to collapse in each other's arms.

As he lay beside her, he kissed her ear. "I'll admit that maybe this reincarnation business just might have something to it, but let's don't tell the kids. Dealing with one set of parents is enough," he whispered.

"There you go with those kids again. Are you trying to propose to me?"

"Definitely. But this time we'll take an airplane on our honeymoon. I'm not taking any more chances on losing you."

"Sounds good to me." But if Rachel did come along as one of those kids—and recent events had proved that anything was possible—she'd have to tell her about "this reincarnation business."

He drew a finger down her bare arm slowly, softly, sensuously. "I don't know about reincarnation, but I know I'll love you for all of this lifetime."

She smiled as she cuddled closer to him. That was all that mattered. They loved each other in the here and now.

But maybe she wouldn't try too hard to get this part absolutely perfect. She wouldn't mind another lifetime or two of loving him, trying to get it right.

* * * * *

ETERNAL LOVE
by Maggie Shayne

Fans of Maggie Shayne's bestselling Wings in the Night miniseries have heard the whispers about the one known as Damien. And now the most feared and revered of his kind has his own story in TWILIGHT ILLUSIONS (SS #47), the latest in this darkly romantic, sensual series.

As he risks everything for a mortal woman, characters from the previous books risk their very existence to help. For they know the secrets of eternal life—and the hunger for eternal love....

Don't miss TWILIGHT ILLUSIONS by Maggie Shayne, available in January, only from Silhouette Shadows

And now for something completely different....

SILHOUETTE

SPELLBOUND
R O M A N C E

In January, look for
SAM'S WORLD (IM #615)
by Ann Williams

Contemporary Woman: Marina Ross had
landed in the strangest of worlds: the future.
And her only ally was the man responsible for
bringing her there.

Future Man: Sam's world was one without
emotion or passion, one he was desperately
trying to save—even as he himself felt the first
stirrings of desire....

Don't miss SAM'S WORLD,
by Ann Williams, available this January,
only from

INTIMATE MOMENTS®
™ *Silhouette*®

SPELL6

Now what's going on in

CONARD COUNTY?

Guilty! That was what everyone thought of
Sandy Keller's client, including Texas Ranger—and
American Hero—Garrett Hancock. But as he worked
with her to determine the truth, loner Garrett found he
was changing his mind about a lot of things—especially
falling in love.

Rachel Lee's Conard County series continues in January
1995 with A QUESTION OF JUSTICE, IM #613.

INTIMATE MOMENTS®
™ *Silhouette*